Also by Gillian Cross

'The Lost' Trilogy
The Dark Ground
The Black Room
The Nightmare Game

A Map of Nowhere
Born of the Sun
Calling a Dead Man
Chartbreak
On the Edge
Pictures in the Dark
Roscoe's Leap
The Dark Behind the Curtain
The Great Elephant Chase
The Iron Way
Tightrope
Wolf

FOR YOUNGER READERS
The Demon Headmaster
The Demon Headmaster and the Prime Minister's Brain
The Revenge of the Demon Headmaster
The Demon Headmaster Strikes Again
The Demon Headmaster Takes Over
Facing the Demon Headmaster

The Tree House

F/CRO

I Belong

Where I Belong

gillian cross

OXFORD
UNIVERSITY PRESS

OXFORD
UNIVERSITY PRESS

Great Clarendon Street, Oxford OX2 6DP

Oxford University Press is a department of the University of Oxford.
It furthers the University's objective of excellence in research, scholarship,
and education by publishing worldwide in

Oxford New York

Auckland Cape Town Dar es Salaam Hong Kong Karachi
Kuala Lumpur Madrid Melbourne Mexico City Nairobi
New Delhi Shanghai Taipei Toronto

With offices in

Argentina Austria Brazil Chile Czech Republic France Greece
Guatemala Hungary Italy Japan Poland Portugal Singapore
South Korea Switzerland Thailand Turkey Ukraine Vietnam

Oxford is a registered trade mark of Oxford University Press
in the UK and in certain other countries

British Library Cataloguing in Publication Data

Data available

ISBN: 978-0-19-275554-4

1 3 5 7 9 10 8 6 4 2

Printed in Great Britain by CPI Cox and Wyman, Reading, Berkshire

Paper used in the production of this book is a natural,
recyclable product made from wood grown in sustainable forests.
The manufacturing process conforms to the environmental
regulations of the country of origin.

This book is dedicated to all nans everywhere, and especially to Winnie Arthur, who knows how to share her passion for reading. Every Saturday afternoon, she took her granddaughter Sharon to the Harris Museum Library in Preston, introducing her to the world of books and stories that has enriched Sharon's life ever since.

There are guns and bandits in this story. And supermodels. And there's drought and starvation too.

Does that bother you? Are you wondering how they can all come together? Well, that's how life is these days. Things don't happen neatly, in separate little places. We're all linked together by emails and phones and the great spider's web of media that spans the world.

That's where this story is set. The world. It's the story of Abdi and Khadija and Freya (that's me) and what happened to us because of Somalia . . .

Abdi

'Spin the globe, boy,' my father used to say. 'Good. Now give me your finger.'

He'd hold it high in the air and then, as the globe slowed and the blurring countries started to separate, suddenly he would—STAB!

And he never failed. Every time, as the world screeched to a stop, my finger was slap bang on the Horn of Africa. Right at the point where letters ran round the coast.

SOMALIA.

'There!' my father would say. 'That's where you belong.'

I'd look down at the jagged, angled shape and think of warlords and pirates. Kids strolling down the streets, with AK47s over their shoulders. Battle wagons with sub-machine guns mounted in the back, and men haggling over ammunition at the arms market in Mogadishu.

You need to be strong to survive in a place like that.

3

You need a good family to back you up, and a pride in your own identity. And Somalis are known for those things—even here. People see how we stand up for each other at school and they say, *Don't hassle him. He's one of the Somali kids.*

That's rooted deep inside me. Every time I look at a globe, every time I read the name of my country or see it on a map, it gives me a feeling I can't describe. I think, *That's me. That's where I belong.*

My father showed me the way there, dozens of times, holding my finger and tracing out the routes on the globe. *Fly to Dubai or Djibouti. And then take a plane straight into Somalia.* It's easy. People do it all the time, in spite of the danger and the guns. Somalis from all over the world go back to visit their families.

But not me. I've never been there.

I was born in the Netherlands. That's where my mother ran to, when things turned nasty in Somalia. And, believe me, they turned *very* nasty.

First there was a dictator, who favoured his own clan, Maamo says. He held down all the others—until Western countries began to play games with the Horn of Africa. Then everything fell to pieces.

And the warlords took over.

What was it like then? Well, imagine living in the middle of a computer game—only it's real. That's how I visualize it, anyway. All the buildings bombed to pieces, grenades exploding every time you walk down the street and machine gun bullets ripping into anyone who gets in the way. Maamo says there was violence everywhere. And corruption. And chaos.

She was pregnant with me then, and my father was desperate to get her away somewhere safe, but his parents were old and sick and he couldn't leave them. So Maamo went abroad by herself, as a refugee. And my father promised to come and fetch her home when the country settled down.

Only it didn't settle down.

My father never lived with us while I was growing up. When I was small, he used to come and visit, filling the whole house with life and energy. He was always full of games and he loved telling stories—especially about the tricks he and his best friend Suliman played when they were young.

We never knew when to expect him. I'd just wake up one morning and find him there, grinning down as I opened my eyes. When I try to remember those visits now, they all merge into one. I see his face and I scream with delight as he scoops me out of bed. Then he throws me up in the air, three, four, five times, catching me in his great strong hands.

'You haven't grown!' he says. Teasing me. 'I thought you'd be big enough to look after Maamo by now, but you're still tiny!'

'No I'm not!' I shriek. 'Measure me! Measure me, Abbo!'

I wriggle out of his arms and slide to the ground, dragging him across to the wall where he marks my height. The pencil lines go up like the rungs of a ladder, one for each time he visits.

Once there were only marks for me, but now there are three ladders next to mine, for my three younger sisters. Fowsia first, then Maryan, then Sahra. But my ladder's the longest, and it goes up very fast. That makes me really happy, because I can't wait to be as tall as my father. He's marked his own height on the wall, so I can see where I'm heading.

Am I near that mark now?

I'll never know, because we don't live there any more. When I was ten, we moved to England—and my father stopped visiting us.

He still kept in touch, though. He'd sent us to the place where Suliman Osman and his family were living, with lots of other Somalis. A part of London called Battle Hill. Suliman was busy opening up a string of internet cafés round there, and every week I went to the one nearest to our flat. There was always an email waiting for me. `Hi, Abdi! How are things going? That was good news about the football match . . .` My father always remembered what I was doing, and what I cared about. And he always ended the same way. `Keep looking after Maamo and your sisters, until I come and see you again. I'm proud of you. Abbo.`

But he never did come.

'He still loves us,' said Maamo. 'It's just that things are harder now. He can't keep travelling backwards and forwards the way he used to. We have to save lots of money to bring him here and then he'll stay for ever—until we go home to Somalia.'

It was because of saving the money that I had to read my emails in Suliman Osman's café. We couldn't afford to buy our own computer, because we needed every penny to bring Abbo to England.

Each Sunday, Maamo and I would sit down and count up what we'd managed to save that week, piling up coins in neat little heaps on the kitchen table. I wrote down the amount in a notebook and added up the total and on Monday morning Maamo took the money round to Uncle Osman Hersi's house, so that he could keep it safe. We did that every Sunday, for three years.

Then, when I was thirteen, we finally had enough, and Uncle Osman came round to tell us it had all been sent off to my father. When he left, Maamo danced round the kitchen, singing Somali songs.

We thought Abbo would email us, of course, to say when he was coming, but we didn't hear from him. In fact, his emails stopped altogether. One week there was the usual message, full of news and questions and funny little stories and jokes. And then—nothing.

I checked my inbox every day, at school, and in the evening I went into the café, to check again. Suliman must have guessed why I kept coming. For a while, he told his manager to give me ten minutes a day free of charge. And that was all I needed—unless I had homework to do—because the message I wanted was never there.

At first, Maamo tried to find out what had happened. Her question went all round the world, passed on from one Somali to another. *Where is Ahmed Mussa Ali?* But no one seemed to have an answer.

And then one day I walked in from school and she told me he was dead.

She didn't make any attempt to prepare me. Just said the bare words. 'Your father's dead.'

When I asked the obvious questions, like when and where—and *who*—her face went blank, as if the story was too painful to tell. She just refused to talk about it.

After that, when I tried to picture my father's face, he was always saying the same thing. `Keep looking after Maamo and your sisters, until I come and see you again. I'm proud of you` . . . And I felt it come down on my shoulders, like a heavy weight.

About six months later, I came home from school and found visitors in the flat. Suliman's father, Uncle Osman, was there, with his wife, Auntie Safia. They were sitting in the front room, drinking tea with Maamo. The flat was very tidy and quiet and there was no sign of my sisters.

Maamo poured me a cup of tea and nodded at the sofa, meaning that I should sit next to Uncle Osman. She and Auntie Safia went on talking and Uncle Osman smiled at me.

'You're doing very well,' he said. 'Your sisters are growing up into good, sensible girls.' I glanced round the flat, wondering where they were and he smiled at me again. 'They've gone to visit my daughters.'

He and Auntie Safia had only one son—Suliman—but they had three daughters, all older than me. We used to see the daughters a lot, when they helped in Auntie Safia's shop, but they were never in there now. They were all studying hard, for professional exams. If they'd taken time off, to mind my little sisters, it could only mean one thing.

Uncle Osman had come round to say something important.

He watched me thinking about it. Then he said, quietly, 'Of course, if you had an older sister, she would be able to keep an eye on Fowsia and Maryan and Sahra. Girls need an older sister when they're growing up.'

Maamo and Auntie Safia stopped talking for a second. When they went on, I could tell they weren't really listening to each other. They both wanted to hear how I was going to answer Uncle Osman. That was the point of this visit.

'Older sisters don't come out of nowhere,' I said.

Uncle Osman studied my face. Then he said, very carefully, 'There's a man in Somalia—a good, hard-working man—who wants his daughter to come to Britain for her education. But he has no relations here to give her a home. He's asked me to find a good family who'll treat her like a daughter—or a sister.'

They were all staring at me now. The three of them

10

must have discussed it already, without me, but it felt as though the decision was mine. As though they were waiting for my permission.

'How old is this girl?' I said.

Uncle Osman shrugged. 'Maybe—fourteen?'

That probably meant she was older. I don't know much about how these things work, but I know that younger is better, because it gives more time for education. And they give you money for longer.

'Who is she?' I said. 'What family is she from?'

Uncle Osman frowned, very faintly. 'It's not good to make divisions like that. Her name is Khadija, and she's your sister. We are all one family now. Your father understood that.'

How could I refuse then? He hadn't chosen us to look after this unknown girl just because we needed the money. He'd chosen us because he knew we were the right kind of people. The wife and children of Ahmed Mussa Ali.

'So what's your answer?' Uncle Osman said.

I lifted my head and looked him in the eyes. 'She can come,' I said. 'Tell her father we'll look after her.'

Khadija

When you say 'Somalia' to *me*, I think of rain on the red desert. Dust spattering up my leg and children screaming with joy as the first fat drops hit the ground. I think of camels lifting their heads, with their nostrils flaring wide. And the scent of the earth as seeds split open and sprout.

When the *gu* rains come, the whole world changes overnight, from red to green, from starvation land to new, fresh pasture. The thorn bushes bud, the trees spread their leaves, the animals start to fatten up again. It's as though everything's been holding its breath, like us, and suddenly all that breath is let out, in a great burst of life.

I never thought I would get to hate the rain.

My name is not Khadija. You need to know that, before you hear my story. Now I am famous, maybe you think you know all about me, but you are mistaken. I am hidden from you, and everything you've heard is wrong.

My little brother Mahmoud calls me *Geri*—giraffe— because I have big eyes and my legs are very long. But that is not my name either. My real name lists my ancestors, going back for thirteen generations. If you heard it, you would know exactly who I am—if you're Somali.

But it may not be wise for me to tell you, so don't waste your time asking. Just listen.

When I was a little girl, my father was a rich man, with a big herd of camels and sheep and goats. He had houses too, and businesses, in Mogadishu and Beledweyne, and he travelled from one to the other and into the Ogaden. His second wife lived in Mogadishu, but we hardly ever saw her. I grew up with my sisters and my brother Mahmoud, moving around from pasture to pasture with my mother and our relations. It was a good life.

But then it changed, without any warning. Or, rather, there were warnings, but I was too innocent to know what they meant. Too trusting.

First, my father came out from Mogadishu and took away three of the camels. We knew he was going to sell them, but he didn't tell us what he was going to do with the money. They were his camels, after all.

And the rains had failed, so I thought he was selling them because of the drought.

Next time he came, he had a camera. My mother didn't like that. I saw her speaking sharply to him, but they were too far away for me to catch any of the words. And when he called to me, she walked off by herself.

He draped a sheet over the side of his car and made me sit in front of it while he took photographs of my face. When he took the first one, I smiled and waved my hand, but that made him shake his head.

'Just look straight at the camera,' he said. 'All I need is your face.'

Perhaps he's finding you a husband, Mahmoud said afterwards. Then he laughed at the expression on my face and I knew he was teasing me. He's too young to be serious about things like marriage. But I wondered whether he was right.

I never thought about passport photographs.

The third time my father came, it was almost dark when he arrived. He and my mother sat by the fire and talked for a long time. Mahmoud didn't say anything out loud, but he looked sideways at me and wiggled his eyebrows to make me laugh. When we went to sleep we could still hear our parents talking.

Next morning, I woke up and found that my mother had bundled up all my things in a piece of cloth. There wasn't much to carry. When you spend your life travelling around, you only take things that are really important.

'You're going to your father's house in Mogadishu,' my mother said. 'Be a good girl and do what you're told.'

'What's happening? Why have I got to go?'

She patted my arm, smiling a narrow little smile. 'You'll know soon. It's a wonderful opportunity.'

Why wouldn't she tell me? I wanted to ask more questions, but there was no time. My father was calling me, and everyone was crowding round his car, waiting for me to get in. Mahmoud was sitting behind the steering wheel, pretending to drive, and Zainab and Sagal were watching me enviously. Mahmoud had been talking to them as well, and they thought there was a marriage in the air.

Everyone hugged me. Then my father turned Mahmoud out of the car and opened the door for me.

'Ready?' he said.

I lifted my head and looked straight back at him. 'Ready!' And I got in and sat down.

Once we were on the way, I tried to find out what was happening. First I dropped hints and then, when my father didn't react to those, I asked him straight out.

'Abbo, are you taking me away to be married?'

He looked startled. 'Who told you that?'

'No one *told* me. But Mahmoud thought—'

'Mahmoud?' My father started laughing. 'What a talented storyteller he is! Remember his song about the goat? *Hey, little she-goat, you are the fairest of all our goats. You are as lovely as a camel, little she-goat. All the he-camels are dying of love for you, little she-goat!*'

He was a good mimic, and sang it in a thin, high voice, like Mahmoud's. It was impossible not to laugh—but I hadn't forgotten my question. 'So, if I'm not going to be married, why are you taking me to Mogadishu?'

My father was silent for a moment. Then he said, 'You're not going to Mogadishu. You're going on a much longer journey.' He looked away from me. 'I've found a place for you in England.'

'*England?*' My voice came out as a croak, as though I was being strangled. 'Why are you sending me away? What have I done?'

'You haven't done anything. If you were a bad girl I wouldn't dare to send you. It's a wonderful opportunity. You'll get a good education—'

'I'm too old for *school*! And how will I understand what they say?'

'You'll have chances—'

16

'I don't want chances. I want to be here, with the rest of you—'

We argued all the way across the desert and out on to the highway. That's my only memory of the rest of that journey. Our voices going backwards and forwards and the desperation that closed me round, like the thorn fence that shuts in the animals at night.

When I think back, I wish I'd kept quiet and looked at the country instead. I shall never travel through the desert like that again—as someone who belongs there. That journey was the end of everything I knew before. But I didn't understand and so I went on shouting and arguing.

At last, my father stopped the car. He turned to look at me, interrupting my complaints. 'Enough,' he said. I could hear in his voice that he meant to be obeyed. 'We are going to meet someone now, and I don't want to be ashamed of you. You will behave quietly and do exactly as you're told. This is the man who will take you to England.'

He pulled out again and drove in silence, with his mouth set grimly and his eyes on the road. It was the first time I felt really afraid. I could see that he wasn't going to change his mind. This thing was really going to happen.

We met the smuggler just outside the town. He was sitting quietly by the road, smoking a cigarette. When the car stopped, he put out his cigarette and stood up and my father told me to get out of the car.

'So this is Khadija,' the smuggler said.

I opened my mouth to tell him he was wrong and that wasn't my name, but he didn't wait for me to speak.

'Here's your passport,' he said.

He didn't give it to me. Just held it out so that I could see my photograph—the photo my father had taken in the desert—with the name written very clearly. *Khadija Ahmed Mussa.*

'That is who you are,' he said. 'I am your uncle, Guleed Mussa Ali, and I'm taking you to your family in England.'

What family?

My father got out of the car and put his arm round my shoulders. 'Listen to your uncle. Remember everything he tells you. If you don't get it exactly right, you could find yourself in trouble.'

The smuggler frowned at the bundle in my hands. 'What's that?' he said.

I couldn't understand why he was asking such a stupid question. 'They're the things I've brought with me.'

He scowled at my father. 'She can't take that on the plane. Have you got what I told you to buy?'

My father nodded. He opened the back door of the

18

car and took out a cheap travelling bag made of plastic. Before I could guess what he was going to do, he had snatched away my bundle—with everything I owned in the whole world. He threw it into the back of the car and put the bag down at my feet.

'Open it,' the smuggler said impatiently. 'You need to know what's inside.'

I undid the zip and peered in. There wasn't much. A few clothes, in dull colours, a little bag of washing things, and a headscarf. Not a big, bright Somali scarf, like the one I was wearing. Just a piece of thin, black material.

'You don't need many things,' my father said. 'You're going to a good family. They'll look after you.'

The smuggler waved his hand impatiently, telling me to pick up the bag. As I reached for the handle, he barked out a question. 'What's your name?'

I guessed he was trying to catch me out, but I was ready for him. 'I'm Khadija,' I said.

'Khadija what?'

'Khadija Ahmed Mussa.' That name was already fixed in my mind.

'And who am I?'

'You're Guleed Mussa Ali.'

'Guleed Mussa Ali—?'

For a moment I didn't understand what he meant.

But he and my father were both watching me, and I knew it was a test. 'Guleed Mussa Ali . . . ' I said slowly. And then I got it. 'Uncle. I must call you uncle.'

'Remember it,' he said. He didn't smile. 'Now pick up your bag and let's get going. It's time to find the boat.'

He started off down the road and I looked at my father, still hoping for a way out. But there wasn't one. My father shook his head at me.

'This is a good thing I'm doing for you,' he said. 'I've paid a lot of money to make sure you get to England. Don't waste it.'

'But I didn't ask you—'

He caught hold of my arms and looked down at me. '*Listen*,' he said. 'You can't do anything here. It's getting harder and harder for people like us, who travel around with our animals. Soon we'll have nothing left. If you go to England, you'll be able to help the whole family. And maybe, one day, you can come back and help Somalia too.'

A week ago, I'd been nothing but a girl minding goats, expecting to lead the same kind of life as my mother. I thought I would have a husband one day, and children to look after and teach. But now, suddenly, I was responsible for my whole family—and the destiny of my country too.

For a moment I was too frightened to answer my

father. But I knew he wouldn't change his mind. He'd chosen me for this task and I had to accept it. So I squared my shoulders and looked back into his eyes.

'Yes,' I said. 'Yes, I will.'

There was no time for anything else. The smuggler was already calling impatiently over his shoulder, worried that the boat would leave without us. My father patted my arm and then jumped back into his car, turning round quickly and driving off with his face set into a mask.

I picked up the plastic bag and walked down the road, to join the man who was taking me away.

He started by taking me to Kenya, in a boat. Those journeys are very dangerous, because the boats are always overloaded and the sea is full of sharks. Hundreds of people have died, horribly, trying to do what I was doing. But I didn't know that until much later. While we were on the sea, I had other things to worry about.

It was a little boat, and I was jammed in tightly, crushed among men I'd never seen before. It was the first time I had ever been in a boat, and Uncle didn't warn me that it would lurch and rock as the waves smashed against it. I was terrified, and I thought every moment that I was going to be sick.

To distract myself, I closed my eyes and concentrated on the things that Uncle had told me to learn, repeating them over and over in my head.

My name is Khadija Ahmed Mussa. I am thirteen years old. I'm going to England to join my mother and my brother and sisters. My sisters' names are Fowsia, Maryan, Sahra. Fowsia is eleven, Maryan is seven and Sahra is four. And my brother Abdi is fourteen.

I didn't try to imagine their faces or what they were like. They weren't people at all, just words that I had to learn. If I got the words wrong, I wouldn't be allowed into England and my father's money would be wasted.

My name is Khadija . . .

Those hours in the boat were the worst hours of my life. I survived by closing myself away from what was happening. And when we landed in Kenya, I truly felt like a different person.

What happened to me is called *hambaar*. Piggyback. Uncle was giving me a 'piggyback' to England in return for the money my father had paid. That was his business, and he did exactly what he'd promised. No more, no less.

Once we left the boat, we travelled by road and then by plane, and every time we went through a checkpoint Uncle smiled at me kindly. That was part of his routine. When we were through, the smile was put away along with my passport and he ignored me again, even when we were sitting side by side.

I could have run away when we changed planes in Dubai. He showed me a seat in the airport and told me to sit there until he came back to collect me. But where would I have run to? I didn't know anything about that place and I had no passport except the one in Uncle's pocket. My father had paid for me to go to England and that was where I had to go. I sat on the seat, shivering in the air-conditioning, and I concentrated on repeating the same words inside my head. *My name is Khadija . . .*

When we landed in England, the sky was grey, and it was raining. Not clean, heavy rain, like the *gu*, but a steady, depressing drizzle. I didn't see how it was going to make anything grow, because everywhere I looked the ground was covered with concrete.

I felt hard and cold, like that concrete ground. If I hadn't, maybe everything would have happened differently. If I'd walked up to the checkpoints with my pulse racing and my eyes full of guilt, maybe the officials would have shut me out of England and sent me home. But inside I was stiff and silent. So they looked at my face and then at my passport and let me into the country.

There were people from everywhere in the world on that train—all taking care not to look at each other. And the bus we took afterwards was just the same. Was the whole city like that? Thousands of people, all pretending that no one else was there?

We travelled through streets of tall, yellow-grey buildings, and all the time the useless rain went on falling. When I looked up at the sky, I couldn't see any sign of the sun. Was it always invisible here?

I thought Uncle would take me to my new family's house. I thought he would introduce me to Abdi and his sisters and present me to the woman who was supposed to be my mother. But what happened was very different.

When we got off the bus, he took some coins out of his pocket and gave them to me. 'Can you use a telephone?' he said.

I lifted my head. 'Of course I can!'

'You see the phone there?' He pointed down the road. 'Put this money into the slot, and phone the number I give you. Then stay in the phone box. The person who answers the phone will come and fetch you.'

I was too amazed to do anything except stare at him.

'Don't waste time,' he said impatiently. 'People will notice you. *Go!*' He pushed a little white card into my hand and gave me a push.

Slowly, I picked up my bag and began to walk down the road towards the telephone. When I was halfway there, I looked back over my shoulder. Uncle had already disappeared. The piggyback was over and I was walking on my own feet down this strange road.

The telephone was different from the phones I had used before, but it was easy to see how to use it. I pushed the money into the slot and pressed the buttons very carefully, checking the number as I went. I had no more money to put in if I made a mistake the first time.

It only rang twice before it was answered. 'Hello,' said a boy's voice. He was speaking Somali, but his accent was very strange. 'Are you in the phone box?'

'Yes,' I said. 'But I don't know where—'

'Just wait,' he said. 'I'm coming.' And he rang off.

I stood with the phone in my hand, looking up and down the road and wondering how I would recognize the boy. But I needn't have worried, because it was easy. I knew him as soon as he came round the corner. A tall Somali boy, heading straight for the phone box.

He opened the door and stared at me. 'I'm Abdi,'

he said. When I hesitated, he said it again, in full this time. 'I'm Abdirahman Ahmed Mussa.'

He was much older than Mahmoud, and tall too, but he was—more of a boy. That was when I really understood how far I'd travelled. I was far away from Somalia, and far from myself, in a place where the people were going to be different. And I had to learn how to live there.

I lifted my head and stared straight back at Abdi. 'And I'm Khadija Ahmed Mussa,' I said.

Freya

I didn't know Abdi or Khadija then. And Somalia was just one name in a list I'd been reciting for most of my life: *My dad's been a war photographer in Darfur and Afghanistan and Rwanda and Somalia . . .*

There were pictures to go with the words, of course, because that's what a photographer does, but they weren't the kind of images you'd show to a little child. By the time I was old enough to see them, Dad's trips were in the past, and I never really sorted out which was which. The photos were all pictures of violence and grief and dust, and the places blurred together in my mind.

It must have been five or six months after Khadija arrived in Britain when I found out *exactly* where Somalia is. It suddenly jumped off the map and into my life. I remember the moment very clearly, because Sandy and I were having breakfast together.

Maybe that doesn't sound special to you. Maybe you have breakfast with your mother every morning of the year. But then your mother's probably not a global brand. I don't suppose she works fourteen hours a day and then staggers back from the workshop with a heap of sketches and a headache.

On normal days, I don't see Sandy until the evening. And sometimes not even then. But that morning was special because she'd just come back from Paris—the Fashion Week and the big fabric fair—and she was sitting opposite me with a tall stack of books in front of her.

Paris always sets her head buzzing. By the time she reaches home, she's already full of ideas for her next collection and they usually spread out on to the breakfast table. But normally she's playing around with photos and fabric swatches, not books. So I wasn't sure what she was up to.

The night before, she'd come to Dad's flat to pick me up, on her way home from the airport. Dad had a meal ready for her, of course, but she hardly ate a mouthful because she was too busy raiding his bookshelves. Without any explanation. Those were the books piled up on the table between us. Heavy, dull paperbacks and second-hand hardbacks with tatty bindings. As I chewed my bagel, I leaned sideways and read some of the titles:

A Modern History of Somalia.

Me Against my Brother: at war in Somalia, Sudan, and

Rwanda (Hm, I wonder if Dad knows the man who wrote that?)

Whatever Happened to Somalia?

None of those sounded like the kind of thing Sandy might read. What on earth was she up to? I craned my neck a bit further, trying to see the book she was holding, but before I could make out the words on the spine, she suddenly looked up. Her face was pink and excited.

'Did you know there's myrrh in Somalia!' she said.

I blinked. 'Yeah? And gold too? And frankincense?'

'Don't be so *religious*.' She pulled a face. Then she looked down at the book and raised her eyebrows. 'Hey! Not sure about gold, but there *is* frankincense. And look at the fabrics! I knew I'd seen those patterns somewhere before.' She leaned in close, peering at a photograph, and then she passed the book across, to show me.

It was a picture of ruin and devastation.

What are you *like*, Sandy Dexter? OK, so, the woman at the front of the picture had a huge, patterned head-scarf and a little heap of myrrh. But was Sandy really expecting me to focus on that? What about the build-ings behind, shot full of holes? What about the boy in the background, holding a gun?

'Who cares about the bloody fabrics?' I said.

Sandy shook her head impatiently. '*Look!* That scarf

is the only colour in the whole place. And why do you think she chose such a bright one? Because that's what people need when life is bad. Colour and pattern—' She waved her hands in the air, launching into a typical Sandy tirade about how important clothes are.

I *hate* fashion. I hate the way it chews life up and spits it out in T-shirts and tailoring and ten varieties of handbag. If you ask me, the whole business is pointless. But not according to Sandy. When she talks about clothes, her face is fierce and intense. She says, *Fashion's a way of understanding the world. It's part of being human—and it's right there, at the cutting edge of culture.*

Well, if fashion's a knife, she's right there at the edge of the blade, slicing into everything that's pompous and settled and smug. That's what makes her iconic, of course. Even my friend Ruby went goggle-eyed when she worked out the connection.

'You mean your mother's—*Sandy Dexter*?'

Yup, that's right. I may not be Style Queen of my school, but I'm the daughter of Sandy Shocking Dexter. Fashion celebrity *par excellence.* The designer who turns headlines into hemlines, and sums up the *zeitgeist* in a zip-all-over dress. And she's not just trying to be clever. That's how things come out when she's really thought about them.

And what she was thinking about this time was that photograph.

She stared at it until her coffee was cold. Then she stood up and muttered something about needing a sketch pad. 'We can go out later on. OK, Freya? I just want to make a couple of notes first . . .'

I knew what that meant. I'd be lucky if I saw her again before supper. Last night, we'd made a plan to spend the whole day together, doing stupid things, like going ice skating, and eating chicken and strawberries in the park. But I knew none of that was going to happen now.

When I'd finished my coffee, I went out to do some basic shopping. It was no use relying on Sandy to remember anything. At least I could make sure there was food in the flat.

I was out much longer than I'd planned. While I was on the way to the supermarket, Ruby called and we met up for lunch. Then we wandered round our favourite shops and I bought a DVD of *Top Hat*. I love old films—and there's nothing like a Fred 'n' Ginger movie when you're feeling down.

When I came back, the whole place was empty and there was a message on the answerphone.

'Hi, Freya. Sandy asked me to call you.' No mistaking that hesitant Estonian voice. It was Stefan, her star apprentice. He coughed apologetically.

'She's . . . er . . . had to go away for a couple of days. I hope you're all right to stay with your dad. Any problems—give me a ring back.'

Your mum's never taken off like that? Well, it's been happening to me all my life. When a new idea hits, Sandy can't bear to stop thinking about it. Either she shuts herself in the workshop all night, or she goes travelling.

When I was little, there was always an au pair living in to take care of me. Usually a new one, who didn't quite know what was what. It worked OK, but life's been much simpler since Dad stopped being a photo-journalist and started teaching instead. He still does some photography—mostly portraits now—but he's always in England. And his flat's just round the corner.

I made myself a coffee and then rang his mobile.

'Sandy's gone off again,' I said. 'Sorry.'

'Hang on a minute.' I heard him muttering briefly to someone else and then he came back to the phone, 'Do you need help carrying stuff?'

I looked at the bags of food I'd just bought. It would only go to waste if I left it in Sandy's flat. 'Yes, I could do with a hand. But there's no rush.'

'How about if I pick you up in an hour?'

'That's fine,' I said. 'It won't take me long to pack.'

How could it? I hadn't even emptied my rucksack

properly. All I had to do was put back the things I'd taken out last night and I was ready to go, in less than fifteen minutes. To fill in the time until Dad came, I sat down at the kitchen table and started leafing through the books Sandy had left there. I was just getting into one of them when the doorbell rang.

Exactly an hour after I'd put the phone down.

There are lots of things I love about my father and one of them is that he is utterly, one hundred per cent reliable. When I opened the door, he was standing in the corridor, grinning.

'I should have watched what Sandy was scavenging off my bookshelves,' he said, as he gathered up my carrier bags. 'What is it this time?'

It's always a huge secret what Sandy's doing, until the models actually come parading down the catwalk. If I pick up any hints, I can't even tell my friends, in case it gets out. But I am allowed to talk to Dad. Even though they've split up—sort of—Sandy still trusts him more than anyone else in the world.

'It's Somalia,' I said.

'*Somalia?*' Dad's eyebrows went through the ceiling. 'What's she going to do with that? She can hardly—'

'Oh yes she can,' I said bitterly. I picked up the rucksack and slung it over my shoulder. 'She's totally callous. This morning she was reading a book about war and saying, *Look at the fabrics*, as if nothing else mattered. She doesn't care about anything except fashion.'

'Yes, she does,' Dad said. 'She cares as much as anyone. But it all goes into silhouettes and texture and colour. That's what she's like, Frey. Can you *imagine* her writing to MPs or leading protest marches?'

'Might be more useful.' I stepped out of the flat and slammed the door, hard. 'Maybe I'll suggest it when she comes back.'

Dad stopped grinning. 'She hasn't *gone* to Somalia, has she?' He was trying to sound casual, but it wasn't a great success. I looked at his face and my heart lurched.

'I don't think so. Why? Is it dangerous?'

'Just a bit.' He turned round and headed for the lift.

That was all he said. He's not the sort of man who goes on and on about things (another reason I love him) but he was very silent as we headed out of the building.

I tried to distract him. 'Hey—I've just been reading one of the books she borrowed. Guess what the Chinese imported from Somalia in the tenth century.'

'Incense?' Dad said vaguely. I could tell he wasn't really listening.

I shook my head. 'Guess again.'

He made an elaborate thinking face and then shrugged. 'No idea. I give up. What *did* the Chinese import from Somalia in the tenth century?'

'Giraffes!' I said with a flourish.

No reaction at all. I waited while we walked down the road and round the corner, but he didn't even look at me.

'Oh, come *on*!' I said, when I couldn't bear it any longer. 'Think about it. Why on earth did they want *giraffes*?'

Normally that's the kind of silly challenge he likes. *Fifteen things to do with a giraffe.* But not today. He gave me a rather pallid smile and I could tell he was trying to think of something funny, but all he managed was one feeble suggestion.

'Maybe they used them for . . . pruning trees?'

No, I didn't laugh either. But I don't think he noticed. He just kept on worrying as we walked into his building and went up in the lift. He didn't say another word until we were inside his flat.

It's very bare in there. Not like Sandy's flat, which is full of pictures and reference books, with scraps of fabric cluttering the worktops and spilling out over the tables. What Dad likes is space and light and air. His only decoration is the huge window wall, with its fantastic view across the city.

It was almost dark when we walked in. Dad made

me hot chocolate with marshmallows and I drank it standing by the window, looking out at the deep blue sky. Staring at the pretty coloured lights that drown out most of the real stars.

When I'd finished my drink I turned back into the room and Dad was standing there with his camera bag in one hand. He was looking thoughtfully at me and the window.

I hate having my picture taken. Photographs are for leggy models and glossy celebrities. Since Dad started doing portrait work, he's produced hundreds of amazing images like that. But I hate it when he points a camera at me.

'Come on, Frey,' he said, wheedling. 'Trust me. It's a fantastic shot.'

I wanted to say no. But at least it had taken his mind off Sandy, so I nodded—grumpily—and turned back towards the window. 'Like this?'

He shook his head. 'Don't force it. Just forget about me and look at the moon.'

I hadn't even noticed the moon, but there it was, way above the tallest buildings. A tiny, pale crescent, like a sliver of cloud just about to dissolve. I stared up at it and for some reason I suddenly thought about Somalia again. The people there were three hours ahead of us, which made it the middle of the night. Was there a Somali girl looking up at the moon as well? If there was, she could probably see a thousand times more stars than I could.

But it was the same moon.

When I turned round, Dad beckoned me across to look. 'It's a good one,' he said. 'I'll make you a print if you like.'

He hadn't photographed me directly at all. It was a shot of the window, with my face reflected in the glass. I was floating in the night sky, looking ghostly and transparent, like the moon. It was a beautiful picture all right.

But the face was still mine. Square and pale, with a little curly fringe.

'I look like a cow,' I said. 'A Charolais.'

Dad pulled a face at me. 'Most people would rather have a cow than a giraffe.'

'Not in Somalia. It's camels or nothing for them.'

Finally I'd made him laugh. 'Then you'll never be a star over there.' He patted my cheek. 'Go to bed, Freya. You're beautiful.'

Mahmoud had a picture too.

It was a picture of his sister Geri, going off in their father's car. She was turning round to wave to the rest of them and there was a wide smile on her face. He could see it clearly, through all the dust that swirled up round the car.

It wasn't a real picture, because it only existed inside his head, but it was always the same. Whenever he thought about Geri, he saw her smiling and waving, all through everything that happened in the months after she went away.

She smiled as the drought shrivelled up the pasture. She smiled as the goats and the sheep were sold to buy food for the camels.

And she was still smiling when the camels began to die.

It was the drought that killed them off. One by one the wells dried up, all across the land they travelled. And sometimes, when there was water, other people were there to claim it, desperate to save their own animals.

All day, Mahmoud's uncles watched the sky, hunting for some sign of rain. But nothing ever interrupted the scorching blue over their heads. So every night they all sat round the fire, discussing where to go next. But there was never an easy answer.

They travelled for a week without water to reach the last place they could try. Mahmoud was walking right at the back, with the goats, and long before he reached the well he knew it was no use. The ground was hard and dusty and his uncles were standing round the hole together, shaking their heads. Mahmoud saw his mother straighten her shoulders, getting ready to carry the heavy bundles again.

No water.

What were they going to do?

They talked about it again that night, going round and round the same hopeless ideas they'd been discussing for months. But the words were as empty as the waterhole, because everyone knew, already, what the choices were. Otherwise they would starve and dry up, like old thorn bushes.

Unless they found water, very soon, they would have to give up and travel away from the places they knew. They would have to go to the camp and ask for food.

Abdi

KKhadija was very quiet when she first came. I think she was struggling to understand English at school, but I didn't see much of her there. Mostly she hung around with the other Somalia girls—always on the edge of a group. And at home, she was busy helping Maamo. She hardly spoke to me at all in the first six months.

And then we began to hear about the drought in Somalia.

There was nothing on the television news, of course. If that was all you had, you'd hardly know Somalia existed. But there are special Somali news websites, and some of the old people read those every day. They crowd into Suliman's café and talk and drink coffee while they try to find out what's going on. Then they tell the rest of us.

Every time I went to the mosque, I heard the men talking about what a bad drought it was. They sounded worried and serious, but they rattled on too fast for me to understand everything they were saying, and I didn't bother to look up the news for myself.

Of course it's sad when your country's in trouble, but Somalia's mostly desert anyway. Everyone knows that. And ever since I could remember the rains seemed to have been failing, so what was the big deal this time? I didn't really get it.

Not until Khadija made me take her to Suliman's café.

Usually, we use the computers at school, because they're free. But that Friday everyone was after computer space, and Khadija must have been crowded out. She didn't speak good enough English to get her own way when that happened. So, on the way home, she came and sat beside me on the bus.

'Have you got any money?' she said.

I looked sideways at her. 'What for?'

'I couldn't check my email today. I need to go to the café.'

I had got a little bit of money, as it happens. But I had other plans for it. 'Can't you wait till Monday?'

She didn't say anything. Just made a stubborn face and shook her head.

I fingered the coins in my pocket. 'What's so urgent, then?'

Her lips pinched together and she gave a funny

little shrug, with one shoulder going higher than the other. 'If you don't know, then you won't understand,' she said. And she got up and went down the bus, to sit beside Fowsia.

Fowsia edged along, to make room, but she didn't stop chattering to the girls in front. Khadija sat without talking, very straight and stiff, and I looked at her back and wondered what I was supposed to understand.

When we got off the bus, Fowsia scuttled away with her friends, beckoning Khadija to go with them. But Khadija shook her head and walked behind, on her own. I watched how she placed her feet, very carefully, as if she was made of glass. As if she was afraid of breaking.

After a moment, I went to catch up with her.

'OK,' I said. 'I'll buy half an hour in the café. As long as you tell me why you need it.'

For a second, I thought she was actually going to refuse. Then she looked sideways at me. 'I can't say it in words. But I'll show you, if you come with me.'

I thought for a second. 'I haven't got time now. How about when I come back from the mosque?'

She hesitated and then nodded. 'All right.'

When I got in, she was waiting, with her coat on.

42

'Don't sit down,' Maamo said, as I opened the door. 'If you're going to Suliman's, you'd better do it before we eat. And take Fowsia with you. She needs something for her homework.'

Sahra and Maryan started clamouring to come too, but I wasn't walking down the street with a crowd of girls.

'Come on,' I said to Khadija. 'Let's go.'

We rattled out of the flat and down the stairs, with Fowsia racing to keep up. The café was crowded with people, some of them using the machines and others just hanging out. I thought we'd have to wait for hours—until I saw that Suliman was there himself. He didn't give me free computer time any more, but I still got special treatment, because of my father. When he saw us, he grinned and called down the shop.

'Hey, Warsame! You've had an hour. Take a break and come and have coffee.'

Warsame flapped a hand, with his eyes still on the screen. *Just five more minutes*. But Suliman wasn't having any of that. He went down the shop and grabbed his ears, dragging him up on to his feet. He was only fooling around, but Warsame knew enough not to resist.

'There you are.' Suliman nodded, holding out his hand for the money. He dragged across a couple of extra chairs, for Khadija and Fowsia, and left us to get on with it.

Within a few seconds, Khadija had pulled up three different Somali news sites. She clicked through the pages, leaning forward and frowning at the screen.

'Thought you'd come to check your emails,' I said.

She made an impatient little noise in the back of her throat. 'You said you wanted to understand and I'm trying to show you. So why don't you *look*?'

You know what it's like. Watching someone else use a computer is one of the most frustrating things in the world. I leaned over Khadija's shoulder and tried to work out the main headlines. But I'm not quick at reading Somali and she was going too fast, flicking from one item to another. I couldn't make sense of half of it.

Fowsia was looking backwards and forwards, from the screen to Khadija's face. 'Is it bad?' she said.

'Very bad,' Khadija muttered. 'Especially where my family is. They haven't had any rain at all. Look.'

She changed to another site and clicked on a video clip. Suddenly we were watching women in dusty clothes, with crowds of staring children huddled round their knees. And then a line of tall men walking aimlessly after some scrawny camels.

Fowsia peered at them. 'Has your family got camels like that?'

'Sssh!' I pulled a face at her. Maamo had told us not

44

to talk about Khadija's family. *You never know who's listening.*

Khadija lifted her head. 'My father had twenty-five camels. But he sold some of them to send me over here. And now, with this drought—' She shrugged her funny, lop-sided shrug.

'Maybe they're still all right,' said Fowsia. She gave Khadija an encouraging nudge. 'See whether they've sent you an email.'

But there were no new messages in Khadija's inbox. 'Maybe they haven't been near any villages,' she muttered. 'Maybe—' She frowned, as though she was thinking, and then began a message of her own in Somali, leaning forward as she typed. Iska waran, Mahmoud . . .

In the other window, I could see the video clip, frozen at the last frame. It showed the back view of a man wearing jeans and a ragged T-shirt. He had a dagger in his belt and his shoulders stooped forward as he walked. It reminded me of the day I'd found my father's dagger lying in the bedroom.

I was lunging forward, pretending to stab at an enemy, and he came in and caught me. *No, Abdi,* he'd said, as his long, strong fingers curled round the hilt of the dagger. *We brought you here so you wouldn't need a knife.* He twisted it out of my hand and slipped it back into its tough leather sheath.

There was a long, jagged scratch down one side of the sheath. I stared at it for a second, wondering whether it was that dagger or another one that had sliced into the leather. I understood, even then, that my father couldn't throw the dagger away. He needed it—because he was going back to Somalia.

That was almost the last time I saw him.

How had he died? Was he murdered by enemies, or shot dead in a fight? Or had he died of hunger and thirst before we sent the money? I didn't know any of the answers. I didn't even know what had happened to the money. Maamo wouldn't talk about that either.

I kept on staring at the skinny man on the screen, walking after his ugly camel, but I didn't really see him at all.

Khadija

Abdi and Fowsia didn't understand.

What was wrong with them? Even if they couldn't read what the websites were saying, they had the pictures to show them what was happening. How could they not understand from those?

Had they never seen a camel before?

Those people in Somalia had nothing. Just a few starving animals, with sunken eyes and ribs that jutted like knives. When I thought of everything there was around me in England—even the horrible dinners they gave me at school—I wanted to gather it all up and send it to Somalia, straight away.

But you can't send potatoes and meat and pots of yogurt. Only money.

Concentrate on your education. That's what my father said when he sent me away. *So you can earn a good living, and help us all.* But how could I wait for that to happen, when people were starving *now*? What use would my money be if everyone I loved was dead?

I wanted to say all that to Abdi and Fowsia, but I knew they wouldn't understand. Not if the pictures didn't mean anything to them. So I turned my back on them both and sent an email to Mahmoud, instead:

Iska waran, Mahmoud . . .

How are you, Mahmoud? Write back as soon as you read this and tell me what's happening. Are Zainab and Sagal all right? Why haven't you emailed for so long? I pray every day that you will find water and pasture for the animals. I know things are hard, but don't be anxious. I will get a job and send some money, very soon. I promise!

From your sister the giraffe.

When I'd sent it, I pushed back my chair and stood up. Abdi had paid for a few minutes longer, but there was no point in sitting around at the computer.

What I needed now was a job.

It took me three days to think of someone who might give me one. And that was only because English Maamo sent me shopping.

She was going to make *lahooh* pancakes, but the flour was all used up, so she sent me running to Auntie Safia's shop on the corner. The flour shelf there was empty too, and Auntie Safia had to go out to the storeroom at the back to fetch some more. She left the door open and I saw her haul herself slowly up a shaky pair of steps, to reach the top of a stack of boxes. As she came down, the flour bag dropped a trail of white dust over the steps and across the floor.

'There's a hole in the bag,' I said.

She glanced over her shoulder and clicked her tongue at the mess. At first I didn't understand why she was making so much fuss about a small thing. Then I saw that it wasn't a small thing for her. She's a heavy woman with a bad hip, and she already looked very tired.

'Give me a brush,' I said. 'I'll do it.'

While I was sweeping, I had the idea.

Keeping the shop was much harder for Auntie Safia now she was getting older. Suliman had his own business, of course, and her daughters were all too busy to help her. So maybe, if I asked . . .

I swept up the flour and threw it into the bin. Then I went up the ladder and took an armful of flour bags out of the box. Carrying them into the shop, I refilled the shelf, stacking it neatly.

Auntie Safia smiled at me. 'Thank you, Khadija. You're a good girl.'

'I could come in every evening,' I said. 'After you've shut the shop, I could sweep up and make sure the shelves are full.'

She gave me a careful look and I could see she was thinking about it. 'Not every evening,' she said at last. 'Twice a week might be useful, for a couple of hours each time. But I can't pay you much.'

'I don't want much,' I said. Very steadily and politely, to let her know she could trust me.

Auntie Safia thought about it a moment more. Then she said, 'Two pounds an hour.'

She was right. It wasn't much. But I worked it out in my head. Two pounds an hour for four hours was eight pounds a week. And in twelve weeks that meant almost a hundred pounds to send to my family. So I smiled and nodded.

And I walked home with a bag of flour and a job.

When I told Maamo what I'd done, she was furious.

'Auntie Safia doesn't shut that shop until ten o'clock. You'd be coming home at *midnight*! Do you think I'm going to let you go wandering around at that time—in the dark? Have you gone mad?'

She ranted at me for almost half an hour, while Fowsia looked on sympathetically and Sahra and Maryan giggled in a corner. Just as she was starting to simmer down, she asked me how much money Auntie Safia had offered, and that caused another explosion.

'Does she think you're a slave?'

I stood there with my head lowered, waiting for her to stop. I was determined not to give in. I had to do something for my real family and this chance was too good to lose.

Abdi was out at his class in the mosque. When he came home, his mother started up again, repeating everything she'd said before.

'Khadija thinks we'll let her go wandering round in the dark, in the middle of the night! And all for two pounds an hour.'

Abdi was just about to agree with her. I could see it in his face. I understood that they weren't just being unkind. They'd promised to keep me safe and they thought the only way to do that was to shut me in. But I needed this job. There had to be a way of persuading them to change their minds.

Suddenly I saw it.

'I don't have to walk around on my own,' I burst out. 'Abdi can take me to the shop—and fetch me when I've finished!'

Maamo hesitated. Then she glanced at Abdi, to see what he thought. He looked—startled.

'It's *important*,' I said fiercely. 'I *must* send money to my family. Auntie Safia's not going to pay me much, but it's better than nothing. Please help me, Abdi. Please!'

Fowsia had been sitting quietly until then. But

51

when I said that she lifted her head and joined in. 'Abdi, you must! Don't you remember how we saved every penny to bring Abbo over here? But we didn't get the money in time—and now he's dead. You *mustn't* stop Khadija helping her family.'

Abdi turned on her. 'Be quiet!' he said roughly. 'We did everything we could.'

'That's right,' Maamo said sharply. 'What happened wasn't our fault. He—' She folded her mouth shut and stood up suddenly.

But I couldn't let the conversation end like that. 'So—is Abdi going to take me?' I said.

Maamo picked up the bag of flour. 'That's for him to decide,' she said stiffly. 'Come on, Fowsia. Help me mix the *lahooh*.' They went into the kitchen and I was left staring at Abdi.

'Please,' I said softly. 'You saw those pictures. You know what my family's life is like in Somalia. I have to help them.'

He looked at me for a moment and then he gave a grudging nod. 'All right. I'll do it for a while. Just to see how it goes.'

Freya

That spring, Sandy must have worked twenty hours a day, seven days a week. I stayed on at Dad's—no point in doing anything else—and I was starting to wonder if I'd ever see her again.

Then one afternoon, just after Easter, I came back from school and found her in Dad's kitchen. She was making French toast. When she heard the door open she looked round at me and grinned.

'Do you want this with cinnamon sugar?'

'What are you doing here?' I said.

'I'm your mother. Remember?' She stood on tiptoe, rummaging in the cupboard. 'I suppose David does *have* cinnamon?'

'He hates cinnamon. How can you not know that?' Sometimes I couldn't believe they were together for ten years. 'Why aren't you at work anyway?' My heart jumped suddenly. 'Nothing's happened to Dad, has it?'

'Of course not,' Sandy said, as if that was impossible. 'I'm just hoping for a bit of help.'

'From *me*?' What could I possibly do to help her? When I was little, I sometimes held the pins while she was draping fabric, but that was the limit of my usefulness. 'What do you want me to do?' I said warily.

Sandy gave up on the cinnamon and shut the cupboard. 'Well, for a start—take a look at this.' She picked up a newspaper cutting that was lying on the worktop. 'How does it make you feel?' She passed it over then put the frying pan on the hob, glancing sideways at me as I looked down.

I was expecting something flamboyant and bizarre. But it was just an ordinary picture of a veiled woman, shrouded in black from head to toe. Only her eyes were showing.

I pulled a face at it. 'You *know* what I think about all that stuff.'

'I'm not interested in what you *think*,' Sandy said impatiently, as if thinking wasn't important. 'I want to know how you *feel*. What was your first reaction when you saw that image?'

What was she after? I stared down at the picture. 'Well—if that's how she really wants to dress—'

'Stop being logical!' Sandy shouted, slapping the bread into the pan. 'I want your gut reaction. When you saw that picture, wasn't there a second—a *split second*—when you felt curious? When you felt: *What's it like wearing one of those?*'

'Of course not!' I said fiercely.

But I wasn't quick enough. I'd hesitated, just for a breath, and Sandy pounced triumphantly.

'Liar! Of course there was. Everyone wants to know what it's like. Because—because . . . ' She frowned and chewed her lip. I could almost hear the ideas fizzing inside her head.

She's rubbish at explaining what she's thinking. Not surprising, I suppose. If she could express her ideas in words, she'd be a poet, not a fashion designer.

'What's all this about veils anyway?' I said. 'Is it part of your Somalia thing? I didn't think they wore veils there.'

'Don't be so literal, Freya. I'm not putting on a Somali exhibition. I'm exploring how we experience our clothes. That's why I made these.'

She darted across the kitchen—forgetting all about the French toast. It was just starting to catch, and I had to go and rescue it. When I turned round, she was holding a fat bundle of black cloth.

'This is for you,' she said. She flicked her hands, like a magician, and the bundle unrolled in front of me, falling in heavy folds.

'You're joking,' I said.

55

'What are you afraid of?' Sandy draped the garments over the back of a chair. 'They're only clothes.'

Only clothes? I wish I had a recording of that. What about: *Clothes are a deep expression of who we are*? What about: *Fashion explores what it means to be human*? With Sandy, nothing was ever *only* clothes. I looked suspiciously at what was hanging over the chair.

'And these are for me.' She bent down and picked up another, identical bundle. 'They won't bite you. Look.'

I watched as she put them on, pulling them over her shirt and jeans. In a couple of minutes she was completely hidden, except for her blue eyes, peering over the edge of the veil.

'Well?' She tilted her head at me. 'How about it?'

What was I supposed to say? OK, she was wearing a long, shapeless garment and her face was mostly covered up. But she was still totally recognizable. I knew exactly how she looked, underneath all that black.

I shrugged. 'It's not really your colour, is it?'

'Maybe it's yours,' she said sweetly. She picked up the other clothes and held them out. 'Why don't you try?'

I backed away. 'Get someone else to do it.'

'No, Freya. I made them for you.'

I looked at the clothes again. She hadn't made me anything since I was four years old.

'It has to be you,' she said. 'Please. It won't take long. We'll be back by half past six.'

'*Back?*'

'We won't go far. I just want to drive up to Battle Hill and walk around for a bit.'

'You want me to put those clothes *and go outside*?'

And she wanted me to do it in a place like Battle Hill? Where there were real women wearing real veils? It was a terrifying idea. And—rude. What would happen when people spotted we were fakes?

'Ask someone else,' I said. 'Ask *Stefan*. He'll do anything for you. He thinks you're the Messiah.'

Sandy shook her head at me. 'This isn't a pantomime. It's a bit of serious research. That's why I thought you'd be interested. But if you're not, I'll go on my own.' She picked up her car keys.

'Don't do it,' I said. 'Please.'

She didn't even listen. Just opened the door and went—leaving me to eat the French toast on my own.

You can guess what happened. As I bit into it, my mind did a complete flip. I couldn't take my eyes off the clothes on the back of the chair. Because Sandy was right, of course. I did want to try them.

I picked them up, one by one, running the material

through my hands and working out where the buttons were. Then I began to put on the long dress.

It fitted perfectly. (Of course it did. Sandy made it
for me.) The seams sat neatly on my shoulders and
the skirt fell heavy and swirling to cover the tops of
my shoes. The neckline was high and snug and the
sleeves just covered my wrist bones.

But it left my head feeling naked and exposed. I
tried to remember how Sandy had fixed the veil, but
it was harder than it looked and my first effort left
wisps of straw-coloured hair sticking out everywhere.
I had another go, and went to check the result in my
bedroom mirror.

As soon as I saw that reflection, I understood why
Sandy had been so determined to go outside. Veils are
all about hiding—and you can't hide from yourself.
There has to be someone else.

That was why Sandy had gone up to Battle Hill. To
look at people who couldn't look back at her.

It was an ideal place—three or four streets lined
with faded blocks of flats, with a mosque at one end
and a community centre at the other. I didn't really
know who lived in the flats, except that most of the
women wore headscarves and a few of them were
completely veiled. You could hide behind a veil up
there without being remarkable.

What was that like?

Well, I'd missed my chance to find out, hadn't I? If I wanted to know, I should have gone up in the car with Sandy. The only way to follow her now was on a bus, and *obviously* I wasn't going to do that. Obviously I was going to take the black clothes off and start on my homework.

I spent five minutes telling myself those sensible things.

Then I picked up my purse and went out.

So how did it feel?

If you're not veiled yourself, that's what you want to know, isn't it? Whether you think it's funny or outrageous, you want to know what it was like inside that black camouflage.

The first answer is—terrifying. When I stepped on to the bus, I thought the driver would call my bluff as soon as I asked for a ticket. *What are you doing in that get-up, love? Going to a fancy dress party?*

He didn't, of course. Just took my money and gave me the ticket, without even looking up. I went awkwardly down the bus and sat next to a window, staring out at the road.

My head was full of paralysing questions. What was I supposed to do if a man sat next to me? If he asked me the time, should I answer? Or show him my watch? Or should I just ignore him altogether? I had no idea of the right way to behave in the clothes I was wearing and I perched on the edge of my seat, almost afraid to breathe.

No one sat down by me. No one spoke. It was like being invisible. The only person who took any notice at all was a woman in a business suit who got on to the bus just before Battle Hill. As she walked past me, her mouth twisted, as though she'd tasted a lemon. She gave me a single glare and then turned her head away, deliberately.

It was trivial, but even that was enough to set me shaking. When I got off the bus, a couple of stops later, my legs felt weak and unsteady. *Don't be stupid*, I told myself severely. I was only going to walk round Battle Hill looking for Sandy. What was so frightening about that?

I turned down the first side street, walking past a shabby little shop, with groceries on the shelves. Next door there was an internet café with a smart new sign: *SO Access*. The street beyond was lined with low-rise blocks of flats, surrounded by balding patches of grass.

I turned another corner—and found myself on a collision course. There was a middle-aged man coming the other way—deliberately not looking at me, as if I didn't exist.

That was how it felt, anyway. And it made me furious, so I scowled and kept on walking. It took me a couple of seconds to realize that the scowl was a waste of energy. My mouth was hidden and my eyes couldn't get the message across on their own. I might as well have been invisible.

For a moment, I wanted to tear off the veil and shout at him. Then it hit me that being invisible meant—POWER. He didn't know who I was. He couldn't tell what I was thinking or what I was going to do. If I chose to hold my ground, he would have to step into the gutter. Unless he was prepared to hit me full on.

I kept him guessing until the very last instant. Until his eyes flickered and I knew he was starting to worry. Then I dipped my head and stepped off the kerb. He went past as though I didn't exist, but I could tell I'd shocked him. His face gave it away.

I'd shocked myself, too. Going head to head with total strangers isn't the kind of thing I do every day. My heart was thudding hard and I was ready to give up and go home. Where on earth was Sandy? I started walking faster, turning down one street after another as I looked for her.

But I couldn't find her anywhere. I did see a couple of veiled women in the distance, but they were walking together, with a gaggle of little children. And anyway they were both half a head taller than Sandy.

I tramped on down the street and round the corner. And on and on, for twenty minutes or more. One or two people gave me odd looks, but no one spoke to me and in the end, I decided that Sandy must have gone home.

That was when I found her, of course. As I headed back towards the bus stop, I turned into the street with the internet café, and there she was, right at the other end, outside the little shop. I recognized her straight away, from the set of her shoulders— and the blatant, unembarrassed way she was staring at a couple of teenagers who were standing in between us.

They were squared up to each other like people having an argument. A girl in a headscarf and a boy with glaring eyes. They were both furious. For a second, I wondered if it was a lovers' quarrel, but somehow that didn't fit. The girl was older than the boy, and a lot taller. From the way she was looking at him, I guessed she might be his sister.

The boy said something sharp and the girl stepped backwards, thrusting her hands out as if she was fending him off. Except that she wasn't quite touching him. It was a startling movement, graceful and aggressive at the same time, and the moment I saw it, I knew why Sandy was staring.

It was the girl who'd caught her eye.

Here we go again, I thought. Sandy's famous for spotting new models to show off her clothes. She discovered Molly Parker and Siobhan a couple of years ago, and she found that trio of Polish girls for her Transparent Winter collection. Discovering amazing new models is part of the Sandy Dexter mystique.

But even by those standards, this girl was special. It wasn't just her face, though that was beautiful, with its sharp, golden-brown angles. It was the dramatic way she moved—and *stood*. Even when she was completely motionless, you had to look at her, because her whole body was alert and alive. Ready for anything.

But there was no kind of showing off about it. From that first glance, I knew she wasn't posing. She simply didn't care whether anyone noticed her or not.

You won't get this one, Sandy, I thought. *Not in a million years.*

We were in the car, ready to go back to Dad's flat, before Sandy spoke to me. As she pulled away from the kerb, she gave me a quick sideways glance.

'Well?' she said. 'How did you feel? What was it like?'

'Horrible,' I said. 'Like being cut off from the world.'

Sandy nodded and for a moment she was silent,

edging her way between two taxis. Then she said, '*Just* horrible? Or something else too?'

'We-ell—'

I didn't want to tell her, because it went against everything I'd always believed about veils. But *just horrible* would have been a lie.

'Being invisible is a kind of power,' I said. 'If people can't see you, it makes them insecure. And if you decide to use that . . . '

I didn't spell it out, because I didn't need to. Sandy was already nodding, as though she understood.

As though that was the answer she'd expected all along.

It was a long walk to the camp. Long and hot, with heavy bundles to carry. Every time one of the pack camels died, Mahmoud had to take his share of the load.

He trudged along, sometimes singing and sometimes making up an email in his head:

You always liked to visit new places, didn't you, Geri? Well, we're travelling to a new place now. And the journey's making me strong. When you come back to Somalia, you won't be able to call me 'little brother' any more . . .

Every time they went through a village, he watched for a place where he could send it, but his uncles wouldn't stop. Now they'd decided to go to the camp, it seemed they had to get there as quickly as possible. And when he asked his mother, she sighed and shook her head.

'Wait until we find out where we're going to be,' she said. 'When we know that, we can email and tell her she has to send us some money.'

So Mahmoud went on walking. On and on and on . . .

Are they giving you lots of food in England? Be careful! If you grow much taller, you won't fit into the aeroplane . . .

Abdi

Yes, I was having a row with Khadija. And she was being completely unreasonable.

OK, I'd promised to take her to Auntie Safia's shop twice a week, and meet her afterwards. Well, I'd done that, hadn't I? For a whole week I'd trailed backwards and forwards on the evenings she was working. The first time I went to collect her, it rained and I got soaked to the skin. And the second time I had to hang around for ten minutes while she finished mopping the floor. And I hadn't even complained.

But that evening was something special. My friend Rageh was off to Somalia the next day. *Being returned to the culture, to teach him better behaviour*, his mother said. He wouldn't be back for four or five months (at least!) and he'd asked me round to his farewell party. It would have been rude not to go.

'You'll have to give the shop a miss tonight,' I told Khadija. 'I won't be around to pick you up afterwards.'

She fizzed like an angry cat—completely over the top. Never mind that we were out in the street, where everyone could see. 'You can't do that to me! You promised you'd come and fetch me!'

'I said I'd give it a try, that's all. I'm not going to let it take over my whole life, am I?'

'But you can't just back out. What am I supposed to do?'

I shrugged. 'I told you. Don't go. One evening won't make any difference.'

'Yes it will. I'm still on trial. I'll lose the job if Auntie Safia thinks I'm not reliable.'

'Don't be silly,' I said scornfully.

But Khadija wasn't going to back down. She glared at me, holding herself very straight, and then took a step backwards, lifting her arms to reject the criticism.

Don't be ridiculous. That's what I was going to say. But suddenly she looked past me, over my shoulder, and her expression changed. She'd been distracted by something behind me. I turned round to take a look and—it was weird.

There was a veiled woman standing at the corner of the road, just outside the shop. She wasn't a Somali woman. And she wasn't like any veiled woman I'd ever seen before. She was standing there staring at us. Not pretending at all, just openly staring. And down at the other end of the road, by the flats where my friend Liban lives, was a second woman. She was dressed in black and wearing a niqab, just like the first one. And she was staring too.

Khadija's eyes were flickering from one woman to the other, trying to keep track of them both. *It's only a couple of women*, I thought. *What can they do?* But I didn't like it either. I stared back at the woman by the shop, trying to make her turn away.

It didn't work. In fact, it had the opposite effect. When she saw us looking, she started down the road towards us, and when she reached Khadija, she stopped and hauled up the long black skirt of her *abayad*. Underneath, she was wearing jeans and she pushed her hand into one of the pockets, hunting for something.

I frowned at her, but she didn't even notice. She was too busy looking at Khadija.

'You're Somali, aren't you?' she said.

No prizes for guessing that. Khadija's everything people think of as Somali—tall and slim, with a fine, confident face.

I stepped in between them. 'So what if we are Somali?' I said. 'That's our business.'

The woman ignored me completely. 'Hang on a minute,' she said, still talking to Khadija. 'Let me give you a card. I think I might have some work to offer you.'

Khadija's eyes flickered very bright, just for a second. But the woman didn't see that, because she was too busy fishing in her pocket. Finally she produced a white business card and held it out. Khadija stared down at the name and I read it over her shoulder— *Sandy Dexter*. The words didn't mean anything to either of us. Not then.

'I'm looking for a Somali model,' the woman said briskly, 'and you could be the person I need. If you're interested you ought to have an agency—it'll be serious money. Try this one if you don't know where to start.' She scribbled a name on the back of the card. 'Tell them I sent you—and take the card to prove it.'

'You really expect us to believe all that stuff?' I said. 'Do you think we're children?'

The woman made an impatient noise in the back of her throat. 'Check me out on the internet if you don't trust me. It's not exactly difficult. There are lots of pictures. Here.' She flipped back her veil to show a narrow, wedge-shaped face with very pale skin. Her hair stood up in short black spikes and there was a tiny blue fish tattooed beside her left eye. 'Take a good look. Make sure you can recognize me.' She let us stare for a second and then held out the card again.

Khadija didn't move.

'Think it over, OK? But don't tell anyone else except your parents. That's very important.' Crouching down, the woman laid the card on the pavement in front of Khadija. Then she straightened up and called down the road. 'Come on, Freya. Let's go home.'

I'd almost forgotten about the other woman. But she was still there. She hurried towards us and when she saw the card on the pavement, she gave a small, impatient snort. And, as the two of them walked off, I heard her mutter, 'You can't go round like that, Sandy! You look ridiculous. Pull your veil down.'

Sandy didn't care. She just laughed and disappeared round the corner with the niqab thrown back over the top of her head.

When they were out of sight, I bent to pick up the card. But I wasn't quick enough. Khadija swooped down and snatched it up, turning it over to squint at the scrawl on the back.

'What does it mean?' she said.

It was a name—*Meredith Fox*—followed by an address, written in energetic black letters. Below that was an odd little squiggle, which could have been a pair of initials. *SD.*

'What a freak,' I said. 'Do you think that's what she does all the time? Wanders round trying to pick up girls off the street?'

Khadija didn't answer. She just went on staring down at the card.

'Hey,' I said. 'Don't take it seriously. It's got to be some kind of scam.'

'But what if it isn't?' Khadija said. 'What if it's real?' She looked at the card again and then put it carefully into her pocket. 'I'm going to check her out tomorrow.'

Khadija

Ever since I arrived in England, I'd been like a frozen girl. When my father handed me over to the *hambaar* man, he sent me into a world where no one knew me, and no one cared who I was. Maamo was kind, but she didn't want to talk about Somalia. If I tried, she shook her head and turned away.

It was the same at school. Even the Somali girls didn't really understand how I felt. Some of the teachers asked me to write it down, but they had to have everything in English and what use was that?

I remember the first time Maamo sent me to fetch some ice from the fridge, I looked at the cubes that were so hard and cold, and I thought, *That's me. That's how I have to be now.*

And I was—until Sandy Dexter spoke to me.

I didn't know who she was, or why she was walking round in Muslim clothes that didn't fit the way she behaved. But when she said, 'You're Somali, aren't you?' she looked straight into my eyes. And she saw me.

No one had told her that I was Khadija, or that Abdi was my brother. She didn't want to see my papers, or ask about my clan. She just wanted—me.

I didn't understand everything she said, because she spoke so fast. But there were two words that jumped out at me. *Work* and *money*. *Shaqo* and *lacag*. As soon as she'd gone, I picked up the card and read her name. Sandy Dexter.

Abdi was very suspicious of her. He tried to say that she couldn't be trusted, but I didn't believe that. She'd looked me straight in the eye and offered me a real job. And she'd given us an easy way to check who she was. Where was the risk in that?

We checked Sandy out together, in the school library. Abdi typed her name into the computer and I leaned over his shoulder, waiting to see what happened. When the search results came up on the screen, Abdi sat up very straight, running his finger down the list.

'Look—she's in *Vogue* and *Elle* and *Grazia* and—'

I could see he was impressed, but those names didn't mean anything to me. 'Look at this one,' I said, pointing to the link at the top of the list. It looked like her own site: www.sandydexter.com

'OK.' Abdi clicked on the link and we both leaned forward as the screen went misty. Gradually— very slowly—it sharpened into words that floated round in the mist: images and storyboards . . . history . . . loose threads . . . Abdi clicked on 'images and storyboards' and the screen filled with a patch-work of pictures and music and little scraps of film.

'I don't understand,' I said. 'What's it all about?'

'Fancy clothes,' Abdi said. He pulled a face. 'For very rich people.'

I didn't see how the mist and the music could have anything to do with clothes. Before I could ask Abdi how he knew, he was back at the search results, clicking again. And again and again. He didn't leave time for me to see what he was doing—until suddenly he let out his breath and sat back in the chair.

And there she was on the screen. The woman from the street, with her pale wedge-face and the fish beside her eye.

'This is crazy,' Abdi said softly. 'She's—*famous*. Look.' He scrolled down the page, pointing at other names. *Stella McCartney. Miuccia Prada, Vivienne West-wood.* I didn't know those names either, but I under-stood from the sound of his voice that these people were very important. They were top fashion design-ers. And Sandy Dexter was one of them.

After that, we found some of the sites where her clothes were sold.

I'd always known there were very rich people in the world, but seeing how they spent their money made me feel weak. That woman, with her spiky hair and her fish tattoo, designed clothes that sold for more money than I could imagine. And she wanted me to work for her.

I could bring my whole family out of Somalia, I thought. And my heart jumped suddenly.

Abdi clicked back to the picture of Sandy's face. Then he swung round in his chair. 'What are we going to do?' he muttered.

I could hardly breathe, but I knew what the answer had to be. Whatever work Sandy Dexter was offering me, I was going to say yes. How could I miss such a wonderful chance?

'Maamo won't like it,' Abdi said. 'Remember how angry she was about your job at the shop. And Auntie Safia doesn't make you parade up and down in front of strangers, showing your legs.'

Why was he looking for problems? 'Maybe I won't have to show my legs,' I said. 'And if you think Maamo's going to be upset, let's find out some more about the job before we tell her anything. Sandy said we had to keep it secret, didn't she?'

Would Abdi do that? Could I trust him? I watched

his face, trying to see what he was going to decide. It seemed a very long time before he looked up at me.

'I suppose . . . it's sensible to find out first. Let's talk about it tonight, shall we? I'll come out of Rageh's party and walk you home from the shop.'

Freya

They decided to go for it.

I don't think I would have dared. They didn't know the first thing about fashion and they had to save up the money for their fares. But a week later they bunked off school and travelled all the way across London. At ten o'clock in the morning, they were walking into the offices of Fox.

I don't know what they expected. A huge atrium full of plants and sofas maybe, or a steel and glass fortress with a six foot doorman in uniform. But Merry doesn't go in for that kind of showing off. Just a couple of smart little offices on the fifteenth floor, and the most efficient receptionist in Europe.

Beth spends her life coping with anyone and everyone, from hopeful sixteen year olds clutching portfolios to shattered supermodels who've forgotten how to eat. They all march into her office demanding to see Meredith Fox. In person. *Now.* Beth has to protect Merry from trivialities and keep everyone happy—without missing out on the next hot thing. (Not easy, in a business where the next hot thing *always* comes out of nowhere.)

Beth's been doing that for twelve years, and she doesn't get fazed easily. But even she was startled when Abdi and Khadija walked in off the street in their school uniform . . .

I wasn't there, of course, and there was no reason in the world for me to get involved. Except that Meredith Fox is my godmother, and she's totally single-minded. Which is why I suddenly felt my phone vibrate in the middle of a boring history lesson.

The message was short and sharp. Typical of Merry. **Where's Sandy hiding???**

I couldn't risk texting a reply while the class was going on. Miss Campbell's on a personal mission to exterminate mobile phones from the face of the earth. So it was lunchtime before I rang back, and by then Merry was volcanic.

'If Sandy *has* to play stupid games, why doesn't she stay in touch? What am I supposed to do if I can't contact her?'

'Have you tried the workshop?' I said. As though Merry was too stupid to think of that for herself.

She snorted, without bothering to answer.

'Sorry.' I tried to think of something more helpful. 'Does Dad—?'

'No. He doesn't,' Merry said shortly. 'Nor does Carmel. Or Stefan. Or Marco. Or Laura. Or—'

She'd obviously made a whole string of calls already. I should have guessed. If she'd phoned me at school, *obviously* there was no one else left.

'Why do you want Sandy anyway?' I said, when she finally stopped.

There was a long, exaggerated sigh. 'One of her little white cards.'

'Oh no!' No wonder she was angry. When Siobhan did that interview for *Hello* magazine, she made a big deal out of how Sandy spotted her in Tesco's. (*She just gave me her card, with Meredith Fox's name scribbled on the back.*) Ever since then, Merry's had an endless stream of girls turning up with cards they've forged themselves. Beth weeds out most of them, but sometimes Merry has to phone Sandy and check.

It wouldn't be good to mess up and send someone away. Not if Sandy had really picked her out.

'Can't you just take some details?' I said. 'And a few photos for Sandy to see?'

'Yes,' Merry said icily. 'That *would* be sensible, *wouldn't* it? Except the wretched girl won't do anything. Not unless Sandy's there. I can't even persuade her to take the scarf off her head.'

Ohhhhhh! went my brain, finally joining the dots. It was *her*. The girl from Battle Hill.

I'd been absolutely certain she wouldn't take the bait. She hadn't looked remotely interested, not even when she saw Sandy's name on the card. I really thought we'd come across a girl who was immune to fashion.

But I was wrong. It made me want to spit.

'Freya?' Merry said sharply. 'Are you still there?'

I dragged myself back to the conversation. 'Sorry. I was just—I think this girl's genuine. I was out with Sandy last week and she did give someone a card—'

There was an impatient sigh from the other end of the phone. 'Why didn't you say so before? Get yourself over here and check her. Maybe she'll settle for you instead of Sandy. I've got a meeting in half an hour, and I don't want the place cluttered up with children.'

'But I'm at school—'

Merry knew that, of course. She just didn't care. Before I could argue, she'd hung up on me.

All right, I didn't *have* to go. I could have ignored the call. But I was curious about the girl and why she'd turned up at Fox. And—if I'm honest—I wanted to try and change her mind and stop her wasting her life on the catwalk. My French class didn't stand a chance against that.

I sneaked away while everyone was milling around buying lunch. It was a long bus journey to Fox and I spent the time working out what I wanted to say to the Somali girl. It didn't even occur to me that I might have to explain myself first. After all, it was only a week since we'd met face to face.

That was how I remembered it, anyway.

It was two o'clock by the time I walked into reception. When Beth saw me, she grinned and rolled her eyes, waving me straight through into Merry's office. As I pushed the door open, I could hear Merry talking in her crisp, no-nonsense business voice. She'd swung her chair round to face the door and she was working flat out, taking a phone call and answering her emails at the same time.

The troublesome little white card was lying in the middle of her desk and the boy and girl from Battle Hill were sitting on the far side of the room, looking awkward and uncomfortable.

And stubborn.

'Hello,' I said cheerfully. 'Remember me?'

They stared back at me, with no sign of recognition.

Merry put the phone down and spun her chair round. 'Well?' she said impatiently.

81

I went to lean over her desk. 'It's her,' I muttered.

Merry frowned. 'She doesn't seem to recognize you.'

'That's because—' *Because she's never seen my face.* I worked it out at last—but I couldn't explain to Merry. She may be my godmother, but she's not part of Sandy's team. And Sandy's always been very fierce about not telling things. *Especially not to Merry. She may be my oldest friend, but she can't resist showing off how much she knows.*

'—because she couldn't take her eyes off Sandy,' I improvised feebly.

'Hmmph.' Merry guessed I was holding out on her, of course. She spun her chair away again. 'Well, I haven't got all day to waste, even for your darling mother. If this girl won't settle for you, she can find another agency to annoy.'

She'd raised her voice, making sure the Somali girl could hear. But there was no reaction. The girl's stubborn expression didn't soften.

'Why don't I take them out for a coffee?' I said. 'If they relax a bit, they might change their minds.'

'They *might*,' Merry said.

'Or I could just go back to school,' I said. Grumpily, to remind her I had a life of my own.

She looked up at me and grinned. 'OK, OK. I know you're being a saint. And the coffee's a great idea. If you can just give me half an hour to deal with Molly, then I'll be free to think about this one. And who knows, maybe Sandy will have turned up by then.'

I grinned back and went across the room, looking as friendly as I could. 'I'm Sandy's daughter, Freya,' I said. 'Sandy won't be here for a while, so why don't we go and wait in Starbucks? I'll buy you a coffee.'

The boy muttered something and the girl frowned for a second. Then she nodded and stood up. I'd forgotten how well she moved. She reached Merry's desk in two long, elegant strides, stretching out an arm to retrieve the little white card. When it was safely in her pocket, she turned towards the door.

Don't lose her, Merry mouthed at me, behind her back.

I bought three cappuccinos and carried them over to the table. The boy had plonked himself into the only armchair, leaving the two of us to sit opposite. I could see our faces reflected in the window behind his head. Next to Khadija's darkly dramatic reflection, I looked pink and fretful. Even Dad couldn't have done anything with that face.

'I'm Freya,' I told them again, putting the coffees down. 'How about you?'

They hesitated briefly, glancing at each other, and then they gave me their first names.

'Abdi.'

'Khadija.'

That was it. One word each. I could see it was going to be tough making conversation. For a moment even French Literature started looking attractive. I took a calming breath and tried again.

'Where are you from? Do you live in Battle Hill?'

More wary glances at each other. Then Abdi said, 'Somewhere around there.'

Did they think I was some kind of spy? And even if I was, what did they have to hide? If they'd treated Merry like that, no wonder she was boiling over.

I could have ploughed on stodgily, asking one dull question after another. But that prospect made me feel so bored I wanted to *die*. Instead, I sat back in my chair and looked at Khadija over the top of my cup.

'What are you doing here anyway? Have you really decided to come and work for Sandy? And spend your life prancing along the catwalk in clothes real people can't afford?'

Khadija frowned. Then she leaned closer to Abdi, murmuring something I couldn't understand. Now I know her better, I'm sure she didn't mean to be rude, but that's how it felt.

'Doesn't she speak any *English*?' I said loudly.

Abdi glared at me. 'Of course she does. She just wants to know why you're so angry.'

That caught me off balance, and I nearly told a lie. *Of course I'm not angry.* But I was—and what did I have to lose by telling the truth?

'I'm angry because you're playing the fashion game,' I said. 'Why does a girl like Khadija want to waste her time on rubbish like that?'

I'd fallen into the trap of speaking to Abdi, because he was the one who'd answered my questions. But Khadija wasn't going to sit here and let us discuss her.

'I want a job,' she said. 'I need to earn money.' Her face was like a mask, but I could tell she was just as angry as I was.

I snapped back, automatically. 'Oh, so this is all about money, is it? You really think that's the most important thing in the world?'

As soon as the words were out, I knew how appalling they were. *Spoilt little rich girl. Sneering at someone who needs to earn a living.* Quickly I tried to repair the damage.

'It's not that simple, you know. Some models earn a lot of money, but most of them don't. And it's a hard life.'

'Hard?' Abdi said. 'What's hard about walking up and down?'

They didn't know anything. How could I make them understand? I was still trying to find the words when my phone rang.

It was Sandy. 'I'm in Merry's office. How soon can you get here?' she said.

I was so relieved that I jumped up straight away, not even waiting to finish my coffee. 'Let's go,' I said briskly. 'Sandy's waiting.'

When we arrived, Merry was still at her desk, but now Sandy was perched on the edge of it, chatting earnestly. As soon as the door opened, she stopped talking and her eyes went straight to Khadija's face.

Merry reached for the phone. 'I'll get Belinda.'

'No photographs,' Sandy said absently.

Merry stared. Even *I* stared. That was like calling someone for a trial at Manchester United and saying, 'No footballs!' What's the use of a model who doesn't come across in photographs? It's the crucial test.

Sandy didn't explain. She just nodded at Khadija. 'Walk for me,' she said. 'Walk up and down the room.'

Abdi stood back, keeping out of the way, and Khadija began, hesitantly at first and then suddenly confident. She stalked backwards and forwards with her shoulders back and her head lifted high on her long, straight neck. Not like a model at all. When models walk, everything about them says, *Look at me!*

Look at the picture I make! Khadija was just using her body to move around.

Merry watched with her lips pursed and her head on one side. Once she tried to catch Sandy's eye, but there was no chance of that. Sandy was totally focused on Khadija. Merry made a quick note on her scratch pad and went on looking.

It was quite different, the way she and Sandy did it. Merry's eyes were very lively, flicking backwards and forwards, and she kept frowning and chewing her lip. But Sandy was completely still and her face was unreadable. I had no idea what she was thinking—but I could feel her concentrating on Khadija as she walked up and down, up and down, up and down . . .

When they finally reached the camp, they were all hungry and exhausted. The rest of the camels had died on the journey and now they had nothing except what they could carry themselves.

Mahmoud's little sisters started whining when they saw the ugly, makeshift shelters lining the road. There were hundreds and hundreds of them, all jammed in close together, with children sitting around them, playing in the dust.

'Uskag,' said Zainab. Dirty. And she started to cry.

Mahmoud watched his mother's face as she gazed at the camp. Did it make her unhappy too? Was she sorry they'd walked so far to reach such a miserable place?

Her expression didn't change. She looked exactly the same as always, strong and determined and cheerful.

'Don't cry about little things,' she said to Zainab. 'This is a good place to be while the drought lasts. Let's put up our houses and then I'll go and find someone to give us food.'

But it wasn't as simple as that. People couldn't put up houses wherever they wanted to—not even little houses like theirs, made of branches and woven mats. Mahmoud's uncles had to spend hours getting permission. And when they were finally allocated a space, it was narrow and awkward, squashed in among dozens of other houses.

By the time that was done, all the food for the day

had already been given out. There was none left for people who'd just arrived.

Mahmoud looked at Zainab and Sagal. They weren't complaining any more, but their faces were thin and tired. 'Is there no food at all?' he said. 'Not even for them?'

His mother didn't answer. But she took the money they had—the little bit of money to email Geri in England—and she set off round the camp.

When she came back, the money was gone, but she had a small bundle of wood and a tiny bag of flour.

'Today—we are going to eat,' she said cheerfully. 'Tomorrow there will be more food. And somehow we'll find a way to earn money for the email to England.'

Abdi

When we went back to the Fox woman's office, I thought everything would be easy. Because the great Sandy Dexter was there—and she wanted Khadija. I walked in with my head high, expecting an apology for the way we'd been treated before.

But it wasn't like that. Instead of welcoming us and talking about work, Sandy made Khadija parade up and down while they all looked at her. There they were in a row, Sandy and Freya and the Fox, all staring.

So who was the most important? The one Khadija had to convince?

Well, it certainly wasn't Freya, even though she was Sandy Dexter's daughter. She was almost as young as Khadija and me. And anyway, she talked like a loser.

How about the Fox woman? She was the oldest, and the most like my idea of a businesswoman. Smart hair. Rings on her fingers. Expensive suit. And she behaved like a businesswoman, too, pursing her lips and narrowing her eyes as Khadija walked up and down—like someone considering a deal.

But she kept looking sideways at Sandy Dexter, waiting to hear what she was going to say. And Sandy was the designer, after all. Surely she had to be the one who gave the orders?

I just wished I could work out what she was thinking. Suppose she offered Khadija a job on the spot? Suppose she wanted a definite answer, then and there? What would we say?

None of that happened. Instead, after ten minutes or so, Sandy held up her hand to stop Khadija. Then she and the Fox went into a huddle, whispering to each other.

'She's very striking,' I heard the Fox say. 'Now if Belinda could just—'

But Sandy shook her head firmly. I missed most of what she said, but I caught the words *awkward* and *trouble-maker*. I edged away from Khadija, sidling close enough to hear properly.

The Fox woman was reluctant to give in. 'I only need a couple of pictures.'

'You'd be wasting your time,' Sandy said. She straightened up. 'I can feel the vibes, Merry. This one's a prima donna, like Veronica. Sign her if you like, but you'll regret it if you do, believe me. I certainly won't book her.'

The Fox muttered something about a waste of time and I could see that she was annoyed. But she didn't argue any more. She was going to stand up, but Sandy tapped her on the shoulder.

'Don't bother,' she said. 'I'll put these two in a taxi.' She nodded at Khadija and me. 'Come on. And you too, Freya.'

She hustled us out of the office, past Beth and into the lift. Khadija looked confused, but I was fuming. *You told us to come*, I wanted to say. *And we spent all our money— for nothing.* But the lift was down in the lobby before I could get out the words, and Sandy went straight out into the street, with her hand up to hail a taxi.

When it drew up at the kerb, she waved at us to get in.

I didn't move. 'We can't afford a taxi,' I said.

'Don't be silly,' Sandy hissed. 'Just get in. I'm coming too, and so's Freya. We need to talk—but not until we're away from here.'

What was there to talk about? She seemed to expect us to do whatever she said—without asking any questions. I frowned at Khadija, to make sure she didn't move.

'We're not coming,' I said loudly. 'Not unless you tell us what's going on.'

Sandy sighed. 'Why can't you *trust* me for a minute?'

I hate being hustled. 'We did trust you,' I said. 'We trusted you enough to skip school and spend all our money on fares. And what have we got for all that? Nothing. You've already said Khadija's no use to you, so why do you want to talk to us? Just give us the fare to get home.'

'You don't understand,' Sandy said. 'Up there in the office, I had a fantastic idea about how I could use Khadija. It's the key to my whole collection.'

I didn't believe her. 'Then why did you say you weren't going to sign her?'

'Because my idea won't work unless it's a secret,' Sandy said impatiently. 'And I can't trust Merry Fox not to give it away. So we have to cut her out, and trust each other. Why is that so difficult?'

'Maybe *you* have to trust *them* first,' Freya interrupted. 'If you take a risk—'

The taxi driver opened a window and leaned across to call through it. 'Look, love, do you want a cab or not? I can't hang around all day.'

Freya pulled the door of the taxi open and looked at Sandy. 'Suppose we go to the workshop,' she said. 'You can show them what you're doing for the new collection.'

Sandy actually went pale. Even paler than she was already. 'You know I can't do that.'

'Why not?' Freya said. 'Don't you trust them?'

She scrambled into the taxi, beckoning us to follow her. Khadija looked at me. Should we go or not? How do you make a decision like that? In the end, it was curiosity that made me get in.

Sandy leaned through the driver's window to give the address and then slipped on to the fold-down seat and closed her eyes. The taxi lurched out into the traffic.

As it pulled away from the kerb, I glanced up at the building we were leaving. At one of the first floor windows I saw a face looking out. A sharp, well-groomed face.

The Fox woman was standing there, staring down into the street.

Had she seen me arguing with Sandy? Had she seen us all going off in the same taxi? And if she had—did it matter?

I nearly asked Sandy. Then I decided to keep my mouth shut.

Things were complicated enough already.

Khadija

I couldn't believe it when Sandy Dexter shook her head, up in the office. But there was no mistake about what she was saying. She didn't want me after all.

So what were we doing now, driving off with her in a taxi?

I leaned my head sideways and whispered to Abdi in Somali. 'What's happening?'

'We're going to Sandy's workshop,' he whispered back. 'And that's some kind of big secret. I don't think she usually lets people see what she's doing. So keep your mouth shut and your eyes wide open.'

It still didn't make sense. 'Why is she taking us there if she doesn't want me to work for her?'

'Of course she wants you,' Abdi said. 'But that's a secret too.'

So many secrets.

It felt as though we'd wandered into another country, with different rules. A small, cramped country, where everything had to be hidden. I closed my eyes, longing for the simple, clean spaces of the open desert.

When I opened my eyes again, the taxi was pulling up outside a tall, grimy building in a narrow street. That wasn't my idea of where Sandy Dexter would work. I thought she would have a wide, airy room, full of glittery mirrors and models like gazelles, with her name written up outside in golden letters.

But there was no sign at all. Just a plain wooden door with a bell beside it.

Sandy paid the taxi driver and jumped out, reaching for her key. 'We're here,' she said. 'Come and meet Carmel.'

Carmel was young and bright, with red hair and long, dangling earrings. She sat at a desk just inside the door, guarding the way through into the rest of the building. She looked up quickly when we walked in with Sandy.

'Hi, Freya,' she said. 'And—?'

'They're called Abdi and Khadija,' said Sandy, 'and they're not here. OK? If you ever see them again you won't recognize them. We're going upstairs.'

Carmel smiled, raising her eyebrows at us. 'Hello,

invisible people. You must be pretty special. Hardly anyone gets to go up there.'

Sandy was already hurrying us past the desk. As she led the way upstairs, Carmel called after her.

'Are you here if anyone phones?'

'Not just now,' Sandy called back. 'You have no idea where I am.'

Secrets everywhere.

The first set of stairs took us up to the main work-room. It was a jumble of tables and racks and machines, with scribbled drawings stuck up on the walls. There were no models. Only a dozen busy women, sewing furiously, with scraps of cloth and thread littered round their feet. And a tall, solemn man at the back, cutting out shapes from a roll of beautiful, bright material.

They weren't expecting visitors. When Abdi and I walked in, they stopped work and looked up quickly, and two of them glanced round the room, to check what we could see.

Sandy waved at them all. 'No worries,' she said cheerfully. 'Abdi and Khadija aren't here. You haven't seen them.' She caught hold of my arm and pulled me towards her. 'Look around,' she said softly. 'You can go anywhere you like. And when you've seen enough we'll go up to my studio.'

At first, I couldn't see anything to look at. Only a

mess of jumbled shapes and colours. The tall man with the scissors was watching me, as if I made him anxious.

'It's all right, Etienne,' Sandy said. 'I'll come and tell you all about it.' She left me on my own and went down the room to talk to him, bending over his table and lowering her voice.

'He's a brilliant cutter,' Freya muttered. 'But he's got Asperger's and he doesn't like surprises.'

I didn't understand what she meant. I didn't understand anything about this place or the way people behaved.

Freya gave me a little push. 'Don't worry about him. Go and look at Sandy's secrets. You'll never get a chance like this again.'

'That's right,' Abdi muttered in my ear. 'Check out what they're doing.'

I felt awkward about walking around and looking at people while they were working. But there was a rail full of clothes on the far side of the room, away from the tables. I went across to look at those. And they were just as strange as everything else.

There were lots of different shapes—dresses and coats and jackets, long and short, wide and narrow— but nothing was finished off properly. All the seams were rough and untidy. And everything was the same colour. The no-colour of unbleached material.

Was this the big secret? No colour? Why would anyone pay for clothes like that?

Beyond the rack, a tall padded dummy stood in one corner of the room. It was draped round and round with a long piece of material. I'd seen my grandmother dressed like that once or twice, a long time ago—but this cloth was different. More like the red and white pattern my father wears when he's in Somali clothes.

I went over and touched it, and the feel of the *suuf* cloth under my fingers made my throat ache with longing. There are things you don't even know you've missed, until you find them again.

On the other side of the room Abdi pulled a face, to let me know he was bored. Sandy turned round and saw him, and she laughed.

'Not what you were expecting? Let's go upstairs now and see if that makes more sense.'

The second staircase took us up into a small, dark passage with a row of closed doors running along one side. Sandy opened the first door and put her head into the room.

'Hi, Stefan,' she said. And a young man looked up and blinked at us.

He was very thin, and so fair that he was almost white all over, except for his pale blue eyes. When those eyes found me, they suddenly filled with light.

'Is this her?' he said.

'This is her.' Sandy waved us into the room—with Freya tagging on at the back—and pulled the door shut behind us. 'She's come to take a look around.'

'Please!' Stefan said eagerly. 'What can I show you? You want to see some sketches?' He opened a folder and sent a pile of scribbled papers spilling across his table. Abdi went to look at them, but I'd seen something else.

On the wall behind Stefan's table was a long board covered in pictures and pieces of material. Familiar things that deepened the ache I'd felt when I touched the cloth downstairs. I recognized the long sweep of a camel's neck, scrawled in black on a sheet of yellow paper. And two photos of nomad houses humped beside a dusty road. What were things like that doing in a fashion designer's studio? Stepping past the table, I went to see what else was pinned up on the board.

There was a scrap of faded blue cloth, like the sail of an old dhow.

A carved wooden comb and an amber necklace, tied up with a piece of string.

A fan of pink hoopoe feathers, tipped with black and white.

And a bright cotton shawl, looped over one corner of the board.

Everything was placed very carefully, so that

the curves echoed each other and the colours sang together. There was a faint smell of incense coming from the shawl. I picked up one edge of the cloth and breathed it in, remembering how my mother's shawl slipped from her head as she leaned over the incense burner, catching the scent in her hair.

The smell pulled at my heart. 'Somali,' I muttered to Abdi, under my breath.

He didn't understand. How could he, when he had never been to Somalia? He'd never sat in the desert under the stars, breathing in the incense smoke while someone began an old, familiar story.

Once there was a man who had three wives . . .

Sandy can't have understood either, but when I spoke, her face lit up with excitement. 'That's right,' she said. 'They're Somali. Do you get it now?'

I didn't know what I was supposed to get. But one thing was clear, from the way she looked at her notice board.

She had fallen in love with my country. And she'd realized how beautiful it is.

Freya

I hadn't been into the workshop for weeks, so it was the first time I'd seen Sandy's Somali mood board. Frankly it was—*embarrassing*. There was hardly anything there. Just a photo of refugee shelters, a crude sketch of a camel (done in ugly black crayon) a bunch of feathers and cheap jewellery, and some garish second-hand fabric that wasn't even cleaned.

What was inspiring about those?

Abdi obviously felt the same. He gave the board one unimpressed glance and went back to sorting through Stefan's sketches. But he didn't say anything.

If I'd walked into somewhere strange, the way he and Khadija had, I would have asked about *everything*. Take the rack of toiles in the workshop, for example. Those look really weird if you don't realize they're just mock-ups—done to test the design before someone cuts into expensive material. *Why are they all the same colour? Why aren't they finished?* Those are the sort of questions Khadija should have been asking. But the only word she said was *Somali*.

I think Stefan was puzzled too. He was watching Abdi leaf through the sketches and it was pathetically clear that they didn't mean anything to him. But still—no questions.

Stefan leaned towards me, whispering like a conspirator. 'These two know what Sandy is thinking? Her idea for the collection?' He has a way of raising one eyebrow that turns his whole face into a question mark.

I shook my head. 'You're probably the only person in the world who really knows that.'

The question mark resolved itself into an expression of luminous joy. 'It is a most beautiful concept. Simple and beautiful.' He picked up his pen and started drawing again, but I could see him watching Khadija out of the corner of his eye, as if she was the incarnation of Sandy's beautiful concept.

Khadija spent a long time looking at the pathetic mood board. When she turned round, Sandy smiled at her. 'Seen enough?'

'It's good,' Khadija said. 'I like these things.'

'So—will you come back and work for me?' Sandy said. 'When I need you?'

Abdi lifted his eyes from the drawings. 'We haven't decided,' he said. 'Are you going to pay her?'

103

Stefan's pale forehead wrinkled, as though he'd heard something rude, but I remembered what Khadija had said in the coffee shop and it seemed like a sensible question.

'Well?' I said to Sandy. 'Are you going to start talking business?'

'I need Khadija's parents here for that,' Sandy said impatiently. She looked back at Abdi. 'Can you bring them next time you come?'

Abdi hesitated and he and Khadija looked at each other.

Sandy frowned. 'You've got a couple of months to convince them. The show's not until September. But remember—this has to be a secret. If you start telling other people about it, the whole thing's off. Understand?'

'Of course we won't tell,' Abdi said, sounding insulted. 'We know how to keep secrets.'

Sandy nodded. 'Good. Because this one's vital. In fact—'

She broke off suddenly and went to riffle through some things on a shelf. When she came back, she was carrying a bundle of black cloth. A bundle I recognized.

'Take these with you,' she said to Khadija. 'And wear them when you come back here. Whenever you're anywhere near me, your face has to be hidden. No one must ever know who you are.'

How was that going to work? Have you *seen* what it's like backstage at a catwalk show? There are people everywhere. Dressers, stylists, hairdressers, make-up people, photographers—everyone you can think of and more. And the models are right in the centre of it all, taking clothes on and off without any inhibitions. Sandy knew that even better than I did.

So how could she say *No one must ever know who you are?*

Abdi didn't get it either. 'If no one's going to see her face, what's the point of it all?' he said.

But Sandy wouldn't explain. She just smiled and picked up the phone. 'Carmel, we need a taxi,' she said. 'To go to Battle Hill.' She gave Abdi a grin. 'Don't worry. I'll pay for this one too.'

As soon as the taxi arrived, she took the two of them down to meet it. And when they'd gone, she came running up again, with a piece of paper in her hand.

'It's going to happen!' she said excitedly. 'I'm *sure* Khadija will do it. Did you see the look on her face?'

She pinned the scrap of paper to the mood board with a scarlet-headed pin. Even from the other side of the room I could read what she'd scrawled in her big black script. A single letter—*A*—and then his mobile number.

'This is going to be good,' she said. 'Stefan—'

She went across and crouched beside his chair, talking very fast in a low voice. For the first few seconds I saw Stefan's question mark expression again. Then his face cleared suddenly and he reached for a sheet of paper. They both began to draw, one at each end of the sheet, glancing backwards and forwards at each other's sketches.

I stood and watched for a moment, but neither of them took any notice of me. So I left, to catch the bus home.

Dad got the backlash, of course. I marched up and down his kitchen, ranting while he cooked my tea.

'It's like a cult in that workshop! All Sandy has to say is *You didn't see these two people* and they all wipe their memories. Without even knowing why.'

Dad gave the stir fry a flip and squeezed on the sauce. 'She's always been big on secrets. People expect a surprise when they come to her shows.'

'But it's not about anything *real*!' I picked out a piece of red pepper and ate it angrily. 'Look at all this Somalia stuff of hers. There's a whole country there— a whole *culture*—but she doesn't care about that. She's just ransacking it for *design ideas*.'

'Well, she is a designer,' Dad said mildly. 'If you

want a human rights campaigner, you'll have to go looking for a new mother.'

'I don't want a new mother! I just want her not to be so—so *self-centred*! She thinks the whole world was made for her to exploit.'

Dad scooped the food on to two plates and put them on the table. 'Don't exaggerate. She doesn't exploit anyone.'

'Yes she does!' I glared at him. 'She exploits *you*, for a start. When she's doing a collection, she expects you to drop everything and look after me. As if you didn't have your own work. As if—'

'Stop,' Dad said. 'Stop it.' He put his hands on my shoulders and pushed me into the chair. 'Now eat your dinner. And listen to me.'

I scowled and picked up my fork.

'That's better.' Dad sat down opposite me. 'You don't remember my sister Meg, do you?'

'Not really,' I said. She died when I was four. There were a few old photos, but no one ever seemed to talk about her. 'She looks nice in the pictures.'

'She wasn't *nice*.' Dad made a funny little sound, half-laugh and half-hmmph. 'She was wild and selfish and self-destructive. Into drink and drugs and big on emotional blackmail. Not like Sandy at all, except—'

Whatever the exception was, it still got to him, even after all that time. He had to stop for a second and

I stopped too, with my fork halfway to my mouth, wondering what he was going to say.

'Meg made all our lives a misery,' he said at last. 'But she was a singer. And when she sang—when she sang *live*, on stage—all the rubbish just dropped away and you heard something that was pure truth. But it came at a price, and she wasn't the only one who paid.'

'And you think Sandy—?'

'Sandy's hard on both of us. I'm not pretending she isn't. But what she does is who she *is*. And if she was different there wouldn't be—' He spread his hands.

'Wouldn't be what?' I was still angry. 'Six more trouser designs and a new bias cut? It's not enough, Dad. And what does it cost *her*? She doesn't suffer like Meg. She hasn't been to Somalia, and seen the children with no legs, and the towns that are shelled to bits. That's what she ought to do, if she wants to be *cutting edge*. If she wants to *explore the interface with reality*.' I pushed my plate away and stood up.

Dad watched me walk towards the door. I was halfway through when he said, 'You know—she does love you.'

'You reckon?' I said, without turning round.

Then I stamped into my room and slammed the door. The laptop was blinking away on my desk and

I sat down and banged out an email to Sandy, letting the words spill out of my head and on to the screen.

```
All you do is use people. You don't
care about Abdi and Khadija. Or Somalia.
You're just a parasite, latching on to
other people's troubles for a cheap fashion
thrill. I'm sick of all those journalists
banging on about the risks you take. Why
don't you go to Somalia? That would be a
REAL risk!
```

I clicked Send without re-reading the message. Sandy wasn't likely to see it anyway. Not when she was designing. Next time Carmel trawled through the inbox, she'd probably just delete it, without even showing Sandy.

It wasn't easy for Mahmoud to send his email. Someone had rigged up a connection, at the other end of the camp, but—of course—you had to be able to pay. And they had no money left, and nothing they could sell.

His mother did what she could. Each time they were given their ration of food, she saved some of her own share and made pancakes to sell, to people who had more than they did. There weren't many people like that, and they couldn't afford to buy much, but every week she managed to save a little more.

Until the fight smashed into their house.

It was a stupid fight—just half a dozen frustrated young men lashing out at each other—but it was enough to wreck the house Mahmoud's family had built. The poles were knocked out of the ground and heavy feet broke the flour bag and trampled the food into the dirt.

Zainab and Sagal screamed and cried, and Mahmoud and his mother darted into the middle of the fight, trying to save their food and their precious water. Mahmoud's face was bruised by a kick meant for someone else, and his mother was knocked sideways against a rock that broke her finger.

The fight was broken up a few minutes later, but by that time most of their flour was spoilt and one of the water bottles was cracked and leaking. They would have to use all the money they'd saved just to keep themselves alive until the next lorry load of food was delivered.

That was a very bad time. Mahmoud was afraid his mother would lose heart and stop struggling. For the first time, he saw how tired she was, and how thin, and he wondered how she could manage to keep going.

But she did. When the fight was settled, she disappeared into the camp to find people who would sell her some of their food. And as soon as she came back, she started rebuilding the house, calling to Mahmoud and his sisters to come and help.

'We'll lose everything if we start complaining,' she said. 'This is a time to work. Don't worry. Things will get better, one day.'

There was no hope of replacing the broken poles that made the framework of their house, but she worked out a way to use them as they were. She and Mahmoud put up the new framework, and she sent the girls to hunt for scraps of polythene, to mend the mats that were their walls.

Then they all sat together, repairing the mats. And while they worked, she told them their favourite stories and reminded them that life was going to get better.

Mahmoud struggled to believe what she said. Ever since he could remember, he'd been hearing about that better life—some time in the past or the future. But it was never now. It was always just out of reach.

The only time he felt hopeful was when he thought about Geri. He knew she wouldn't forget them. One day she would come back and rescue them from the camp, with enough money to buy new camels, and guns to keep them safe.

Of course she would rescue them.

Why else had she gone away?

Abdi

Driving home in the taxi was like travelling from one life to another. When we left Sandy's workshop, I was actually thinking about how to tell Maamo where we'd been. Surely she would understand what an amazing opportunity Khadija had? And it wasn't just Khadija. The link with Sandy could transform everything, for our whole family. All I had to do was make Maamo see that.

But that was just a fantasy, of course. When we reached the road to Battle Hill, I was still struggling to think of a plan. Maybe it was better to keep the secret a little longer. To avoid ruining everything.

'Drop us off here,' I said to the taxi driver. 'We can walk the rest.'

He shrugged and drew up where I pointed—round the corner from where the school bus stopped. If we walked from there, it would look as though we'd come home on the bus, the way we usually did.

That was what I thought, anyway. But it was too

late to be clever, because one of the teachers had noticed that Khadija and I were both absent. She'd asked Fowsia if we'd caught the bug that was going round—and Fowsia hadn't had enough sense to keep her mouth shut when she got home.

When we walked into the flat, Uncle Osman and Auntie Safia were sitting in the kitchen with Maamo. There was no sign of the girls. Just the three adults, waiting for us to come home. As soon as I saw them, and the way they looked up at us, I knew there was going to be trouble.

'Where have you been?' Uncle Osman said.

'We've been to school,' Khadija said quickly.

How stupid can you be? Why did she think they were waiting for us? They were bound to know she was lying.

I did what I could to repair the damage. 'Khadija went off site—to the library,' I gabbled. 'She wanted something for a project, but I saw she hadn't signed out. So I went to get her back and—'

I had the whole story in my head, and it was almost convincing. But Uncle Osman looked me straight in the eye and the words evaporated.

'Sit down,' he said. 'In that chair. And you there, Khadija.'

We sat beside each other, facing him across the table. If only we'd had the sense to make up a proper cover story! It was too late for lies now—but we couldn't tell the truth either. *Remember—this has to be a secret*, Sandy had said. *If you start telling other people about it, the whole thing's off.*

It had seemed such an easy thing to promise. *Of course we won't tell.* But I hadn't reckoned on having to face Uncle Osman. And seeing Maamo shake her head at us, as if we'd robbed a bank. What were we going to say to them?

Auntie Safia leaned across the table. 'Where did you take Khadija?' she said gently. 'You must be careful, Abdi. Remember—she's not really your sister.'

That hadn't even occurred to me. It was so ridiculous that I almost laughed out loud. 'It was nothing like that.'

Khadija looked outraged. 'Me and *Abdi*? How could you even think—?'

'It's not what *we* think,' Maamo snapped, the way she does when she's worried. 'It's what everyone else thinks. Your father's trusting us to look after you.'

Khadija slapped her hand down on to the table. 'You do look after me. And I haven't done anything.'

'So—where have you been?' Uncle Osman said again.

Have you ever been cornered by a gang, in a blind alley? That was how I felt. There was no way out.

Uncle Osman wasn't going to give up until he knew where we'd been—and we couldn't tell him that. I looked desperately at Khadija.

She did the one thing I hadn't thought of. She told the truth. 'I've been offered some really good work. It's honest and well paid and I think I can earn enough to bring my whole family over here.'

'All of them?' Uncle Osman raised his eyebrows. 'I didn't know honest money was so easy to earn.'

'What have you got yourselves mixed up with?' said Maamo.

Khadija sat up straighter. 'It's a secret.'

That was like setting off a bomb, of course. Auntie Safia gasped with shock and Maamo went crazy.

'How can you be so *foolish*!' she shouted. 'Why would anyone honest ask you to keep a secret from your mother?'

Don't lose your temper. I forced myself to stay ultra-calm. 'I know it sounds bad, Maamo, but that's what we promised. And there is a good reason. Just trust us. Please.'

Maamo snorted, as though I'd said the most stupid thing in the world, but Uncle Osman looked at me thoughtfully.

'Promises are serious things,' he said. 'And I know you're a sensible boy, Abdi. So maybe we *should* trust you.' He chewed his lip for a moment and then

116

nodded at Khadija. 'Why don't you go and fetch your sisters? They're round at our house.'

Was he saying we could keep our secret? I was astounded. Khadija looked startled too, but she got to her feet and headed for the door.

I stood up to go with her, but Uncle Osman stopped me, with a tiny movement of his head. He waited until Khadija was out of the flat and then his eyes sharpened and he held out his hand.

'Give me your phone,' he said.

'What?' I stared at him.

He didn't say it again. Just sat there, with his hand out and a grave, patient look on his face. I wanted to refuse, but I knew he was only trying to do what was right. Since my father disappeared, he'd helped us dozens of times—without asking for anything in return.

I took out my phone and balanced it on the palm of my hand. 'I have to keep my promise,' I said feebly.

'I'm not asking you to break it,' Uncle Osman said. 'Just looking for another way to protect you. And it's not just you, Abdi. What you do affects the rest of us too.'

I knew what he meant. Whenever a Somali does something bad, people stick a label on the whole community. *Somalis are proud . . . Somalis stick up for each other . . .* There are dozens of them. Working for

Sandy wasn't exactly bad, but it could certainly add a new label to the list. *Somalis are great on the catwalk.* I couldn't see Uncle Osman going dizzy with delight about that.

I dropped my phone into his hand and his fingers closed round it. 'You're a good boy,' he said. 'Make sure you stay that way. And I'll see what I can do to help Khadija's family.'

A few days ago, I would have believed him. Until then, I'd thought he was a really powerful, important man who could make big things happen. But that was before I'd stuck my nose into Sandy Dexter's world. Now I knew that I'd spent my whole life inside a narrow box. All the real power and money were outside—and that was where I wanted to be.

So I smiled at Uncle Osman as he put my phone in his pocket, and I tried to look as though I'd given in. But all the time, my brain was working hard, trying to work out a way round this latest problem.

How could Sandy find me now I'd lost my phone?

Khadija

Maamo and Uncle Osman were angry, but they didn't shout and scream. No one hit us, or locked us up in the house. They just took away Abdi's phone.

And rearranged my life.

It was all done very calmly. The next day, Auntie Safia came round with a pair of trousers she wanted Maamo to alter. I was washing up at the sink and, while Maamo looked at the trousers, Auntie Safia sat down at the table—slowly and comfortably, the way she did everything.

'You're a good girl,' she said, after a moment. 'I'm pleased with how you work in the shop. If you want to make some money for your family, I'll pay you to do a bit more.'

'But—' It was only a few days since she'd said *Twice a week is all I need.*

She was watching my face. 'If you come in every day, I'll pay you—thirty pounds a week!' She beamed, as though she was offering me a bucket full of gold.

I almost laughed out loud. *Thirty pounds a week? Don't you know how much I could be earning soon?* But I understood what she was doing. She and Maamo were trying to fill up all my time. I was going to be shut away from trouble, like a rackety she-camel behind a thick thorn fence. And thirty pounds was the juicy bait they were dangling, to make me agree.

I almost refused. But, just in time, I realized that would be stupid. If I wanted to keep any freedom, it was important to make them trust me. So I smiled back eagerly at Auntie Safia.

'Yes, I'll do it. Thank you very much.'

The next moment, Maamo came bustling back into the kitchen. She glanced at us both and Auntie Safia gave a quick little nod. So I was right. They'd planned it together. *Abdi's not going to be pleased*, I thought. *Now he'll have to fetch me every night.*

Whenever I went to the shop, I could feel Auntie Safia watching me. Looking for clues to help her guess what *good, honest work* I could have been doing instead. But I didn't give anything away. I just did whatever she asked—and there was plenty of that. When Abdi came to collect me, he always had to wait by the door while I finished cleaning windows or stacking shelves.

Every Saturday evening, for three weeks, Auntie Safia paid the money she'd promised. She counted out one twenty pound note and ten pound coins, laid them on the counter and checked them carefully. Then she snapped her purse shut.

'You're a good girl,' she said. 'I'm sorry I can't afford any more.'

On the fourth Saturday, there was a surprise. Auntie Safia didn't close her purse when she'd taken out the money. Instead, she looked up and smiled.

'I was telling Suliman how hard you work,' she said, 'and he thinks you deserve a bonus. So there's something extra for you this week.'

What was she going to do? Give me a tin of beans?

She took a folded piece of paper out of her purse. 'If you go into the café when Suliman's there, he'll give you a free hour on one of his computers. Monday evening's the best time, he says. Because it's quiet.'

I took the paper carefully. It wasn't money, but I'd be glad to have a whole private hour on the internet, with no one peering over my shoulder. *Hey, Khadija, are you a fashion geek?* I didn't dare to visit Sandy's website on the school computers, in case people started asking questions. All I could do there was send emails. And once the summer holidays started I wouldn't even have that.

Abdi was already waiting outside the shop. I slipped the money into one pocket and the folded paper into another before I went to meet him.

'Did she pay you?' he muttered under his breath.

I nodded and patted my pocket, but I didn't tell him what else I had—in case he had other ideas about how to use my precious sixty minutes. Those were for me. I'd earned them. All I had to do now was find a way of going to the café on my own, without having to explain.

I thought that would be a problem, but when I walked into the shop on Monday evening, Auntie Safia had already washed the floor. It was glistening wet and she was kneeling on a rubber mat, refilling the shelves.

'Please,' I said. 'That's my work.'

She looked up and smiled. 'I've done some for you—because Suliman says this is a good time for you to use a computer. So—off you go. You can come here afterwards.'

'But—' I wasn't quite sure what she meant.

'Don't worry. You won't lose any money.' She smiled again, waving me away.

It was almost too good to be true. I wanted to get on

to the computer. I slipped out of the shop, as quickly as I could, and went next door to the café.

Suliman was there himself. He has four or five shops, I think, all run by managers, but that night he was the only person working there, with just a couple of customers sipping coffee and checking their email. When I walked in, he was busy on his own computer and he kept me waiting while he finished a message. Then he jumped up and waved me to a seat right at the back.

'This one's for you,' he said. 'Do you need any help?'

'Of course not!' Did he think I was a fool? I sat down and logged in straight away. Before he was back at the front of the shop, I'd started typing my email.

```
Iska waran, Mahmoud?

It's so long since you wrote to me!
What's happened? I hope and pray you are
all well and that you have found some
pasture for the animals.

I have a job working in the shop here,
which means I can send some money soon.
It's not much, but—
```

But.

My fingers hung in the air over the keyboard. *Don't tell anyone*, Sandy had said. But Mahmoud was far, far away in Somalia—where no one had ever heard

123

of Sandy Dexter. And I wasn't going to give her name anyway. Not even to Mahmoud. I just wanted him to know that there was hope. That, very soon, I might be able to take him away from the drought and the fighting.

The other customers had started talking to each other. When I looked round, I saw that Suliman was right at the front of the café, bent over his own computer. No one was near enough to read my screen as I went on typing. I felt very safe.

```
-but I've been offered another job
too. Much better. You know Iman, the
famous Somali model? Well, I have been
offered work like hers! By a very VERY
famous fashion designer. Now I know you
are laughing to think of your sister the
giraffe being like Iman, but believe me
it's true. I can't tell you more now,
because it's a big secret, but I think it
will really happen because she wants me,
this designer, and she is a person who
always gets what she wants. It's best if
you don't tell anyone about this, but I
wanted you to know that it won't be long,
insh'Allaah, before I can give some real
help. So go on making your terrible jokes
to keep everyone happy, little brother.
```

THINGS ARE GOING TO CHANGE!!!
From your sister in England.

It was done. Before I had time to think any more, I'd pressed the button and sent it. Suliman looked up suddenly, almost as though he'd seen me do it. That had to be impossible, but it reminded me to take care. I opened up a Somali news page and kept it minimized, ready to pull up if anyone came snooping down the café. Then I found sandydexter.com and clicked on *collections*.

I wanted to know some more about the clothes Sandy made. Not what they cost—I'd seen that already—but how she liked them to look. It took me a while to find the right part of her website, but when I did it was all there. Pictures of every collection she'd ever made.

They were strange and amazing. Beautiful, wild clothes, completely different from anything you'd see out on the street. And the girls who wore them were different too, with narrow, bony faces and distant, proud expressions. White skin and black skin, lips coloured yellow and purple and blue, hair twisted into elaborate fantasy shapes.

I tried to imagine myself walking like them, with my head uncovered and my legs long and bare. I hated the idea. Sandy had said, *No one will see you*, but what did that mean? I didn't understand any of it.

It had to work, though—somehow. Because the time was seeping away, like water into dry earth.

I was still staring and wondering when Suliman stood up suddenly and came down the café. *Jump!* went my heart. Quick as a hawk dropping out of the sky, I shut down Sandy's page and pulled up the news site.

It was a good thing I did. A second later, Suliman was standing right behind me. The shadow of his face fell across my computer, with his big nose pointing straight at the screen.

'Your time's just about up,' he said, looking over my shoulder at pictures of pirate ships in the Gulf of Aden.

'I've had a whole hour?' I couldn't believe it, but when I looked up at the clock I saw he was right.

'That's a lot of time to spend reading bad news.' He nodded at the headlines.

'It's our country,' I said, shutting down and pushing back my chair. Not a full-face lie, but enough to make him think that's what I came for. 'We should know what's happening. I just wish there was something better.'

'That day will come,' Suliman said fiercely.

It almost sounded like a promise, and he looked down at me as though he expected a reply. But what could I say? None of us knew what was going to happen. I stood up, without answering, and he stepped back to let me go.

* * *

The next day, Auntie Safia said something strange.

I was kneeling in front of a low shelf, filling it up with packets of rice. She came up behind me and leaned over my shoulder to straighten one of the packets.

'What would you do,' she asked, 'if I paid you five hundred pounds?'

I twisted round to see her face, because surely she was joking. But no. She looked into my eyes, as if she wanted an answer.

'Five hundred pounds?' I couldn't think how to reply. It was such a strange question.

'Or a thousand.' She shrugged, as if the difference was nothing. 'What would you buy?'

'I wouldn't buy anything,' I said. 'I'd send it back to my mother. For Mahmoud and my sisters.'

It was the first time I'd spoken Mahmoud's name out loud since I came to England. It made me feel like crying and I turned back quickly towards the shelf, to hide my face. When I pushed at the packets of rice, one of them burst open, spilling hard white grains across the floor.

'I'm sorry,' I said hastily. 'I'll sweep it up.'

I started scrambling to my feet, but Auntie Safia had fetched the broom before I could reach it. She began sweeping up the rice herself and I knelt down again and brushed the loose grains off the shelf with my hand, keeping my head bent low.

Suddenly the broom stopped.

'What do you really want?' Auntie Safia said softly.

I want to go home, I thought. *I want to be back in Somalia.*

But if you speak words out loud, you can never take them back. And what's the point of longing for something impossible? I straightened the last packet and sat back on my heels.

'I want to get a good education,' I said. 'So I can help my family.'

I heard Auntie Safia take a long, deep breath. 'Of course you do,' she said. 'You're a good girl, Khadija. And we'll do our best to look after you.' For a moment she just stood there behind me. Then the swish and scrape of the broom started up again.

When Abdi came for me, the sky was dark. And it was raining so hard that the gutters were streams of water.

Freya

I spent the next couple of months living with Sandy. At least, I went back and stayed in her flat. She came there to sleep—most nights—and she sometimes ate the odd meal, if there was food in the fridge. But she was designing hard and spending all her spare time in meetings, so I didn't see her very much.

I'm not griping. That's par for the course. She's worked ten times as hard as everyone else, since before I was born. That's why I chose to live with her when I was old enough. If I'd moved in with Dad, I might not have seen her for weeks on end.

So living with Sandy is my choice—but it can be lonely. I don't miss the gruesome au pairs, of course, but I spend a lot of time on the phone to my friend Ruby. And Dad usually asks me round for a meal two or three times a week.

That's where I was when Sandy finally connected with my email.

I'd almost forgotten it by then. When she bounded into Dad's flat, waving a hard copy, I was so surprised that I nearly fell off my chair.

'This is brilliant!' she said. She was so excited she was shouting. 'You're a bloody *genius*, Freya! I was driving myself mad trying to work out a way of grounding this collection—and then I found this in my inbox. It's the perfect idea!'

She flapped the paper and I glimpsed a few stray words—and remembered my furious ranting.

. . . don't care . . . just a parasite . . . a REAL risk . . . But I still had no idea what she was talking about.

Dad didn't even try to understand. He grabbed hold of her elbow and pulled her into a chair. 'What you need is some food,' he said. 'You look as though you haven't eaten for days. *Weeks.*' He started spooning pasta into her mouth, as fast as he could—to make up for all the time she'd spent living on smoothies and crisps.

Sandy swallowed impatiently, waving her hands and talking with her mouth full. 'It wasn't comfortable reading this,' she said, flapping the wretched email again. 'But I know what you mean. I *really do know*, Freya. It's about being authentic, isn't it? About confronting reality, not just playing around with ideas. And that's right at the *heart* of what I'm doing at the moment. Showing and hiding, veils and faces . . . '

She went on and on and on and after two or three minutes, I lost the will to live.

' . . . the clothes will have ten times as much impact in their true context,' she was saying now.

What was that supposed to mean? I saw her mouth opening and closing, but I let the words flow into my ears without bothering to decode them.

Until Dad suddenly dropped the spoon and said, 'You're going to do *what*?'

My brain jolted back into gear, scanning the last fragments of sound, and I realized what Sandy had just said. *We're going to do the catwalk show in Somalia.*

There was a terrible silence, like a black hole. Then Dad said, 'How can you? No one will come.'

Sandy looked smug. 'They won't need to. We'll be streaming it live into London Fashion Week.'

'Right,' Dad said. I could hear him struggling to keep his voice light. 'And where *exactly* were you thinking of doing it from?'

'I thought Eyl would be good,' Sandy said calmly.

I didn't know then that's where the pirates are based. But Dad did, and he went pale. 'Don't be stupid. You're not a reporter, Sandy. You're a designer. You make *frocks*.'

Sandy didn't answer. She just sat there, looking quiet and determined. When Dad tried to feed her another spoonful of pasta, she shook her head politely—and Dad did something I'd never heard before.

He *shouted* at her.

He banged the spoon into the pasta, spattering tomato sauce all over the table. Then he stood up and yelled down at her, with his voice cracking and his face turning red. 'What's happened to your brain? You've got a great career and a fantastic daughter. And you've got me, wound round your little finger, supporting every crazy idea you dream up. So what do you want to do now? You want to go off and *die*! Just for the sake of a bit of cheap publicity. Great! Thanks, San. *I'll buy your ticket, shall I?*'

She let him shout himself hoarse and then she picked up the email again. 'You've got it wrong,' she said. 'It's not about publicity. It's about what Freya said.'

He took the paper and I watched him read it, wishing I could wipe the words off the page and out of Sandy's brain. But it was too late for that. All I could do was wait for Dad's reaction.

He finished reading and looked up at me. 'Why do you have to take everything so *seriously*?' he said.

It would have been easy to say, *I didn't really mean it. I was just pissed off because Sandy ignored me.* But suddenly I knew that wasn't true.

'It's got to be serious,' I said. 'Otherwise, why have I spent my life taking second place?'

Dad looked down at his hands for a second. Then he said, 'You won't find it easy, Sandy. Have you thought about how you're going to organize the Somali end of this ridiculous plan?'

For the first time, Sandy hesitated. 'I thought—maybe I could use some of your contacts?'

'Most of my contacts are dead,' Dad said brutally. 'And anyway, I'm not going to help you risk your life. Don't even waste your time asking.'

Sandy took a long breath. 'Then I'll just have to use my own contacts, won't I?' she said. She reached in her pocket and took out another piece of paper. It was badly crumpled, but I recognized the big capital A and the mobile number.

'Suppose that doesn't work,' I said. Before I could stop myself. 'Suppose she's changed her mind—or she can't get her parents to agree?'

'She'll manage it somehow,' Sandy said. 'Trust me.' She spread out the paper and reached for Dad's telephone.

But before she could pick it up, he slapped her hand away. 'I told you,' he said. 'I'm not going to help you do this.'

Sandy shrugged. 'Please yourself.' She took out her own phone. The room was so quiet now that we heard the *tap tap* of the keys as she typed in the number.

And we heard the answering service cut in at the other end.

'Damn,' Sandy said softly. She waited a minute and then tried again. And again.

Nothing. Either the phone was flat or Abdi had switched it off.

I felt Dad relax. But he was wrong if he thought she was going to give up. She rang the number again, and this time she left a message on the voicemail. *This is Sandy. Call me. As soon as you can.*

That was all she said. Just ten words, thrown out like stones dropped into a lake. None of us guessed— none of us even dreamt—how far the ripples would spread . . .

When the men came, Mahmoud was sitting behind the tent with his sisters, scratching numbers into the dust. Sagal was struggling, but Zainab was very quick. She solved the puzzles as fast as he could write them down.

The men stopped behind Mahmoud and their shadows fell on the ground in front of him. He turned round and saw there were two of them. Tall men in jeans and T-shirts, with guns slung over their shoulders.

A second before, a dozen other children had been hanging around, watching the numbers. Suddenly they'd all vanished. Mahmoud and his sisters were alone with the strangers, hidden in an angle between two tents.

One of the men said his name. Before he had time to frown, Sagal was nodding, and it was too late to pretend he was someone else. The man flicked at the air, telling the girls to leave, and Mahmoud signed to them to go. Whatever was going to happen, they would be safer out of the way.

Until the last moment, he was waiting for a chance to run. Surely the men would relax, just for an instant, and when they did he would jump up and disappear between the tents. He knew exactly how he would do it, dodging through the narrow, twisting spaces and ducking his head until they'd lost track of him.

But they didn't relax. They kept their eyes on his face and their hands on the triggers of their guns. And, in less than a minute, they were hustling him into their car, pushing at his back so that he sprawled on to the floor. One of them jumped in after him, using his feet to keep Mahmoud's head down, and the other one leapt into the front and started the engine. The car lurched away down the road, but Mahmoud couldn't see where they were going. All he could see was the sunlight glinting along the barrel of a gun.

Abdi

Life without my phone was a nightmare. I missed out on everything.

'Course I didn't mean to leave you out,' Liban said when the others met up without me. 'Sent you a text, didn't I?'

'But I told you—I've lost my phone,' I said. 'You could have come down to tell me, couldn't you? It's not exactly a long walk.'

'OK, OK,' Liban said easily. 'But—you know how it is.'

I was finding out fast. Without a phone or a computer, it's as if you don't exist. And no one's even sympathetic. They just keep grumbling at you.

'It's a real pain not being able to call you,' Liban kept moaning. 'You have to get yourself a new phone, man. Top priority.'

That was easy for him to say. His dad was in England with a good job and Liban got whatever he asked for. He didn't understand what it was like to be hard up. Maamo was saving all our spare money for a computer now (*to help with your education*) and there was no point in asking for a phone.

Even if Uncle Osman hadn't forbidden it, by taking my old phone away.

I wasn't going to tell Liban about *that*, of course. But I kept thinking about it. Every time I went to Uncle Osman's house, I kept my eyes open, hoping to see my phone lying around. If I knew where it was, I might be able to sneak it away when Uncle Osman wasn't looking. I imagined my fingers closing round it and the familiar weight as I dropped it into my pocket.

But I never discovered where he'd put it.

Sometimes I lay awake at night, tormenting myself by wondering how many times Sandy Dexter would call before she gave up. What would she do when she didn't get an answer? Would she keep trying, or would she find another girl, instead of Khadija? I imagined a dozen different possibilities.

But not what really happened. That was totally weird.

One morning at the end of June, we were all waiting at the bus stop—Khadija and the other girls in a neat line and the boys all over the place, as usual. People are always complaining about it, because they have to push past us, and that morning, there were all the regular grumblers, like Rabi's mother and the old man with the shopping trolley.

But there was an extra one too.

Just before the bus came, Suliman's wife Amina pulled up at the kerb. She jumped out of her car and started telling us off, as if we were little kids.

'Don't you realize how dangerous it is, blocking the pavement like that? People can't get past without stepping into the road. What's that woman supposed to do with her pushchair?'

She flapped her hand, pointing behind us and we all turned round to look, but I don't know what she was fussing about. The pushchair was miles away.

'And look at all this litter!' she snapped, when we turned back. She was bending down to pick up a crisp packet. 'It ruins the whole neighbourhood. Come on. Clear it up!'

We picked up a few things, to humour her. But only while she was looking. When she drove away, Hassan dropped it all again and pulled a face at the back of her car.

'She thinks she can order everyone around. Just because she's Suliman Osman's wife.'

'She is a doctor,' I said, trying to be fair. 'Maybe she sees a lot of accident victims. That would make her a bit—'

And then my phone started ringing.

When I didn't react, Liban gave me a nudge. 'Aren't you going to get that?' he said.

I took off my backpack and there it was. In the side pocket, where I'd never have put it myself. I must have stared like an idiot, because Hassan started laughing.

'All that fuss about losing it, and it was only in your bag. Time you had your eyes tested, Abdi.'

I was only half listening, because by that time I was answering the call. But it was only a couple of voice-mail messages. Hassan was close enough to hear the first one.

Where are you, man? How many times do I have to call you?

He crowed out loud. 'Hey, that's Rageh! Phoning from Somalia!'

Suddenly everyone was crowding round to listen to my voicemail. That didn't seem like a very good idea, so I turned the phone off and slid it into my inside pocket. Luckily the bus turned up at that moment. By the time we'd all got on, Liban was jabbering about his band and the others had forgotten my phone.

But I hadn't.

How had the phone suddenly appeared in my bag? It couldn't be anything to do with Uncle Osman. If he'd wanted me to have it back, he would have given it into my hand—along with a lot of talk about trusting me to use it properly.

But if he hadn't given it back—who had?

It was break before I had a chance to listen to my messages in peace. Once the others were safely out of the way, in the queue for the drinks machine, I slipped back to the classroom.

Both the new messages were from Rageh. They were very predictable. *Come on, Abdi, phone me back. I want to hear about the football.* (Nothing about what it was like in Somalia. Which was what *I* wanted to hear.)

But there was a saved message, as well. I nearly rang off without listening to it, because I thought I must have heard it before. But something made me keep listening. And suddenly there was the voice I'd been hoping for. Very clear and businesslike:

This is Sandy. Ring me. As soon as you can.

I listened three times, just to be sure I wasn't imagining it. Then I headed off to find Khadija. She was hovering on the edge of a crowd of Somali girls and it only took a nod from me to make her peel away.

'Look what I've got.' I held up the phone to show her. 'And guess who's left a message.'

We hadn't talked about Sandy at all, not since the day my phone was taken away. But Khadija understood instantly. She went very still for a moment, and then she held out her hand. 'Let me hear it,' she said calmly.

None of the *Oh, I can't believe it!* screams you'd have got from other girls. It was as though she'd never doubted, for a moment, that Sandy would call. She took the phone and listened to the message and then she gave a small, satisfied nod.

'We should ring her back. What are you waiting for, Abdi? Do it now. That's what she says.'

'Wait a bit.' I'd been thinking hard. 'Someone saved that message—and it wasn't me. That means someone's been listening to my voicemail. And they know about Sandy.'

'*What* do they know about her?' Khadija said scornfully. 'She's not the only Sandy in the world, is she? Stop worrying about stupid things and phone her!'

It would have been crazy to do it there, where anyone could listen in, so we went back to our classroom and shut the door. I played the voicemail through again, for Khadija to hear, and then I rang Sandy's number.

She answered almost immediately. 'Abdi? Is that you?'

My heart thumped in my chest. 'Yes, this is Abdi,' I said. 'You wanted me to call you?'

'Of course I did. What took you so long?'

'I've been having a few problems with my phone.'

'Well, we need to get a move on.' I could hear the impatience in Sandy's voice. 'And I want to talk to your parents. Can we meet up on Sunday afternoon? About four?'

I imagined what Maamo would think if she met Sandy. 'Maybe,' I said carefully.

'I *have* to see your parents,' Sandy said, insistently. 'You will bring them, won't you?'

'Yes of course.' I didn't want to do anything that would put her off. 'We'll be there on Sunday.'

'Good,' Sandy said. 'But remind them it has to be secret. If they talk to anyone else, then I can't use Khadija. Got that?'

'Got it,' I said. Because that was the answer she wanted to hear.

But I couldn't help wondering what her life was like. Didn't she have any friends? Any *family*? If Maamo heard what Khadija was being offered, of *course* she would talk to other people. She'd want everyone's advice before she made up her mind.

But she wasn't going to hear. That would ruin everything.

Sandy had already moved on. 'I don't think you'd better come to the workshop. It would be better to meet somewhere more anonymous. I'll text you an address. OK?'

'OK,' I said. 'We'll be there at four.'

143

'Great,' said Sandy. And she rang off without even saying goodbye.

It was a breathless moment. Khadija and I looked at each other, and I knew we were both thinking the same thing. *What are we going to do?*

But before we could talk about it, the phone rang again. I didn't recognize the number, so I thought it must be Sandy, ringing back, and I answered straight away.

'Yes? Hello?'

It wasn't Sandy. And there was no kind of greeting. Just a rough, deep voice speaking very fast, in Somali.

'This is a message for the girl you call Khadija Ahmed Mussa. Tell her that we have her brother Mahmoud. The price for his life is ten thousand dollars.'

For a moment I couldn't say anything. My brain was staggering.

'Do you hear me?' the voice said again. 'The price is ten thousand dollars.'

There was a blare of noise in the background. Maybe a radio. And I could hear the rumble of other men talking, somewhere close by.

'Khadija hasn't—she hasn't got any money,' I said, almost choking on the words. 'She's only a student.'

At the other end, the man laughed scornfully and his voice blurred as he turned away to repeat my

144

words to the others. I heard them jeering at me from four thousand miles away.

Khadija was saying something as well, asking a question, but I couldn't cope with that. I put a hand over my ear, blocking her out, and spoke frantically down the phone. I knew they wouldn't listen, but I had to try.

'Look—Khadija goes to school with me. And at night she works in a shop, for around—' I work it out roughly, '—around fifty dollars a week. That's all she's got. How can she possibly—?'

The harsh voice interrupted me, dismissing everything I'd said—in two words. 'Sandy Dexter!'

The Somali accent was so thick that I didn't understand for a moment. When I did, my stomach lurched and I nearly threw up. Suddenly I realized how serious this was.

The man was talking briskly now, snapping instructions at me. 'In ten minutes I shall call this phone again, and I want to speak to Khadija. You understand? Make sure she's there when I ring.'

Ten minutes. We had ten minutes to think.

'I'll make sure,' I said.

'That's good.' The phone went dead in my hand and I leant against the wall, because I couldn't stand up any more. But there was no time for sitting down. We only had ten minutes.

Khadija

Abdi looked dreadful. I thought he was going to faint.

'Sit down,' I said quickly. 'I'll go and fetch you some water.'

'No!' he said. 'Don't go—'

But I was already halfway through the door. I had no idea who'd just phoned, but whatever he'd heard, it could wait a couple of minutes. He needed water—fast.

There was a queue at the water cooler in the canteen and no one seemed to be hurrying. I waited for a little while and then took a paper cup and went to fill it in the cloakroom. When I went back, Abdi was sitting down on one of the tables. He jumped up quickly.

'Listen, Khadija—'

'Have some water first,' I said. I held it to his mouth, so that he had to drink. He swallowed a couple of gulps and then pushed the cup away.

'Listen,' he said again. 'That phone call—it was from Somalia. Your—' For a moment there were no more words. Whatever he needed to say, he was struggling for a way to tell me.

And before he could find it, his phone started ringing again.

I saw his hands shaking as he picked up the phone and answered. 'Yes,' I heard him say. 'Yes, she's here.' He pushed the phone at me, without any explanation, jamming it against my ear.

And the voice at the other end said my real name.

It was like having someone grab hold of my head and wrench it round the other way. A shock went right through my body.

'Who are you?' I said. Automatically, I was speaking Somali.

'I'm the man who can save your brother's life.' It was an ugly voice. Cruel and harsh. And I didn't understand straight away. Because I was in England, I thought he was threatening Abdi.

Then there was an odd little gasp and a different voice spoke down the phone. Saying a different name.

'Geri!'

Only one person in the whole world has ever called me that. 'Mahmoud! Is that you?'

I heard him gasp again and then the words came

147

spilling out, like water overflowing from a bucket. 'They took me out of the camp. Two of them—with guns. I couldn't fight back, Geri. I *couldn't*. If there'd been only one man, then I would have tried—'

I didn't understand, but already I wanted to cry. Does he really think I'd expect him to fight a man with a gun? *Ssh*, I wanted to say. The way I used to, when he was little and he fell over. *Ssh, you're the bravest boy I know.* But he was too old for that.

And the thing that had happened was worse than tumbling over.

I interrupted his apologies, because I had to. 'Just tell me what's happened. Who are these men, and what do they want? Mahmoud?'

He didn't reply, because they'd taken the phone away from him. The cruel, ugly voice came back, and it was shouting at me.

'You want to see your brother safe? Then you must pay. We'll give you three months to get the money.'

'What money?' I said frantically. I was thinking of the little stack of coins in my room and wondering whether Auntie Safia would pay me in advance. I still didn't understand.

'We want ten thousand dollars,' the man shouted. 'When you've got it together—text this number. Then I'll phone again and tell you how to deliver the money.'

I couldn't breathe. 'Ten thousand—?'

'US dollars.'

'But I haven't got—'

'Then ask *your friend* Sandy Dexter,' said the voice from Somalia. 'Let her give it to you. Let her pay—if she wants a Somali girl to show off her body in front of the world!'

What he said after that was insulting and disgusting. The words crawled over me like insects. But I couldn't ring off, because that didn't matter. None of it mattered—except the most important thing.

'Don't hurt Mahmoud!' I shouted down the phone. 'Don't you dare—'

The man repeated my words, in a stupid, squeaky voice, and I heard all the others laughing as he rang off.

As soon as I could think, I knew I had to send a message to my family in Somalia. The computers in the library were all being used, but Abdi went and muttered something to the librarian. I don't think he told her the truth, but whatever he said must have sounded convincing because two minutes later I was sitting in front of a screen.

When I opened my inbox, there was an email there from my father. It was short and raw.

Your brother Mahmoud has been taken by
some men. We are looking everywhere to find
him, but it is impossible. They will ask
for money, and we have nothing left. You
must send what you can.

And pray that we find him soon.

I forced myself to type a reply, shivering as I
pressed down the keys. I told my father about the
men who'd phoned, but I didn't explain about
Sandy. *If you start telling other people,* she'd said, *the
whole thing's off.* I couldn't take a risk like that. Not
now I needed the money so much.

But I couldn't help remembering the last email
I'd sent, to Mahmoud. I shouldn't have done it. I'd
known that, even while I was typing the words. But
I'd sent it anyway. And—somehow—the kidnappers
must have seen it, and found out about Sandy.

It was all my fault.

Freya

I 'd had an exhausting day at school. It started when I arrived, just before nine. My friend Ben was waiting for me, with a face like a wet dishrag.

'Alice,' he said. That was all, but I heard his voice shake and I knew what was coming.

'She's dumped you, hasn't she?' I said. Preparing myself for a *lot* of listening. When Ben's miserable, being his agony aunt is a full time job.

By the end of the day, I was shattered. It wasn't one of my evenings for going round to see Dad, so when I got home (finally!) I made myself an espresso and a cheese toastie and settled down to watch a DVD of *West Side Story*. (OK, I know that's really sad, but I needed some fast calories and a sentimental fix.)

Just as the Jets and the Sharks were getting ready to meet head to head, the phone rang. I nearly didn't answer, but then I thought it might be Ben feeling suicidal. So I turned down the volume and picked up the telephone.

It wasn't Ben. It was Dad.

'Hi, Freya,' he said. 'Do you fancy a trip to Sandy's workshop? She's got something she wants to show us.'

My whole body groaned at the thought of going out again. 'Does it have to be now?'

'That's what she wants,' Dad said. 'I think she's after a bit of feedback and she can't really ask anyone else. I can pick you up in a couple of minutes. Please, Freya.'

I should have said no. But I was already pulling on my trainers. As soon as Dad rang off, I lifted the remote control and said goodbye to the Jets and the Sharks. Then I went downstairs, to be ready when Dad drew up outside.

'This had better be more exciting than *West Side Story*,' I said, as I got into the car. 'What's Sandy up to?'

Dad shrugged as the car pulled away. 'It's what she always used to do, back in the beginning when she made all the clothes herself. She kept everything super-secret until the collection gelled. But as soon as it did, she was desperate for a reaction. I've had calls at three in the morning before now.'

I stared out of the window. 'And you always went?'

He nodded. 'Yes, I did. Until—well, you know.'

Until I was born. Yes, I did know. I'm not a fool. And Dad's not a fool either. He didn't make things worse by trying to pretend it didn't matter. He just gave my hand a quick squeeze and turned on the radio.

The street door buzzed open as soon as we rang the workshop bell. Inside, everything was dark and I reached up to flick the switch. But Dad caught at my arm.

'It's not accidental,' he said. 'If the lights are off, it's because she wants it like this. Come on.' He took my hand and led me towards the stairs.

'Where are we going?' I said, as we felt our way up.

'She wants us to stop when we get to the cutting room.'

'And then?'

'We wait,' said Dad.

So we waited. For three or four minutes, we just stood in the dark at the entrance to the room.

Finally, a light came on at the far end. A space had been cleared in front of the back wall and standing right in the centre of it was a tall figure, veiled in black from head to foot. It was a powerful silhouette, with wide, strong shoulders, and for a second I thought it was too tall to be Sandy. But then she moved and I heard the click of her high heels on the hard floor.

She took two steps towards us and then twisted sharply, and the whole long dress flared suddenly bright, slashed diagonally with bold reds and greens and yellows. For a second, as she spun round, the colours took over completely, forming shimmering patterns as they blurred together.

Then she stopped. The dress shivered for a second and the colours disappeared as the folds fell back into place. Once again, all we could see was steady, unbroken black.

I let out my breath. 'How did she *do* that?'

It wasn't really a question about dressmaking, and Dad didn't bother to answer. We both waited to see what she would do next.

She stood perfectly still for a moment. Then she unfastened the dress and unpinned the veil, letting them both fall to the ground. It was like watching her disappear. Underneath the black dress, she was wearing another one, the same reddish-brown colour as the wall behind her. The material was very fine, but it was cut so that it stood away from her body, disguising her shape. The change was so startling that it was a few seconds before we realized that she was still veiled.

'What's all that about?' Dad muttered.

It wasn't like him to miss the point. 'She's hiding,' I said.

We were speaking very softly, but Sandy heard us and laughed. 'That's how the show's going to start,' she said. 'With Qarsoon the Hidden One.'

'That's what you're going to do with Khadija?' I said.

Sandy nodded. She came across the workshop like a ghost, with the second dress whispering around her. 'And there won't be any unveiling at the end. She's going to stay hidden for ever. Invisible. No one will ever know who's under that veil, except Khadija and her brother. And us.'

'Is this the Somali girl?' Dad said. 'The one from Battle Hill?'

His voice was tense and Sandy stood up straighter, holding her veiled head high. 'Yes,' she said. 'And before you ask the real question—no, I haven't changed my plans. We're still going to do the whole show from Somalia.'

'You've got no idea what you're playing around with.' Dad's voice was low and angry. 'If you'd seen the things I've seen—'

'I *have* seen them,' Sandy snapped. 'You showed me every single picture you took. Remember? And you talked too—on and on and on, as if you were trying to empty it out of your head. But that was *fifteen years ago*, David. Things change in fifteen years.'

'Don't meddle with what you don't understand,' Dad said. 'Please, Sandy. What goes on there is serious stuff.'

'And all I do is *make clothes*?' Sandy said. Suddenly she sounded just as angry as he did. 'Is that what you're trying to say?'

She lifted her head and stood there, defiant and immovable, invisible except for her eyes. I found myself thinking, *If only Dad could see her face, he'd be able to persuade her*—as though the veil was a barrier between their minds as well. And I could feel how it was frustrating him.

He stood looking at Sandy for a whole minute, with his face pale and his fists tightly clenched. Then he turned away towards the door.

'Please yourself,' he said shortly. 'Just don't expect me to come and bail you out. I'm going home. Are you coming, Freya?'

He was challenging me to take sides. After all these years, I know how to recognize that—but I'm quite good at compromising, too. Call it experience.

'I won't be long,' I said. 'Can I come to your flat tonight? And have some hot chocolate before I go to bed?'

That raised a wry grin. *Nice one, Freya.* But he

didn't say no. He just shrugged and went off on his own.

Sandy began to undo the next set of buttons and, just for a second, I felt as though she might go on taking dresses off, one after another, until she disappeared completely. But when she slipped off this one she was in her underwear. She kicked the high heels away and reached for her jeans.

Standing like that, with her hair sticking up at funny angles, she looked small and very vulnerable. Before I could stop myself, I said, 'You will be careful, won't you? Please.'

She looked up. 'It's OK, I promise. I'll have a serious talk with Khadija and Abdi's parents. And if *they* say it's too dangerous—then I will change my mind. Trust me, Freya.'

And when she put it like that, I did. She wasn't a child, after all. Or even a romantic singer with a suicidal drinks-and-drugs habit, like Meg. She was a highly successful fashion designer, in touch with what was going on all over the world.

I grinned. 'Sounds great. Maybe I'll come along for the trip.'

It was just a joke, but she looked thoughtful as she buttoned up her shirt.

* * *

157

We left a few minutes later, and she dropped me off outside Dad's flat. Neither of us suggested that she should come inside. She just gave me a quick kiss and drove away, and I went up in the lift on my own, looking forward to hot chocolate and bed.

But it wasn't time for bed yet. When I walked into the flat, Dad was waiting for me. And there were photographs lying all over the coffee table. Face down.

'You need to look at these,' he said grimly. 'So you understand what it was like.'

He didn't say what kind of photographs they were. He didn't need to. I knelt at the table and he began to turn them over, one by one.

You've seen them too, those images of hunger and violence and death. They're always wrong. Always horrible. But these were even worse, because Dad knew the people. As he turned over each picture, he told me about it, in a few harsh words.

'This little girl's father carried her for twenty miles to get her to the camp. But she was too far gone to eat. She died the next day . . . This man had been managing on one leg for almost a year. It was losing the other leg that finished him off . . . And this is the boy that shot him. His gun was older than he was . . .'

Dad knew them all. Their stories, their injuries,

sometimes even their names. He told me about them, in a flat, unemotional voice, turning over one picture after another. On and on and on.

He was showing me what he saw in his mind, every time Sandy talked about Somalia. The kind of pictures you never forget.

I couldn't forget them either. That night, they forced their way into my dreams, with a terrible, added twist, morphing into the faces of people I knew and loved. And, all the time, I could hear Dad's relentless commentary.

Merry stepped on a landmine. Half an hour after I took the picture, she died from gangrene . . . That was Ben. He'd walked a hundred miles to the feeding station, but when he got there he was too weak to eat. I saw him die . . . Sandy was abandoned out in the desert . . .

In the dream, I was shrieking for him to be quiet. And when I woke—at last—my mouth was open in the same silent scream. *Make it stop! Make it stop!* It was three o'clock in the morning and I knew I wasn't going to sleep again.

As soon as I could move, I sat up and pulled on my dressing gown. My mouth was very dry and I fumbled my way into the kitchen for some water. Cupping the mug in my hands, I walked slowly across the hall and into the sitting room. Because the flat's so high, Dad doesn't bother with curtains and it was light enough to see the photographs, still spread out on the coffee table.

They pulled me across there.

You know that sick feeling when something's so terrible that you have to go back and look again? Mostly, it's not so bad the second time, because your memory was exaggerating. And if not—well, the human brain can get used to all kinds of horrors, can't it? It's a survival mechanism.

But it wasn't working that night.

The second time round, the photographs were even more devastating. Because of my dream. In six months' time, would someone be looking down at another set of photographs and saying, *This was Sandy* . . . ?

Cupping the mug of water in my hands, I looked down at those faces and cried.

It was almost morning when Dad found me. I didn't even know he was there, until he squatted down beside the chair and put his arm round my shoulders.

'I'm sorry,' he said. 'I didn't mean to give you nightmares. I just wanted you to know why I'm worrying. But Sandy's right. All these pictures were taken fifteen years ago.'

I went on staring down. 'And has anything got better since then?'

Dad hesitated. I knew he was tempted to tell me a comforting lie, but he didn't. 'I just don't know,' he said at last. 'Not without going there.' He pulled me on to my feet. 'Come on, Freya. If you go back to bed now, you can have another two hours' sleep. You're too tired to deal with this kind of stuff.'

'Those people have to deal with it. However tired they are.'

'You won't help them by falling asleep at school. Come on.' He put an arm round my shoulders and steered me back to my bedroom.

I was still clutching my mug and before I got back into bed, I drank the rest of the water straight down, in one gulp. Then I climbed into bed and lay down.

'You never know,' Dad said gently, as he tucked the duvet round me, 'Sandy might even make some people think. And that's always a good thing to happen. Now sleep . . . '

When Mahmoud asked for water, one of the men laughed and told him to be quiet.

They drove him to a village he didn't know and shut him up in a room with no windows. There was nothing in the room, except an empty bucket, and he was hungry and afraid. He couldn't guess why the men had captured him.

After a day and a half—or maybe longer—a man came to haul him out of the room. There were three men now, and one of them was talking on the phone. He stopped when Mahmoud appeared and pushed the phone at him.

'It's your sister,' he said. 'Your sister in England. Say something to her—so she hears your voice.' His eyes were hard and cold and Mahmoud wondered if it was some kind of cruel trick. But he did what he was told and spoke into the phone.

'Geri?'

He heard her speak his name.

Suddenly he was talking as fast as he could, trying to explain what had happened to him. But the man with the cold eyes snatched the phone away before he'd finished, because he wanted to talk to Geri himself. And what he said then was the most frightening thing of all.

Ten thousand dollars.

Mahmoud couldn't even imagine so much money. How could one person—one poor Somali girl—ever find so much, even in a rich country? It was impossible.

But if she didn't, he was going to die.

Abdi

I thought Khadija would scream and cry when the kidnappers rang off. But she didn't. She closed her eyes and stood without speaking, so still I couldn't even see her breathe. Was she thinking? Praying? Or just frozen with shock?

'You could ask Sandy for the money,' I said. It was the only thing I could think of. 'You never know, she might give you ten thousand dollars, if you tell her why you need it.'

Khadija opened her eyes. 'What? If we tell her that every kidnapping *budhcad* in Somalia knows she's given me a job? Don't be stupid. We're supposed to be keeping that secret. If she finds out about this, she won't want me any more—and there'll be no chance of saving Mahmoud's life.'

'We must be able to do *something*,' I said. 'If the kidnappers were in this country, we could go to the police. But in Somalia—'

No need to spell it out. *In Somalia there are no police.*

163

There's no government, no law and order. Just budhcads and warlords and pirates. Kids strolling down the streets, with AK47s over their shoulders. Battle wagons with submachine guns mounted in the back . . .

Khadija rounded on me. 'In Somalia we have family! My father and my uncles are all out hunting for Mahmoud! And if I was there, I could ask them what to do. But I'm on my own in this country. There's no support!'

'There's *my* family!' I said hotly.

'That's not the same!' Khadija cried out. 'How could it ever be the same?'

And she was right. Of course she was right. *Me and my clan against the world*, Somalis say. *Me and my family against my clan*. How can you rely that much on anyone else?

'We promised to look after you,' I said. As the next best thing. 'We'll do everything we can.'

Khadija shrugged. 'Are you going to find the money for me? Or take me to Somalia, to hunt for Mahmoud?'

'You know we can't do that.' I was thinking desperately. 'But there must be someone who can help.'

We were on the bus home before we worked out who. Logically, it had to be one of the people who knew the truth about Khadija. One of those was Maamo, and I didn't see how she could possibly do anything. But maybe there was another one who could . . .

He was in the little room at the back of the mosque, discussing something with the imam. We looked through the glass door and saw them together— old Uncle Osman, with his grey beard and wise, wrinkled face, and the fierce young imam, with his passion for goodness and truth. I thought it would be bad to interrupt them, but Khadija knocked on the door and opened it without waiting for an answer.

Uncle Osman looked up. When he saw Khadija's face, he beckoned us inside. 'What's the matter?' he said.

'Something's happened,' I whispered. 'Something bad.' I looked at the imam.

'Whatever it is, you can tell us both,' Uncle Osman said gravely. 'We have no secrets from each other.'

Khadija hesitated for a moment, then she said, 'My brother Mahmoud has been kidnapped in Somalia. They want ten thousand dollars for his life.' Her voice was flat and unemotional. 'And they've given us three months to find it.'

She sounded so matter-of-fact that I wondered whether they would believe her. The imam closed his eyes for a second, and Uncle Osman sat very still, looking down at his hands.

Khadija ran her finger backwards and forwards along the edge of the table. 'Well?' she said. 'Are you going to help me?'

Uncle Osman frowned. 'I'm not a rich man, Khadija. And even if I had the money—'

Khadija tapped her hand on the table. 'I'm not asking you to give all the money yourself. But you could ask everyone else. They all trust you. If you tell them there's a need—and ask them all to give what they can—then maybe—'

She paused, looking from him to the imam and back again, trying to work out what they were thinking. But they didn't say anything. They just waited.

'Ten thousand dollars isn't *so* much money,' Khadija said desperately. 'Only a hundred dollars each for a hundred people. What's that? Sixty pounds? Seventy? If every family gives seventy pounds—if they *lend* it—'

Uncle Osman's face was full of pity, but we could both see that he was going to say no. Khadija dropped her head.

'Please help me,' she said. '*Please*. I don't know what else to do.'

Uncle Osman sighed, so hard I could almost feel

the weight in his chest. But it was the imam who answered.

'I know this is hard,' he said. 'But we mustn't give in to wicked men, Khadija. If these kidnappers get the money they've asked for, they'll do it again. And again and again and again. Lots more people will suffer.'

'At least Mahmoud will be safe!' Khadija was trying to be defiant, but she just sounded forlorn.

'No one will be safe,' Uncle Osman said. 'Even if you manage to find the money, you can't be sure they'll give your brother back. Much safer for them to kill him.' He was being as kind as he could, but I saw Khadija flinch as he said it.

The imam leaned forward. 'There's one thing that puzzles me,' he said thoughtfully. 'Why would those men think it was *worth* kidnapping Khadija's brother?'

It was such an obvious question that it sent a chill into my bones. And the one he hadn't asked was even worse. *How did the kidnappers know?*

'We tried to tell them she's only a schoolgirl,' I said. 'But they didn't take any notice.'

'They're cruel, wicked men,' Khadija said. 'And they don't care about anything except money. What can we do to stop them?'

Uncle Osman lifted his head. 'Let me talk to my son, Suliman. He's in touch with people all over

Somalia. Maybe he can find out something about your brother.'

That didn't sound very hopeful to me, but Khadija sat up suddenly and her eyes sharpened. 'Yes,' she said. 'Maybe he can. I hadn't thought of that.' She stood up, without warning. 'Thank you for listening to me.'

I scrambled up too, muttering my own thank yous. We were both in the doorway when Uncle Osman said suddenly, 'Tell me—how did the kidnappers contact you?'

I dared not tell the truth. I had to hang on to my phone. 'They emailed me,' I said quickly.

'You? Not Khadija?' Uncle Osman raised his eyebrows.

It was too late to correct myself. I gave him a weak smile and shrugged stupidly. 'I can't explain any of it.'

Then I left and ran after Khadija.

Khadija

That old man couldn't do anything to save Mahmoud and nor could the imam. Time was too short to waste it on talking to them. I walked out of the mosque and by the time Abdi caught up with me I was halfway down the street.

'What are you doing?' he said. 'Slow down.' My legs are longer than his and I was walking very fast.

'If we're too slow,' I said, 'my brother Mahmoud will die.'

'You heard Uncle Osman. He's promised to talk to Suliman.'

'When? Tomorrow? The next day?' I kept on walking. 'I can't wait *one extra minute*. If Suliman can really help, I need to be talking to him now.'

The internet café was the first place to look, but we could see through the window that Suliman wasn't there. Just the manager, dealing with a crowd of customers. We could have asked him whether Suliman was at one of his other shops, but I couldn't bear the idea of waiting to speak to him. I needed to be *doing*. So I walked past the café and on down the road, without explaining to Abdi.

But he guessed where I was going. 'Can't you wait till tomorrow?' he said. 'You'll annoy Suliman if you go bothering him at home.'

'If you don't like what I'm doing, don't come with me,' I said, without slowing down. He should have understood how I felt. If someone had kidnapped one of his sisters, would he have waited until tomorrow?

Suliman Osman didn't live in a flat, like most of the other Somalis in Battle Hill. He had a smart, white house on the far side of the main road, with three rows of windows and steps up to the front door. I marched up the steps and caught hold of the knocker. It was made of yellow metal shaped like a clenched fist and it hit the door with a good, loud sound.

When Suliman opened the door, I thought he might be surprised to see me, but there was no sign of that. Just a second when his face was very still and controlled. And then a smile.

I spoke quickly, before he could say anything. '*Assalaamu alaykum*, Uncle Suliman! Please help me. My brother has been kidnapped!'

Suliman's eyebrows went up and he turned his head to look at Abdi. Quite slowly, the way a storyteller does when he wants you to understand a hidden meaning. *Not this brother*, said Suliman's face. He stepped back, waving us into the house.

'Let's not discuss family matters in the street,' he said. 'Come in, and Amina will make you some tea.'

Amina bobbed out of one of the doors, smiling and tying her headscarf. Suliman showed us into the front room and within a few moments Amina was there with tea and biscuits, and a little dish of dates. But she didn't stay to hear why we'd come. She served the tea and then went out, closing the door behind her, as though she was used to people coming for private conversations with her husband.

Suliman waited until we picked up our cups and drank. Then he said, 'Now, tell me about your brother.'

'Not Abdi,' I said.

'Of course not.' Suliman waved his hand as though that was understood. 'Another brother, maybe. But not in England?'

Abdi joined in, leaning forward to interrupt me. 'Her brother's been kidnapped in Somalia. I had a phone call—'

'—and they're going to kill Mahmoud!' I had to say that myself, to make sure Suliman understood how serious it was. 'The only way to save his life is to send them ten thousand dollars.'

171

'—they wouldn't listen when I told them Khadija was a student—'

'—and it's not a trick, because they made Mahmoud speak to me—'

Suliman listened, sipping his tea and waiting for us to run out of words. When we did, he put his cup down, very carefully, and said, 'That's a terrible thing. You have my sympathy, Khadija. But why have you come to me?'

'Ask your friends in Somalia to find the kidnappers!' I said fiercely. 'Make them let Mahmoud go.'

'*Make* them?' Suliman's eyebrows went up again. He put his hands together and looked at us over the tips of his fingers. 'Do you mean you want my friends to find the kidnappers—and then *bargain* with them? How is that possible? What have you got to offer?'

'She hasn't got anything,' Abdi said.

Suliman looked at me. Suddenly his eyes were very sharp. 'Maybe not ten thousand dollars. But you must have something. Or why would they take *your* brother? Somalia's full of boys with relatives in England. Why did they choose *yours*?'

Abdi looked at me.

I looked at Abdi.

Suliman picked up his cup again and drank the tea, quite slowly. Waiting for us to speak. But what could

172

we say? If we told him about Sandy, our one hope of raising the money would disappear.

When the cup was empty, Suliman put it down and looked at Abdi. 'You mustn't make the mistake,' he said softly, 'of thinking that people in Somalia are stupid. There's no room for stupidity there. All the stupid ones died, a long, long time ago. No one could survive without being clever.'

His eyes glinted black, like beetles in the sun. When he turned to me, I felt as though he was staring into my heart.

'Your brother hasn't been taken by ignorant men,' he said. 'You can be sure they know all about you. They know that you came to Britain with a *hambaar* man, to get a good education, and you won't earn any real money until that's finished. Yet they've chosen *this* moment to kidnap your brother. There must be a reason for that.'

I looked down at my feet. 'No reason they could possibly know.'

'And what about the reason they *couldn't* know?' Suliman murmured.

'There is—something,' Abdi said slowly. 'But it's a secret. And if it stops being a secret, then it's not going to happen.'

Suliman got up and walked across the room. He stood looking out of the window, with his back to us.

After a moment he said, very softly, 'I think you can trust me with your secret. Who do you think it was who had the phone put back in your bag?'

I heard Abdi gasp. When I looked at him, his face was full of shock, but there was something else too. He'd started believing that Suliman could make things happen.

I hoped he was right. 'I've been offered a job,' I said. 'There's a famous fashion designer called Sandy Dexter—'

Suliman didn't turn round, but he made a little movement with his head, to show that he knew about Sandy.

'And she's offered me a job.' I took a deep breath. 'She wants to use me as a model. To wear some of the clothes in her show.'

It was the first time I'd spoken about it and saying the words out loud made me realize what a huge thing Abdi and I had done. I started to tremble, expecting a storm of angry questions. *What makes you think you can trust this woman? Does she want you to wear short skirts and uncover your head? How can you be sure she really is Sandy Dexter?*

But Suliman didn't ask any questions at all. He went on staring out of the window for a moment. Then he turned round and said, 'That's why your brother's been kidnapped. I don't know what this woman has offered to pay you, but there's a lot of money in that kind of fashion. Why don't you ask *her* for help?'

'We can't,' Abdi said. 'Not without letting her know that the kidnappers have found out the secret.'

'I don't know how they know,' I said desperately. 'I haven't told *anyone*. And I must earn that money—'

'Don't get worked up,' Suliman said. But he wasn't really thinking about me. I could see from his eyes that he was concentrating on something else. 'Maybe you can't talk to Sandy Dexter about this, but she's still the key. Are you going to see her soon?'

'That's another problem,' I said hopelessly. 'She wants us to go on Sunday at four o'clock—and we're supposed to take our parents. But I don't think Maamo—'

Suliman's head lifted suddenly and his eyes brightened—like my uncles' eyes when they see the clouds that mean rain. He came back across the room and sat down beside us.

'Better not to worry Abdi's mother,' he said smoothly. 'Just tell her your brother's been kidnapped, Khadija, and say that I'm going to try and help you. Then call Sandy Dexter—and tell her you're bringing your father.'

Abdi understood straight away. 'Cool!' he said.

Suliman stood up and opened the door. 'I'll pick you up at three fifteen. Make sure you're ready.'

175

Abdi was grinning, as though that solved everything, but I couldn't feel like that. As we went out into the hall, I looked back at Suliman. 'Please—don't forget about Mahmoud,' I said. 'We must find him *quickly*. Ask all the people you know in Somalia—'

Suliman bent his head. 'Of course I will. I promise you that everything possible will be done for your brother. Everything.'

He opened the front door and watched us as we walked away down the steps.

Abdi's mother was sewing when we got home, rattling long pieces of material through her battered old machine. When Abdi told her about the kidnap, she sat up sharply and her face was shocked and sad.

'Who's taken him?' she said.

How could we know that? Did she think the men on the phone had given us their names?

'Uncle Suliman's going to try and find out,' Abdi said. 'On Sunday we're going to talk to some of his friends.'

'What use will that be?' Maamo said. 'What does Suliman know about any of this?'

'He knows *people*,' I said. 'Lots of people, in England and in Somalia. He must be able to find out something.' I was trying to stay calm and steady, but my voice told how I was struggling.

Maamo put an arm round my shoulders. 'Don't worry,' she said. 'Your brother's bound to be safe. When they realize you're just a poor ordinary girl, they'll let him go straight away.' She gave me a squeeze.

I opened my mouth and then shut it again, without saying anything.

'Everything will be all right,' Maamo said, turning back to her sewing. She spread out the material and clicked the lever down fiercely, to hold it in place. 'There's no need for Suliman Osman to start interfering in our family affairs.'

'It's not interfering,' said Abdi. 'Of course he wants to help us. He was one of my father's best friends, wasn't he?'

The sewing machine stopped dead. For a second, Maamo's hands were very still. Then she shrugged. 'Well—Suliman Osman will do as he likes. The same as always. Let's hope it's good for your brother, Khadija.' She set her needle whirring along another seam and the conversation was over.

Or that's what we thought.

Freya

Sunday was my birthday party.

Not my actual *birthday*, mind you. I was born in September—slap bang in the middle of London Fashion Week. That got Sandy some great publicity at the time (what other designer came out to take the applause with her newborn baby in her arms?) but it's been a problem ever since.

Especially when it comes to parties.

In the beginning, when Dad still had a serious career, he was often away on the other side of the world. So Sandy had to organize my parties, and my friends got invited to all kinds of strange places, at a moment's notice. Like Starbucks, at half past nine on a Monday morning. Or the garden in our square, at midnight. (That one was popular.) Or on a train to Manchester. (*Of course they'll enjoy it*, Sandy said. *All children love trains.*)

When Dad finally gave in and turned himself into a teacher, he decided I needed an official birthday in

July. When Sandy could count on being there. And he dreamt up the idea of a Grown-up Luncheon Party, with a surprise new dress for me and caterers to do the food. No children—in case something went wrong. Just Dad and Sandy and me. And my godparents, Merry and Spike.

It used to be hilarious seeing those two side by side. Every year, Merry was sharper and more well-groomed than the year before, with rings glinting from every finger and hair like a hard golden helmet. And every year Spike was paler and thinner, with ever-scruffier clothes and a yellower face. They never stopped teasing each other.

Until two years ago, when Spike died. After that, it wasn't funny any more.

We still lay his place and pour him a glass of brandy.

This year's party looked like being the best one ever. Dad and I had spent a week dreaming up the menu, and when I unwrapped the dress, on Sunday morning, it was perfect. Neat and casual, with no pretentious twiddles—and no label, of course. Dad always cuts them out and swears he bought the dress in Marks & Spencer.

At eleven o'clock, on the dot, I went to have a bath and Dad phoned Sandy—to make sure she hadn't forgotten. There must have been some kind of hiccup, because I heard a bit of shouting, but by the time I'd dressed Sandy was there, with a big bunch of white roses and a tiny parcel wrapped in a Japanese gift cloth. Everything looked good.

And when Merry walked in, that seemed like the finishing touch.

My party is the only time she lets herself go. Everywhere else, she has to be smart but restrained, keeping up her professional image. For my party she always wears a dress that's totally over the top, like an explosion of scarlet taffeta or a shower of metallic beads. This year, it was slinky emerald green satin, with a huge ruffle all the way down the front.

Sandy put her hands to her head. 'No, Merry!' she screeched. 'No, no *no*!'

Merry looked smug, because that was the reaction she wanted. My birthday party is one of the few places she can play her favourite game of Shocking Sandy. She wiggled her hips, to make the ruffle shake, and then kissed me and produced my present (a Mara Hennessy bag that anyone but me would die for).

Dad pretended to reach for his camera and Merry smacked his hand. 'Don't you dare! One photograph and I'll sue!'

For the first hour, we had a fantastic time. Sandy and Merry set each other off as usual, swapping outrageous rumours that got more and more surreal. By the time we reached the strawberry profiterole gateau that was my birthday cake, they'd lost all connection with reality. (*'And you'll never believe who the other woman was!'* 'No! In a BALLOON??') All four of us were laughing hysterically.

Then, just as Dad was spooning out the profiteroles, everything suddenly changed.

Merry opened her handbag to find a tissue, because she had tears rolling down her face. As she wiped her eyes, she said—quite casually—'Oh, while I think of it, Sandy—you've forgotten to book Siobhan for your show this year.'

Sandy looked down at her plate, pushing a strawberry around with her spoon. 'Actually, I don't think Siobhan's quite what I want. Not this year.'

Merry dropped the tissue into her handbag and lifted her head, very slowly. Staring. We were all staring. But Sandy just went on pushing that tiny strawberry round and round her plate.

'What?' Merry said. Very short and sharp, with all the laughter drained out of her face.

Everyone always wants Siobhan. She has one of those wonderful Irish faces—white skin, blue eyes, and very black hair—and the camera loves her. Until that moment, ever since Sandy had spotted her working on the cheese counter, she'd been The Face of Sandy Dexter.

And she was Merry's star client.

Sandy didn't look up. 'This collection's a bit different,' she said. 'I need a different kind of model to open and close the show. And Siobhan won't want to take second place.'

(She was right about that, at least. Siobhan must be the most touchy, self-obsessed, arrogant nineteen year old in the entire world.)

Merry snapped her bag shut. 'So—are you just making a change for the catwalk show? Or do you want to talk about a new face for this collection?

'I think we've found someone already,' Sandy murmured. She lifted her head and looked innocently at Merry. 'We're calling her Qarsoon.'

'*Carsone?*' Merry looked as though she'd bitten into a lemon by mistake. 'What kind of name is that?'

'It means *the hidden one*,' Sandy said. With a quick little laugh. 'Not her real name, of course.'

'Of course not.' Merry swallowed hard. 'So who's her agent?'

Sandy opened her eyes even wider. 'I'm afraid that's a secret.' She spooned up the strawberry at last and started eating it as though there was nothing wrong. As though she hadn't just snubbed her oldest friend.

Dad had been standing like a statue, with an empty bowl in his hand. He blinked and then served himself some of the gateau. 'This is supposed to be a fashion-free zone,' he said brightly. 'Remember? It's Freya's birthday party.'

He was doing his best to get the party back on track, and he almost succeeded. Merry pulled herself together and did a good imitation of godmotherly jollity and Sandy told a funny story about Vivienne Westwood that I'd never heard before. But nothing quite lifted the chill from the room.

I stared at Spike's glass. He was the best company there, even though he was dead.

Gradually the conversation died, in spite of all Dad's efforts to keep it going. By three o'clock, Sandy wasn't even pretending to laugh at anyone's jokes and Merry gave up and clapped a hand to her mouth.

'I must be going senile!' she said. 'I've just remembered something I need to sort out in the office.'

Dad frowned. 'Merry, you don't have to—'

Merry gave him a wide imitation smile. 'Busy days!' she said lightly. 'Fashion never stops. Bye, darlings!'

She pushed her chair back, aiming a couple of air kisses at Sandy and Dad. I went to the front door with her, to say goodbye, and as she slipped on her jacket, she leant towards me and whispered, 'Sandy's looking very *thin*. Is she under a lot of pressure?'

'She's fine,' I said stoutly. Sandy was always under pressure. She liked it. Merry knew that as well as I did.

'Problems with the collection?' Merry's voice was like a scalpel, feeling its way under my skin.

I opened the door. 'Everything's fine, Merry. Really. I know it's rough on Siobhan—'

'Oh—*that*.' Merry flapped a hand, as though Siobhan's tantrums were insignificant. 'Siobhan can take care of herself. No, I was just worried. But if you think everything's OK . . . ?' She raised an eyebrow at me and then—just as the question began to feel awkward—gave me a quick butterfly kiss and wafted away down the corridor.

I wanted an explanation just as much as she did. As soon as she'd gone, I went marching back to the table.

'Well?' I said angrily.

Sandy opened her eyes very wide. 'You know I couldn't tell her, Freya. You *know* why it has to be a secret.'

'But you didn't have to do it like *that*,' I said. '*Why*?'

Sandy stood up. 'I couldn't let her stay any longer. Qarsoon's bringing her father here. It's a very important meeting.'

'*What?*' said Dad.

Sandy looked faintly apologetic. 'I didn't want anyone to see them going into my flat. I meant to tell you, David.'

'How could you arrange a meeting now?' I said.

Sandy pulled a face. 'Look, I didn't *mean* to be doing it today. But I'd almost given up hope of finding her again. And when Abdi phoned up, I just—'

'You just forgot it was my birthday,' I said flatly. 'Didn't you?'

Sandy sighed. And then nodded. 'I'll make it up to you, Freya, I promise. But I have to get the show sorted. You do understand?'

'Oh yes,' I said. 'I understand all right.' I ran into my bedroom and slammed the door behind me.

As quickly as I could, I kicked off my smart shoes and undid the dress Dad had given me, letting it lie on the floor where it fell. Then I pulled on jeans and a T-shirt and pushed my feet into my oldest pair of trainers.

When I opened the door again, the meal was all cleared away and Sandy and Dad were in the kitchen, washing up the glasses. I could see Dad was angry—but he wasn't angry enough to forbid her to have her meeting in his flat.

'I'm going out,' I said.

'You don't have to do that.' Sandy put down the cloth she was using. 'If you stay—'

I didn't wait to hear what she was going to say. I just marched out of the flat and headed down the stairs without waiting for the lift. It didn't matter where I went, but I needed to be walking.

Mahmoud was asleep in the dark when the door opened. He sat up suddenly, before he was properly awake, and stared at the patch of yellow light.

One of the men came in, carrying a plate of maize and bananas and a cup of hot tea. There was a gun slung over his shoulder and a torch sticking out of his pocket. He put the plate down carefully on the floor. Then he turned on the torch and held out the cup, waiting for Mahmoud to take it.

Mahmoud was hungry and very, very thirsty. But how can you trust someone who's stolen you away from your family? He stared at the cup and then at the plate on the floor, trying to think clearly.

'Come on. Drink.' The man squatted down beside him, still holding out the cup. 'If you don't drink, you'll get ill.'

Mahmoud looked at the tea. 'And if I do drink?' he said.

For a second the man stared, not understanding what he meant. Then he laughed. 'It's good tea. Don't be afraid.' He held the cup closer.

Mahmoud swallowed, feeling the dryness in his throat. 'You drink first,' he said.

For another, long moment the man held the cup where it was, watching Mahmoud's face to see if he would weaken and drink. Mahmoud looked back at him steadily, without wavering.

At last the man laughed and tilted his head back, tipping a little of the tea into his own mouth so that Mahmoud could see him drink and swallow. Then he held out the cup again, smiling as Mahmoud took it. 'You're a good boy,' he said.

Mahmoud smiled back, to show he was grateful. '*Bismillaah*,' he said. And drank.

Abdi

Maamo didn't say another word about Suliman. Not until he pulled up outside our flats at quarter past three. Not until he'd hooted and Khadija and I were picking up our coats. Then she lifted her head and looked round at us.

'I need to go out in a minute,' she said. As if it was no big deal. 'You'll have to take Sahra and Maryan with you.'

'What about Fowsia?' I said. 'Can't she—?'

'No she can't.' Maamo looked back at her sewing. 'Fowsia's coming with me.'

'But we're going out with Uncle Suliman,' I said.

'He's got room for two more, in that big car of his.' Maamo nodded at Sahra and Maryan. 'Fetch your coats. You're going with Abdi.'

'They can't come,' I said. 'Tell her, Khadija.'

But Maamo didn't give Khadija time to back me up. 'Please yourself,' she folded up the dress she was sewing. 'If you can't take them with you, then you'll have to stay here and look after them.'

What choice did we have? If we took the little girls, they'd come back babbling about where we'd been and who we'd met. But if we went without them, Maamo would know we had something to hide.

I looked at Khadija, but she just shrugged and picked up her bag. 'Come on,' she said. 'He's waiting.'

We trailed down the stairs with Sahra and Maryan skipping ahead of us. The closer we got to Suliman Osman's car, the harder it was to imagine it full of children. I thought he would take one look at the four of us and shake his head.

But he didn't. When he first saw us coming, he pulled out his phone and called someone and by the time we reached the car he was smiling.

'What a close family you are,' he said.

I pulled a face. 'Maamo said we had to bring them. I couldn't—'

'No worries.' Suliman waved me into the front seat and let the girls crowd into the back. 'Let's go. Faarah's waiting.'

I had no idea what he was talking about. Who was Faarah? I would have asked, but when I opened my mouth Suliman looked sideways at me, pursing his lips. 'It's all right,' he said. 'Stop fretting and find us some music.'

I flicked through the radio stations, but I couldn't stop fretting. I didn't know that we were about to have a perfect demonstration of how Suliman operated. No fuss. Just a smooth operation, with everything sorted in advance.

We hadn't been travelling for more than ten minutes when we pulled up outside a furniture warehouse. As Suliman was turning off the engine, the owner came out to meet us. He was a brother. A Somali.

But he frowned at the little girls in a very un-Somali way. 'What are they doing here?' he said stiffly.

'Well—you know.' Suliman spread his hands and smiled. 'They have to be with someone, Faarah. They're good girls. They won't be a problem.'

'They can't come in here,' Faarah said stiffly. 'You know what it's like. Furniture piled up everywhere. I'm not insured for children.'

Suliman looked concerned. 'But we need to talk to you. What can we do?'

Faarah bent down to peer through the window at Sahra and Maryan. Then he smiled suddenly. 'No worries. Jaz can look after them. She loves children.' He turned and called into the warehouse. 'Hey, Jaz! How about taking a break from stock-taking? Mr Osman's brought two nice little girls for you to play with.'

It was as easy as that. Out came a pretty Asian girl,

with a clipboard in her hand and a grin all over her face.

'I've got business with Mr Osman,' Faarah said. 'Just keep them entertained till we've finished. OK?'

'OK.' Jaz grinned cheerfully at Sahra and Maryan. 'Come on, you two.'

Sahra and Maryan jumped out of the car and started fighting to hold her hand.

'None of that,' she said. 'Here.' She gave Sahra her clipboard and Maryan her pen. 'Carry those for me, and then you can both hold my hands.'

They went off without even looking back at us, and Faarah grinned. 'You see? The girls will be fine. But just before you go . . .'

They walked aside together and began to talk in low voices, and I sat back and watched them. I had the comfortable feeling that we were in safe hands. Suliman wasn't like his father. He really knew how to make things happen.

I couldn't wait to see how he dealt with Sandy Dexter.

Khadija

I didn't like it at all. Suliman had fixed our problem with Sahra and Maryan, but he'd done it too easily, as if he played tricks like that all the time. He hadn't asked us whether we were happy to let Sahra and Maryan disappear with a complete stranger and even though I knew they would be all right I felt—unsettled.

But I had to go along with anything that gave me a chance of saving Mahmoud. So I pushed the girls out of my mind and opened my bag. It was time to put on the black clothes Sandy had told me to wear.

I tipped them out and started putting them on. Even in Uncle Suliman's big car, there was hardly enough room to wriggle my arms into the sleeves of the *abayad* and I had to lift myself off the seat to tug the long skirt down over my jeans. When it was straight, I wound the black scarf round my head, over my own *hijaab*, and reached out for the little *niqab*, to cover my face.

But it wasn't on the seat. I guessed that I'd knocked it off while I was struggling to dress, but I couldn't see it, so I bent down and felt around my feet. When I didn't find it, I reached further forward, under the driver's chair.

And I felt cold metal.

There was something hidden there, taped to the underside of the seat. My fingers felt their way over its ugly angles, recognizing the shape. I knew what it was—but I'd never expected to find one in England.

Guns are part of ordinary life in Somalia. How else can a man protect his animals and his family, out in the lonely desert? How can he keep them safe in the towns where people ignore the laws of God? Nomads need guns and I've known how to use one for as long as I can remember.

But why should a man like Suliman need a gun?

The *niqab* was lying right underneath it. I pulled it out from under the seat and sat up with it. As I tied it over my face, I said, very softly, 'Abdi—there's a gun under Suliman's seat.'

He lifted his head, but before he could even look round Suliman and Faarah had turned towards us and Faarah was nodding goodbye.

'No worries, bro,' I heard him call as Suliman walked away. 'Just don't be gone too long.'

Suliman raised a hand, half-turning back. 'A couple of hours, that's all. And then I'll take care of your little problem. OK?'

He opened the car door and glanced in. When he saw what I was wearing, his mouth twisted into a sarcastic smile. He laughed as he started the engine.

'Is this the great secret? A fashion for veils? Are you sure Sandy's not teasing you, Khadija?'

'You don't understand,' I said. '*I'm* the secret, not the clothes. No one must know who I am.'

His eyes flashed up to the mirror again, trying to tell whether I was serious. But he couldn't see my face, of course. As I stared back at him, I saw his smile disappear, but he didn't say anything as he pulled away from the kerb. And I didn't say anything either. I just watched the back of his head and thought, *Why do you need that gun?*

Fifteen minutes later, we pulled up outside a tall, new block of flats with glass security doors across the entrance. Suliman nodded at Abdi. 'Call her, to say we're here.'

Abdi was already tapping in Sandy's number. When she answered, he turned round to tell me what she said. 'You must go in on your own, Khadija. She'll send someone down to let you in—a man called David.'

'What about us?' Suliman said quickly. 'Is she try-ing to shut us out?'

His voice must have been loud enough for Sandy to hear, because there was another rush of instructions down the phone.

'OK, fine,' Abdi said. 'We'll see you in ten minutes. And Khadija's coming now.'

He flapped his hand impatiently, hurrying me out of the car, and I opened the door and shot out. My trainers got caught in the hem of my *abayad* and I almost fell over.

'You'd be better off in a mini skirt, love,' shouted the driver behind us.

I lifted my head and crossed the pavement quickly, in long strides. As I reached the glass doors, the lift came down on the other side of the foyer and a tall man stepped out and raised his hand, very slightly, to show he was coming to meet me. A second later, the glass doors glided apart and I stepped into the building.

'Hello,' said the man. 'I'm David. Freya's father.' I think I might have guessed that without being told, because he was very like her. Fair and pale, with a square face and light blue eyes.

I lifted my head, to tell him my name in return. 'I'm—'

But he interrupted before I could finish. 'You're

Qarsoon,' he said. 'That's what Sandy wants you to tell people if they ask.'

Qarsoon. *Hidden.* Another new name, to cover up the one the *hambaar* man told me to use.

Layers and layers of hiding.

'I'm Qarsoon,' I said, obediently.

David nodded and smiled. Then he led the way to the lift. As we went up, he began to talk in a quiet voice, preparing me for what was going to happen.

'This may not be a peaceful meeting. Marco insisted on coming. He's Sandy's business manager, and I don't think he's very happy with her plans. But don't let him scare you. He'll probably do a lot of shouting and stamping around, but Sandy usually gets her own way in the end.'

We came out of the lift into a bright, carpeted corridor and David took out his key. 'This is where I live,' he said. 'And Freya stays here too, when she's not with Sandy. Welcome.' He unlocked the door of the flat and took me across the little entrance hall to the main room.

It was like stepping into the sky. We were in a wide space, full of air, with windows that stretched from the floor to the ceiling. All the shapes in the room were pale and simple, and there was a long view across the darkening city. Everything was calm and light.

Except the thin, dark-haired man sitting on the couch. When he saw me, he scowled.

'Is this it?' he said, in a sulky, impatient voice. 'The great secret that's going to drive the whole collection? Come *on*, Sandy! It's never going to work.'

He wasn't my idea of a businessman. More like an angry, spoilt child with no manners. But Sandy was laughing at him.

'Give it a chance, Marco. Say hello to Qarsoon.'

Marco slid off the desk and held out his hand. He was a head shorter than I was, and his arms were strong and very hairy. 'Hey there!' he said. 'Don't mind me. I'm suffering from twenty years of working with Sandy Dexter. The doctor says the scars are permanent.'

I looked down at his hand. I didn't shake it—that's not what we do—but I bent my head politely. 'Good evening,' I said.

Up went his eyebrows and he took a step forward. 'OK, let's take a look at you then.' And he reached out to pull the scarf away from my face.

Sandy's arm shot out and she slapped his hand away. 'No you don't! *Nobody* gets to see who she is.'

Marco stared at her. And I stared too. Did she really think she could keep that up? What was I supposed to do if he tried again, when she wasn't there?

But he didn't try again. He took a few steps

backwards and looked me up and down. 'Can she walk?' he said.

'Of course she can.' Sandy nodded at me. 'Show him please, Qarsoon. Walk up and down, the way you did in Merry Fox's office.'

I straightened my shoulders and began to walk up and down in front of the great glass window, with my head high and the long skirt of the *abayad* swirling around my feet. I was determined that this Marco wasn't going to laugh at me. Let him watch, and understand how much I knew about walking.

And he did watch. He stood still and silent, tugging at his earlobe and turning his head to follow me as I went up and down. I walked proudly, without letting my eyes stray towards his face, imagining that I was on the other side of the glass, stepping from cloud to cloud as I strode across the sky.

I must have been moving for five minutes or more before he held up his hand for me to stop.

'Not bad,' he said, grudgingly. 'She'll be very striking on the catwalk.' He whirled round to face Sandy. 'And that's all you need. There's no sense in scurrying off to some bandit-ridden desert. You have to be here, in London, with the clothes. That's where your customers are going to be.'

'I'm not showing in London,' Sandy said calmly. 'I've told you what I'm doing, Marco.'

Marco's face went very red and his eyes bulged. He came striding across the room and pushed his face up close to mine, so that he was staring straight into my eyes, through the slit in my veil. 'And what do *you* think of that, Qarsoon? Are you ready to miss London Fashion Week—just so you can spend twenty minutes parading up and down in *Somalia*? Of all the horrendous places in the world. Does the idea fill you with delight?'

What did he mean? Was it really possible . . . ?

Before I could ask, he was shouting at Sandy again. 'It's a great collection! A *brilliant* collection! And you want to throw it all away because of some ridiculous notion about visiting the most godforsaken country in Africa!'

The shouting didn't have any effect on Sandy. She sat down on the couch and looked up at him, folding her hands in her lap. I think she was waiting until he was too hoarse to shout any more, so that she could say *No* again, without raising her voice.

But I couldn't let him go on with the terrible, wrong things he was saying. I took a step forward and tried to interrupt.

'Excuse me—' I said.

I don't think he even heard. He just went on bellowing, with his face growing darker and darker.

'—it's no good behaving as though you don't need to sell the clothes—'

'EXCUSE ME!'

I hadn't meant to shout, but it came out very loud indeed. Even louder than Marco's voice. He stopped yelling and turned round, with his mouth open.

'I have to tell you,' I said politely, 'that Somalia is not forsaken by God. And it is not horrendous. It is a beautiful place and if Sandy asks me to go there, I shall be very happy.'

For a moment, there was complete and utter silence. As though everyone was surprised that I should love my country.

Then Sandy said, very softly, 'You see? You *see.*' Not to me, but to the two men. 'How can you talk about Somalia at all, unless you've been there? How can I sell this collection—how can it have any authority at all—unless people know that I'm not just playing around? Of course I'm going there.'

The way she said it made an end of the argument. The time for changing her mind was over. Her plans were set.

I thought it was Marco who would speak, because he was the one who'd done all the shouting. But I was wrong. It was David who answered Sandy. And his face was even paler than before, as though all the blood had drained away from it.

201

'If you're going to Somalia,' he said, 'then I'm going too.'

Sandy blinked at him. She looked very surprised. 'What about Freya?'

'I can't—' David closed his eyes and put a hand on the sofa, as though he needed to hold himself up. 'Do you really think I'm going to choose Freya instead of you? I can't let you go without me, Sandy.'

I knew it was a terrible thing he'd said. I didn't understand why, but I could tell from the sound of his voice, and the expression on Sandy's face. For a moment, the room was full of a fierce, sharp silence.

And then a harsh voice from the hall said, 'Well, you needn't think you're leaving me behind. If you're both swanning off to Africa, then I'm coming too.'

And there was Freya in the doorway, in shabby old jeans and a pair of dirty, battered trainers.

Freya

D id I hear what Dad said? Of course I did. I'd been standing there for at least a minute, with Abdi and Suliman behind me, and I heard it all. So did they.

And how did it make me feel? Don't expect me to go on about that. What's the point? I know. You know. La-di-da-di-dah. Let's get on with the story.

My dramatic entrance knocked everyone speechless, but I carried on talking cheerfully, as though nothing had happened. 'Look who I met outside the front door. I've brought them up to join the party.'

I waved Suliman and Abdi into the room and stepped back to see how they fitted in. There was one of those split second pauses when anything seems possible. Then Sandy stepped forward, with her hands held out. 'Welcome,' she said to Suliman. 'It's a pleasure to meet you. You have a very special daughter, Mr Mussa.'

She'd obviously got something wrong, and Khadija and Abdi both opened their mouths to correct her. But Suliman was too quick for them. He came forward and gave Sandy a little bow, with one hand on his chest.

'Please,' he said. 'Somali names are very complicated. Just call me Suliman. What can I do for you?'

He looked as though he spent his whole life walking into stunning city flats and meeting celebrities. And maybe he did. How would I know?

'I want to take my catwalk show to Somalia,' Sandy said bluntly, 'but David keeps telling me it's much too dangerous. What do you think? Is it possible to go there?'

Suliman was very still for a second. 'Going to Somalia isn't like going to France,' he said carefully. 'It's important to take—certain precautions. But if you do that, yes, of course it's possible. People go there all the time.'

Sandy gave a little satisfied nod. 'And can I afford to do it? I'll need to take around ten models—at least—plus all the hairdressers, make-up artists and dressers. Then there's me and David and Marco—'

'I'm not coming,' interrupted Marco.

'But I am,' I said. I glared at Sandy. 'Don't even *think* of leaving me out.'

Dad opened his mouth—and then shut it again. I

knew what he thought, but he'd obviously decided not to have the argument there.

Sandy waved her hand vaguely. 'This is just broad brush stuff. We'll firm up the numbers later.' Then she carried on quizzing Suliman. 'We'll need a place to put on the show, and I want to do live streaming—'

Suliman didn't blench at any of it. He didn't even look surprised when she started on money. Everything to do with the fashion industry involves *obscene* amounts of money, but he took it all calmly. Either he'd done some very good research, or he was used to people who dealt in hundreds of thousands of dollars.

Abdi wasn't, though. I saw his eyes widen, and he began whispering to Khadija. If she replied, her voice was too quiet to hear, and her expression was hidden behind the black veil.

I edged across to them. 'What are you thinking?' I said.

Abdi shrugged, trying to look cool, but he didn't say anything. It was Khadija who answered.

'When I left home this morning, ten thousand dollars was a very big sum of money,' she muttered. 'But now it seems—nothing.'

'Don't you believe it,' I said harshly. 'Ten thousand dollars is still a lot of money in the real world. Fashion's a land of its own.'

Khadija's eyes glittered through the slit in the veil. 'Do you think Sandy will pay me ten thousand dollars?'

It seemed a weirdly precise amount. I wanted to say, *Of course she won't! Why should a schoolgirl earn ten thousand dollars for half an hour's work?* But I knew better than that. Fashion is a crazy, unbalanced business, and there was no way of guessing how far Sandy would go when she'd set her mind on something. 'What's special about ten thousand dollars?' I said.

'It's what I need,' Khadija murmured. That wasn't really an answer, but I couldn't ask anything else because she turned away to listen to Suliman and Marco.

There was some serious bonding going on there. Somehow, Suliman had become an insider, in about fifteen minutes, and he and Marco were sitting side by side on the sofa, with their BlackBerries out. I don't think Marco could believe his luck. There aren't many people in the fashion world who are as practical as he is. The two of them were making lists and working out ballpark figures, while Sandy and Dad stood over them, listening to every word.

'Why spend so much money shipping people into Somalia?' Suliman said. 'Would you take so many if you were doing the show in New York?'

'Of course not,' Marco said impatiently. 'We'd hire local people. But New York's completely different.'

Suliman frowned. 'Do you think all Somalis are terrorists herding camels? We have hairdressers and make-up artists too. And the whole country's full of beautiful women.'

'This is very specialist work,' Marco said. 'I'd be very surprised if anyone in Somalia has the right kind of experience.'

Sandy leaned over his shoulder. 'The show has to be perfect,' she said fiercely. 'I'm ready to pay for that.'

'Of course you are.' Suliman gave her a calming smile. 'But there's no point in paying for things you don't need. Just give me a few days to talk to my contact in Eyl. I think he'll be able to find the kind of people you need. There's a lot of money there at the moment.'

'Pirate money,' Dad said bitterly.

Suliman looked up at him. 'Pirates are the same as other men with money. They like to spend it on luxuries, and so do their wives. If my friend finds us some Somalis to do the make-up, and act as dressers, then this whole trip becomes more . . . economic.'

'We'd need someone to manage it all,' Marco said carefully. 'Someone who understands how things work here, as well as in Somalia.'

207

He and Suliman exchanged glances. 'I could do that,' Suliman murmured. 'If you like.'

Marco gave a little nod and the two of them bent over their sums again. *It's going to happen*, I thought. *It's really going to happen*.

I wasn't sure how I felt about that, but there was one thing I knew for certain.

I wasn't going to be left behind.

The next time the door opened, the men were very excited, laughing and joking together. They grinned at Mahmoud as though they expected him to be laughing too.

'Get up,' said the young one the others called Rashid. Usually he was silent and nervous, but today he grinned as he dragged Mahmoud to his feet. 'We're going on a journey.'

This is it, Mahmoud thought. This is the day they're going to kill me. And he lifted his head and stood straight, so they wouldn't see that he was afraid.

They took him up the concrete steps and out of the building. Their battered Toyota truck was parked outside and Rashid pushed him into the front and climbed after him, so that they were both squashed into the passenger seat. He could feel the barrel of Rashid's gun against his ribs.

Two of the men jumped into the open back of the truck and another one slid in at the driver's door. He was the friendly guard who brought the food, the one they nicknamed Sanyare—Littlenose.

Sanyare frowned when he saw Rashid's gun. 'No need for that,' he said. 'The boy's not stupid.' He stared until Rashid dropped the gun barrel down towards the floor and then he started the engine.

They drove for most of the day, bumping over rough roads and roaring through small dusty villages. Twice they stopped, once to buy food and Pepsi and once to fill up the petrol tank from cans in the back of the truck. Mahmoud could see they were travelling north-east, but he had no idea where they were or what their destination might be.

It was almost dark when they reached the coast. The truck stopped again and Sanyare opened his door.

'I have to call Sanweyne,' he said. 'Keep quiet all of you.'

Rashid clamped a big hand over Mahmoud's face, almost suffocating him. He was muttering under his breath—something about why was it always Sanyare who phoned the boss in England. Mahmoud listened to Sanyare's voice outside and thought what childish nicknames they used. Sanweyne and Sanyare. Bignose and Littlenose. Like two children playing together.

Sanyare finished his call and climbed back into the truck. 'Sanweyne's arranged a place for us,' he said. 'We have to ask for a man called Yusuf.'

They bumped along the coast road for another ten minutes or so and then Sanyare pulled up outside a line of buildings. Rashid opened the door and jumped out, waving his gun at Mahmoud.

'Walk!' he said.

Mahmoud's legs were shaky from sitting so long. He stumbled out of the truck and Rashid's gun prodded him towards a big, single-storey building across the road.

A man lounged in the doorway, chewing qat leaves, with green juice trickling from the corner of his mouth.

'Yusuf knows we're coming,' Sanyare said.

The man jerked his thumb. 'In there,' he said.

Inside, the building was full of noise and bright, blaring light that hurt Mahmoud's eyes after the darkness outside. Two men were sprawled in chairs, watching motor racing on a wide screen. There were cans of beer on the table and plates of rice and stewed meat left half-finished on the floor.

'Sanweyne sent us,' Sanyare said, above the noise of the television. 'We're looking for Yusuf.'

'Here I am,' said one of the men. His eyes were narrow and sharp. 'So this is our little pot of gold, is it?' He peered at Mahmoud and prodded him in the ribs with a sharp finger.

'We need a room to keep him hidden,' Sanyare said.

Yusuf nodded impatiently. 'Don't worry. It's all fixed. I'll show you the place as soon as the Grand Prix's over.' He turned back to the television, taking a long swig of his beer.

Rashid shrugged and flopped into a chair, pulling Mahmoud down to the ground. 'Keep your mouth shut and enjoy this,' he muttered. 'You won't see any more for a long time.'

Warily, Mahmoud settled himself on the floor, watching the cars as they raced round and round the circuit.

Abdi

Suliman was very pleased with himself. When we left the meeting, he sang under his breath, all the way back to Faarah's warehouse. Once or twice he glanced at me, out of the corner of his eye, and I knew we had things to discuss, but not yet.

We collected Sahra and Maryan and headed home. As I was getting out of the car, Suliman leaned across and said, in a low voice, 'Call round at my house tonight. When you've taken Khadija to the shop.'

I didn't know what he wanted to say to me, but I felt my pulse speed up. As the big car glided away, I thought about how Suliman had taken charge of the meeting that afternoon. And I thought about the gun taped underneath his seat.

Things were starting to happen, just as I'd hoped. I could feel myself moving beyond the tight little neighbourhood where I'd grown up, out into the current of the wide, wild world. And I knew where I wanted to go.

* * *

When we walked into the flat, Maamo was clearing up her sewing. 'What took you so long?' she said to Khadija, as though we'd just been shopping. 'Where have you been?'

Sahra and Maryan burst out excitedly, telling her all about Jaz's computer and her photocopier and the ten different colours of nail varnish she kept in the filing cabinet.

'Look! A different colour for each nail!' shrieked Maryan, waving her hands in front of Maamo's face. 'And she said—'

'She showed us how to *draw* on her computer!' Sahra was determined to have her say as well. 'And she let us print it out. Look, Maamo!'

I was filled with admiration for Suliman all over again. There was no way Maamo could question Khadija and me. Every time she asked us a question, one of the girls interrupted with a new detail about the wonders of Jaz and her office.

But that didn't stop her worrying. And she didn't like it when I told her I was going round to Suliman's house.

'I suppose you'll be round there all the time now,' she said. 'I knew this would happen if he started interfering.'

'He's not interfering,' I said. 'He's trying to help. Don't you care about Khadija's brother?'

'Of course I do,' Maamo said impatiently. 'But what can Suliman Osman do to help him?'

I wanted to tell her everything, just to see her eyes widen when I shouted words like *model* and *fashion* and *photography*. I wanted to tell her about all the arrangements and how much money Khadija could earn. But all I could do was shut myself in my bedroom until it was time to go out.

Even Khadija didn't seem to understand how fortunate we were. As we walked to the shop, she suddenly said, 'Do you think we're right to trust Suliman?'

'What do you mean?' I was baffled. 'Of course we're right.'

'Why do you think he has a gun?'

'So people don't mess him about,' I said. 'That's what we need, isn't it? Someone strong, who can sort out the kidnappers.'

'If he can,' Khadija said. 'I was just thinking . . . before he gave your phone back, do you think he listened to the message from Sandy?'

'So what if he did?' I said impatiently. 'There are lots of people called Sandy. No reason for him to link that to Sandy Dexter, was there? Not until we told him.'

'No-o, I don't think so.' Khadija frowned.

For a moment I thought she wanted to say something else, but I didn't hang around to find out what it was. We'd reached the shop by then and I wanted to get to Suliman's house.

'Stop worrying,' I said. 'OK? We'll get Mahmoud back—and a free trip to Somalia as well. See you later.'

And I went.

I think Suliman was waiting for me to come. When I knocked, he opened the door straight away, with a smile that made me feel I'd suddenly grown older and taller.

'So,' he said, 'are you ready for some hard work?'

I almost stopped breathing. 'You want me to work for you?'

'This trip to Somalia is going to take a lot of organizing. I need an assistant to make phone calls and keep track of everything. Someone I can trust.' Suliman looked me up and down. 'Do you think you can do it?'

'Of course I can do it,' I said. (What was so difficult about phoning and making notes?) 'Do I—' I hesitated and then said it anyway. 'Do I get paid?'

'Better than that.' Suliman's nose sharpened like a beak as he smiled. 'If you work hard, I'll make sure you come with us. Will that do? Do you fancy a free trip to Somalia?'

That was more than I'd hoped for. As soon as he said it, I knew I had to go.

'Do you think you can fix it?' I said.

Suliman laughed. 'Of course I can fix it. But you'll need to start working *now*. Is that a deal?'

I took a long breath, to steady myself. 'It's a deal,' I said. And I walked into the house.

Khadija

From that day on, Abdi always seemed to be round at Suliman's house. What were they *doing*? The time slid past—three weeks . . . four weeks . . . five weeks—and all I heard was busy talk about arrangements for Sandy's show. Lots of time and money were being spent on those, but what good would that do? Didn't Suliman *understand* that Mahmoud's life was in danger?

The emails from my parents kept getting more and more frantic: . . . No one knows anything about Mahmoud . . . We've tried everything we can think of . . . Why did the kidnappers choose our son . . . ?

The questions were like knives, twisting into my heart, because I knew the answers—but I couldn't tell them. It was all my fault, but I didn't dare to say anything, in case it caused even more trouble.

When I tried to talk to Abdi, he just told me not to be impatient.

'Suliman knows what he's doing,' he said. 'The important thing is to get Sandy into Somalia. When she's there—when she sees what it's like—she'll give you ten thousand dollars without even blinking. It's nothing compared with the money she's spending on her show. But Suliman says we need to get her there first.'

It was all *Suliman says* now. Especially once the summer holidays started. I hardly saw Abdi after that, and when I asked him what they were doing, all he would say was, 'Contacting people. Making arrangements. There's a lot to fix up.'

So why didn't anything *happen*?

We still hadn't talked to Maamo about it and I dreaded telling her. *Leave it to Suliman*, Abdi said. *He'll fix it.* But I didn't see how anyone was going to persuade her.

And then one day I came back from doing some shopping and found Suliman's wife Amina sitting in the lounge. She and Maamo were talking, very politely, and drinking cups of tea.

When I walked in, Maamo gave me a wooden smile. 'You're very lucky,' she said. 'Auntie Amina and Uncle Suliman have offered to take you and Abdi to Somalia. They think they may be able to help find your brother, Khadija.'

She said it as though she'd learnt the words by heart and I could see she wasn't happy. But what did that matter? Somehow, Amina had persuaded her to let us go. That was the important thing.

Amina put down her teacup and stood up, smiling brightly. 'We have a lot of things to do and not much time. The first thing is—you and Abdi need passport photographs. Let's go and do that now. My car's outside, and we can pick Abdi up on the way.' She gave me a long look as she picked up her bag. 'What do you want to wear for the photographs? Maybe— something special?'

Understand me, said her eyes. For a second I was puzzled. Then I realized she was lying about the passport photographs. We were going to see Sandy.

The black clothes were in my school bag, because that was the only place where Maamo never looked. By the time I'd fetched it, Amina was already at the front door.

'You'll have to change in the car,' she said, as we went down the steps. 'Suliman told me to make sure your face was hidden. I don't know why.'

She opened her car and I slipped into the back seat. 'I'm Qarsoon,' I said lightly. 'The Hidden One. Nobody must ever see my face.'

Amina started the engine. 'So what's the point of

today? I'm supposed to be taking you to a photo shoot. What's the point of that if your face is hidden?'

I unrolled the *abayad* and shook it out. 'Don't ask me. I don't even know where we're going.'

But Abdi knew all about it, of course. Amina stopped outside her house to pick him up and he had all the instructions we needed.

'We're meeting Sandy at David's flat. She wants some pictures—to get people talking about Qarsoon—and David's going to take them. Do you know how to get there, Auntie Amina?'

'Maybe you should set the satnav,' Amina said gravely.

I think she was teasing him, but he set it anyway, fiddling around until he found out how to do it. Then he pulled out his phone and rang Sandy, to say we were on our way.

When we reached the flats, David was waiting in the entrance hall. He opened the doors straight away and whisked us into the lift.

As we went up, he raised his eyebrows at me. 'Ready for some hard work?'

I thought it was a joke. 'What's so hard about being photographed?'

He laughed and rubbed a hand across his head, where the hair was growing thin. 'You'll know soon enough. By the time this session's over, you'll think

I'm a monster. And you'll find that Sandy can be very demanding too.'

'Sandy's here?' Amina said. As though she couldn't quite believe it.

David grinned. 'Come and meet her.'

Sandy wasn't just there in the flat. She'd taken it over. The main room was set up ready for the photographs, with lights and screens, and she'd turned David's bedroom into a changing room. There was a long rail of clothes that she'd brought for me to wear and she was busily sorting through them.

Amina went straight into the bedroom to meet her and Sandy lifted her head from the clothes and grinned.

'You must be Khadija's mother.'

'It's a pleasure to meet you,' Amina said eagerly. 'I love your designs.' She glanced past Sandy at the clothes on the rail—and her smile faltered slightly.

Sandy grinned even more. 'Did you think I was going to dress your daughter in puff skirts and boiler suits? Fashion's all about change, you know.'

'Especially yours,' David said drily, sticking his head in at the door.

Sandy pulled a face at him. 'Go away. No one's allowed in here except me and Qarsoon and—?'

'Amina,' said Amina. She smiled politely at David. 'Maybe Abdi could make himself useful out there with you?'

'Maybe Abdi would like a coffee.' David grinned at him. 'Let's take a break while we can.' He shut the door and Sandy pulled a hanger off the rail.

'Shall we begin with these?' she said.

I nodded, almost without looking. What did it matter which clothes I wore? I was doing this for Mahmoud, not to please myself. I began taking off my black clothes, but Sandy shook her head firmly.

'It's easier if we do it for you. All right, Amina?'

'Of course.' Amina looked delighted.

I stood straight and still and the two of them moved round me, fixing and fastening, like women preparing a bride for her wedding. They weren't just putting on clothes. The long dress had to be adjusted with hidden pins, until it hung exactly right. The shoes needed padding with tissue paper to stay on my feet and my hair was pulled back tightly and fastened in a knot.

Then Sandy made up my eyes.

'Normally I'd have a professional in for this,' she said as she chose the colours. 'But we don't want anyone else to see your face, so I'll do it myself. But I'll keep it fairly simple.'

Fairly simple meant black lines all the way round

222

my eyes and deep purple eye shadow on my eyelids. I could feel it every time I blinked.

Sandy twisted the *hijaab* over my head and tied the veil into place. Then she stepped back and looked at me, with her head on one side.

'Wow,' Amina said. 'That's *awesome!*' She sounded more like a sister than a mother.

When I turned round, to see my reflection, my breath stopped for a moment. What I saw was a pillar of gold. As I moved, the light rippled down my body, beautiful as water, fragile as a bubble in the air. Through the slit in the golden veil, my eyes were dark, like night on the heels of sunset.

'Let's get started,' Sandy said.

David was right when he warned me it would be hard work. For three hours I stood and lounged and walked and sat, doing everything he told me, as exactly as I could. Twice I changed into other clothes and each time the positions were different.

'That's good,' he kept saying under his breath. 'You're very good at this.' But I understood that he wasn't really looking at me. This was all about Qarsoon. She was an image we were making together and each of us had a part to play in that.

Once or twice Sandy muttered a question or an

223

instruction, but mostly she sat very still, concentrating hard. David hardly ever answered when she spoke, but I could see they were working together all the time. And I was part of that.

Amina sat watching everything, almost without blinking, and Abdi disappeared into the kitchen. I think he was mostly watching television, but every hour or so he emerged with coffee and biscuits.

I couldn't believe how hungry it made me, just having my picture taken.

Finally, David nodded and put down the camera he was holding. 'That's it,' he muttered. 'I think we've got all we can out of those clothes. Thanks, Qarsoon.' He hesitated and then went on. 'I know I've given you a hard time, but could you manage one more thing?'

Amina glanced down at her watch and coughed. 'I really think—'

'Only ten minutes,' David said. 'I just want a couple of shots in those black clothes she came in.'

'*Those?*' Sandy looked as though she was going to argue. Then she shrugged. 'Well—I don't see why not. She has to put them on anyway, before she goes.'

There was no fussing this time. Sandy took off the clothes I was wearing and left me to dress myself in the black ones. I was ready in a couple of minutes.

David had opened the big glass doors that led on to

224

the balcony. He beckoned me to join him out there. It was starting to get dark by then and the tall city buildings stood out black on the skyline. Behind them, the sky was a bright red-gold.

He knew exactly what he wanted and it was all done very quickly. I leaned against the corner of the balcony, with the sunset behind me, and he took the photograph that was going to make me famous. A strong black shape, looking down on a twilight city, with the sun dying in the west.

The picture that comes into everyone's mind when they hear *Qarsoon*.

I was back in time to go to Auntie Safia's shop. I was very tired, but it was a relief to be doing familiar work, in a place I knew.

Auntie Safia was specially kind to me that evening—in an odd, nervous way. I think she was puzzled about the trip to Somalia, but she didn't ask any questions. Maybe she didn't want to know the answers. Anyway, she just made me a cup of tea and gave me biscuits to eat while I swept and dusted. And when the work was over, she followed me to the door when I went to meet Abdi.

'So,' she said to us both, 'you're off to Somalia in a fortnight.'

'Ten days!' Abdi said, with a fierce light in his eyes.

'And you're going to Dubai and then flying into Hargeysa?'

Abdi shook his head. 'No, we're not going that way. We're flying into Galkayo,' he said.

I hadn't heard that before. My heart jumped to think that we were going so close to the places where my family travelled, but Auntie Safia frowned.

'That's not what Suliman told me. Has he changed his mind? Or maybe you've made a mistake.'

Abdi hesitated. Then he nodded slowly. 'Yes,' he said. 'I must have made a mistake.'

But I knew he was lying.

And so did Auntie Safia. She didn't say anything, but when we left she stood and watched us, all the way down the road.

Freya

And why wasn't I at Khadija's earth-shattering photo shoot? Because I was with Merry. She'd phoned me, out of the blue, while I was wandering round the shops with Ruby and Ben. Ruby and I were trying to sort out Ben's love-life—as usual—but we had different ideas about what he ought to do. (And, no, that has absolutely nothing to do with this story. But I want you to know that I'm not a loser. I have dozens of friends and especially Ruby and Ben.)

'*Tell* her,' Ruby was saying. 'She needs to know how you feel. Honestly, Ben—'

When my phone rang, I answered it, but I went on listening to Ruby as well, the way you do. That's why it took me a moment to tune in to what Merry was saying.

'Darling, I'm sorry I made such a soap opera out of your birthday. Can I make it up to you this afternoon?'

'You don't need to do that,' I said absently. 'Honestly, Merry, it's fine.' *It's just good to hear your voice, and know you haven't really stepped on a landmine.* (No, I didn't say the last bit out loud. My brains weren't quite that scrambled.)

'Don't worry,' Merry chirruped. 'I'm not going to come round in sackcloth and ashes, or anything embarrassing like that. But I've got a *delicious* idea—'

I should have listened to what she was suggesting, but just at that moment I heard Ruby whispering to Ben again.

'Look, there she is—going into Next! Follow her and *tell* her you still love her! Before you lose your nerve.'

No! That was terrible advice! I knew I had to get off the phone and stop Ben getting hurt all over again. So when Merry said, 'Shall I pick you up from your dad's in half an hour?' I didn't take it in at all. I just muttered, 'Thanks. That'll be great—' and grabbed hold of Ben's arm, a split second before he launched off into trauma and disaster.

'Wear something pretty,' Merry trilled as she rang off.

It was five minutes before her words sank in properly. When I realized what I'd done, I felt like ringing her back and saying I couldn't do it, but I was afraid of upsetting her.

'I've got to go,' I said to Ruby and Ben. 'Don't do anything dumb while I'm not here. OK?'

I must have sounded very fierce, because I could hear them laughing at me as I shot off back to the flat.

That was all before the famous photo shoot, of course. Much earlier in the day. When I let myself into the flat, Dad was off at Sandy's workshop, collecting the clothes, and I was all alone.

I stood in front of my wardrobe and panicked. What had I agreed to do? And what had I got that Merry might possibly accept as *pretty*?

I wore my birthday dress in the end. It was the only thing. I just had time to put it on and pull a brush through my hair before Merry rang to say she was parked outside.

'I'm on my way!' I said into the phone. Pushing it in my bag, I raced out of the flat, slamming the door behind me.

We were driving away before I remembered that I hadn't left a message for Dad. I should have done it from the car, but Merry was rattling on about tea and cake and wonderful light scones, and I suddenly realized she was taking me to Benson's. (Thank goodness I'd chosen the birthday dress!)

'I've arranged a little party,' she said. 'Just people you know. Nothing to worry about.'

Oh God, I thought, *don't let it be models.*

But it was models, of course. Who else does Merry know that's remotely my age? They were there in the hotel lounge when we walked in. Siobhan and Lorelei, Molly Parker and Nadya K, and half a dozen others, all lounging on the big, squashy sofas and chattering away like a flock of long-legged birds.

Cranes, maybe, or flamingos.

When I came in, they all jumped to their feet and burst into 'Happy Birthday', singing at the tops of their voices. 'Not my idea', Merry muttered under her breath. 'But you have to say it's nice of them.'

And that wasn't the end of their niceness. They'd all brought presents, too. Bags and scarves and neat little bangles too small for my wrist. Probably all free from somewhere, but they were still things most girls would die for. Siobhan had even found a pair of Vivienne Westwood shoes that were almost my size.

I pulled all the presents out of their bags, going 'Ooh!' and 'Aaah!' in the right places, and I squeezed my feet into the shoes and showed off my ankles as if they were worth it. The girls shrieked as each new thing appeared, knotting scarves through my belt and arguing about which bag went best with my frock.

And all the time, Merry was being the fairy

godmother, ordering up Earl Grey tea and hot toast and little iced fancies as well as the scones she'd promised. The models all ate like horses—those who weren't anorexic—and when all the other food had disappeared a birthday cake materialized. Nothing blatant. Just a feather-light sponge, with crystallized violets around the edge and a silver candle in the middle.

I was bending forward to blow out the candle when Siobhan said, 'So—tell us about Qarsoon. Who *is* she?'

I spluttered and missed the candle completely. *So that's what this is all about.* 'I can't tell you. It's a secret.'

'So you *do* know!' Molly said triumphantly. 'Merry *said* you were there when Sandy spotted her.'

'Oh, *that* girl,' I said, as nonchalantly as I could. I picked up a knife and sliced into the cake. 'What makes you think it's her? When Sandy saw her walk, she said she was no good. Didn't she, Merry?'

Merry arched her eyebrows. 'So why did you all go off in the same taxi?'

It's no fun discovering that your fairy godmother is really a wicked witch. I cut a huge slice of cake and plonked it on to her plate. 'Ever heard of red herrings?' I said sweetly. That got a laugh from the girls.

Merry nodded, as if to say, *Quick thinking!* but I could see she wasn't taken in. I picked up another scone, taking a huge bite, so that my mouth was full. If they were going to bombard me with questions, I needed time to work out my answers.

But there weren't any more questions. Instead, Merry looked over my shoulder and beamed. 'Tony! You made it!'

From behind me came a familiar, greasy voice. 'Merry—*darling*—when have I ever let you down? You know you're my favourite woman in the whole wide world.'

It was Tony Morales. The most annoying, posturing, slimy-tongued photographer in the entire world. He's mainly a fashion photographer, but he's not above selling candid celebrity snaps to the tabloids if he sees a chance to make some money. Everything about him is repulsive—except the pictures he takes. At least two of the girls there owed their careers to a brilliant Tony Morales photo.

'Surprise!' Merry trilled, giving me a huge smile. 'This is an extra little birthday present, Freya darling. Tony's going to take your picture.'

There was no chance of escaping. The girls crowded round me so tightly I could hardly breathe, and Tony narrowed his eyes and looked up at the light. Then he began to prance around, crouching on the floor one moment and leaping on to a sofa the next.

'It's the angle,' he was chanting. 'You know I have to find the right angle. And maybe a few tiny adjustments—' He darted forward, tweaked at the neckline of my dress and brushed my fringe sideways with his fingers. '*Much* better. Now all look left—and think of chocolate cake.'

All the faces around me took on expressions of hopeless longing and Tony was just lining up the shot when my phone rang.

I had to wriggle sideways to squeeze a hand into my pocket. As I answered the phone, everyone pretended to look away, but I could feel them listening avidly. They were hoping it was Sandy. Hoping to pick up a clue about the mysterious Qarsoon.

They were out of luck. It was Dad.

'Where are you?' he said. 'I thought—'

I interrupted, before he could give anything away. 'Hi, Dad. I'm at Benson's!'

'You're *where*?'

Time for a bit more quick thinking. I put on a silly, excited voice and prayed that he'd understand. 'Merry's arranged a *fantastic* tea party. With Siobhan and Lorelei and—everyone. *And Tony Morales has come to take my picture!*'

Dad got it straight away. He positively bellowed

down the phone. 'Have you forgotten you're supposed to be here? I want you home IN TWENTY MINUTES!'

He rang off immediately, and I put my phone away, trying to look embarrassed. 'I'm sorry, I've got to go now.'

But it's not that easy to ruin Merry's plans. She was just too quick for me.

'Don't worry, darling,' she said smoothly. 'Tony can drive you home—can't you, Tony? It'll only take fifteen minutes if they bring his car round.' She nodded to a waiter to arrange it and clapped her hands. 'There's still time for the picture if you're quick. Chocolate cake, girls!'

All the models turned their heads obediently and put on the longing expression again. I just stared stolidly, straight ahead, until Tony had taken the photograph and then I jumped to gather up all my things, with lots of smiles and thank yous.

Lorelei had given me one of those gigantic Jennifer Chan totes and I crammed everything else into it. Then I started on the goodbye kisses, backing away at the same time. When I reached the door of the lounge I slid through it and scuttled across the foyer, hardly giving the doorman time to open the big glass doors.

All the way back to the flat, Tony tried to trick me into saying something about Qarsoon. That was obviously the point of the whole tea party. Merry was desperate to know who was going to be behind the veil, so she'd surrounded me with people who were sure to ask. Hoping that I'd let something slip.

Well, she was going to be disappointed. I slumped down in the passenger seat and clamped my mouth shut, trying not to listen to Tony's wheedling voice.

'Just a little *hint*, Freya darling,' he kept saying. 'To make the whole thing more interesting. Just a *morsel*.'

I was determined that he wouldn't get anything out of me and I nearly made it. I didn't let my guard down until we were pulling up outside Dad's flat. As Tony braked, the glass doors opened suddenly and out came three figures. A woman. A boy. And a tall figure veiled in black.

'Is that her?' Tony said sharply.

'No!' I said.

But I wasn't fast enough. And my voice was too loud to be convincing. Tony took one look at my face and grabbed his camera. We both jumped out of the car at the same time, me shouting, 'No! Don't let him see you!' and Tony snapping away even before he hit the pavement.

Abdi heard my shouts first, and he reacted very fast. He muttered at the woman and they both put up hands to shield their faces. Catching hold of Khadija, they began to run, with Tony racing after them like a paparazzo.

It only lasted a few seconds. Then they were in their car and driving away and Tony was coming back towards me, flicking back through the shots to see if he'd got a picture he could use.

It was in the paper the next morning. A sharp, dramatic picture of a tall black figure poised against a pale, reflective wall. *Mysterious Qarsoon—the face everyone wants to see.*

Sandy was ecstatic. She came round at breakfast time, waving the paper and beaming all over her face. 'You're so *clever*, Freya! How did you manage it?'

'It was just an accident,' I said.

Sandy hugged me. 'Well, it wouldn't have happened without you. This is absolutely perfect timing. It's just the kind of thing the media adore—and the story's got almost two weeks to build before the show.'

Dad was already laying her a place at the table. 'Do you want toast?' he said.

She flapped a hand, as though food was insignificant. 'I want a *picture*,' she said. 'Can you let me have it now? I think it has to be the one in black, that you took on the balcony. That ties in with what she's wearing in Tony's photo. We can release that in a couple of days, to give things a boost, and then I'll get Carmel to leak our flight details. And the fact that Qarsoon's coming separately, but on the same flight.'

'Be careful,' Dad said. Making the toast anyway. 'It's risky playing games with the media.'

'Not this time!' Sandy said. 'This is going to be perfect. And nobody—*nobody*—will dare to miss my show. Even if the real clothes *are* on another continent!'

I don't think I've ever seen her look quite so happy.

I think Tony Morales was pretty happy too. A couple of days later, he sent me a big print of the photo he'd taken in Benson's. *Two great shots in one day!* said the message on the back. *Thanks, Freya. xxx* (Kisses from Tony Morales! How gross is that?)

It was a vile picture. It made me look like a freak. There were all the models, with their bony, beautiful faces, staring off wistfully to one side. And I was in the middle, looking square and stubborn and gazing straight into the camera.

I was just going to tear it up in disgust when Dad came and looked over my shoulder. 'How can a man as unpleasant as Tony Morales produce such great images?' he said.

I pulled a face at him. 'What's great about it? He's made me look an idiot.'

'No he hasn't,' Dad said. 'He's made you look like yourself. Stubborn and independent—and completely beautiful.' He kissed the end of my nose. For a second it was almost as though nothing had changed between us.

Then I dropped the photo on the table. 'You can have it,' I said. 'As long as you take me to Somalia.'

'Freya, we've talked about that. It's too risky.'

'You just don't want me there, do you?'

'It's not that—'

'Yes it is,' I said fiercely. 'You want to concentrate on keeping Sandy safe—without me hanging round to distract you. Well, what if something does happen? If you both get killed, do you think I'll be *pleased* I was left behind?'

'Now you're being melodramatic,' Dad said. But he was on the defensive and I knew he understood exactly how I felt. Wasn't that why he was going with Sandy?

I had no intention of backing down and neither had he. We were glaring at each other, on the edge of saying hurtful, unforgivable things, because this was about much more than a trip to Somalia.

But then—just before the argument exploded into a real fight—I saw the way to get what I wanted. I was wasting my time trying to convince Dad, but I could make Sandy take me. If I was prepared to be ruthless.

'Have it your own way,' I said with a shrug. I pushed the photo across the table. 'Just get this thing out of my sight.'

Dad looked as though he was going to hug me, so I went away quickly before he had a chance. And as soon as I was alone in my bedroom I sent Sandy a text.

Take me to Somalia or I'll tell Tony Morales about Qarsoon. Really.

My hands were shaking as I sent it. I knew it would work. When Sandy and Dad flew off to Dubai, they wouldn't leave me behind. I'd be travelling with them, all the way to Somalia.

I couldn't think about anything after that.

Mahmoud's new room was light and airy, with a mattress to lie on and a soft, new blanket. And he was almost never alone. Now Sanyare sat with him, telling stories and chanting poems and songs to pass the time. They shared meals and prayed together and Mahmoud laughed at Sanyare's jokes.

Sometimes he even made jokes of his own.

'What is it today?' he said, when Rashid came in with the food. 'Goat stew? And camel milk?'

Sanyare laughed and leaned forward, ruffling Mahmoud's hair like a father with his son. And Rashid grinned as he held out the plate of maize porridge.

'This is better than goat stew,' he said. 'It's from the best restaurant in Eyl—Makhaayad Rashid!'

'Rashid's cooking is like no other,' Sanyare said gravely, pulling a face at Mahmoud. 'And the tea too. It has a very special taste.'

They went on teasing Rashid until he pretended to lose his temper and stamped out of the room. Then they sat side by side, talking and sharing the food.

It would have been easy to think of Sanyare as a friend.

But a friend doesn't hold on to his gun while he talks to you. And when he has to go out of the room, he doesn't lock the door behind him. No amount of jokes and poems could change those things and Mahmoud didn't stop noticing them.

He knew he was only there as part of a plan, and when the time came, Sanyare and the others would use him without caring how he felt, the way men use a knife or a gun when they go hunting. All he could do was watch and wait.

And try to spot the mistake that would let him escape ...

If you work hard, Suliman had said, *I'll make sure you come with us*. That was the deal—and he made sure I kept my side of the bargain. I've never spent so long hunched in front of a computer as I did in the two weeks before we left. There was an endless stream of arrangements to make, and never enough time.

But I wasn't grumbling. Every time I sent an email to Somalia, I thought, *I'll be there in a couple of weeks. I'll see what it's really like.* I could still hardly believe it.

As long as the holidays lasted, I spent most of the days at Suliman's house, keeping records while he phoned and phoned and phoned. And after the beginning of term, I was still there for hours every evening, making copies of documents and typing up checklists for everyone.

We were travelling in two groups. Suliman, Amina, and I were leaving first, with Khadija. We were going to change planes at Dubai and go straight on to Galkayo, where Suliman would start contacting everyone he'd lined up to help with the show. The drivers and guards would meet us in Galkayo, but everyone else—dressers and make-up experts, carpenters and computer technicians—would be waiting in a village near Eyl.

The equipment for live-streaming the show was being hired—at huge expense—and Suliman was responsible for checking it through Dubai and picking it up when it arrived in Galkayo. That meant even more phone calls.

Sandy and her group were setting out two days after us and making their own way to Dubai. From there on, Suliman was responsible for them as well. And for getting everything together in time. Sandy was expecting to land in Somalia, travel straight to the village, and set up the show in three days flat.

My brain couldn't take in the whole picture. I just sat in Suliman's house, doing the paperwork he gave me and listening to him talking to relations and friends and friends of friends of relations, arguing and haggling and making promises. His conversations were sharp and serious, like something out of an action movie. Only he wasn't pretending. This was real—and we were going into the middle of it all.

On the evening before we left, I was in Suliman's

house, checking us in on line. When I stood up to go, he held up a hand to keep me there.

'Just a minute,' he muttered. He ended his phone call, very quickly, and then he spun round in his chair to look at me. 'So—we're off tomorrow,' he said. 'At last. Are you feeling anxious?'

'I'm fine,' I said quickly.

He gave me a wry smile. 'How can you be *fine*? You've spent your whole life hearing bad things about Somalia. Things about warlords and pirates and a totally failed state. We get the worst press in the world. You wouldn't be human if it didn't affect you.'

I avoided his eyes, to stop him seeing how right he was and he laughed and punched me gently on the shoulder.

'It's normal, OK? But don't let them frighten you. In a couple of days, you're going to see the truth with your own eyes. And the truth is—our country is beautiful. Full of space and light and courage. You know the song?'

I shook my head, and he closed his eyes and began chanting it softly, in Somali.

> *'The boys who herd camels*
> *and ignore their own hunger*
> *hold the spirit of our country.*

244

The red earth where I sleep,
with no mat to cushion me,
holds the spirit of our country.

The tents of the nomads
and the bright shields of warriors
these all hold our spirit.

Keep us strong, keep us free
Victorious God!'

I knew the song was making pictures in Suliman's head and I thought, *Soon, I'll be able to see those pictures too. Soon I'll be there.*

He opened his eyes and smiled at me. 'It's a great place, Abdi. It's where we belong.'

The words sparked up a precious, painful memory. 'That's what my father always used to say.'

Suliman nodded. 'That sounds like Ahmed. He's rooted in Somalia.' He turned back to the phones, leaving me to see myself out of the house.

I shut the door quietly behind me, thinking about my father. Suliman had spoken about him as though he was still alive. I felt like that too, even though it was over a year since he'd died. How *could* he be dead? Where had all that energy gone? As I walked down the road, I imagined a tall, green tree growing out of his body and spreading a shade of cool air over the desert sand.

Was that what Suliman meant by *rooted in Somalia*?

It was early in the morning when we started out. But, even though it wasn't really light, Maamo and my sisters came down to watch us load our bags into Suliman's car. Half a dozen neighbours rolled up too, to give us messages to pass on to their families. And even Liban was awake enough to send me a text— enjoy returning 2 ur culture bro.

The neighbours were all chatting and smiling and Fowsia, Sahra, and Maryan were jumping up and down with excitement. Only Maamo held back— until the very last moment. Then, as Suliman started the engine, she suddenly dived forward and tapped on the window to make me wind it down.

'Remember who you are,' she said fiercely. 'And come back safe.' She reached through the window, to pat my hand, and then she dived back again, with her lips pressed tight as though she was holding back tears.

And that was it. We'd left.

The journey was a kind of magic nothing-time that flew by too quickly to grasp. I thought it would be boring and full of hassles, but with Suliman all the difficulties were smoothed away. The flight was exactly on time and once we'd eaten the meals and watched the movies we were almost landing in Dubai.

There was a delay then, while we waited for our plane to Galkayo—but who could be bored in the airport at Dubai? I walked up and down, staring at all the luxury in the shops and choosing the clothes I would have bought if I'd had enough money. And Suliman came up behind me, while I was staring at a rack of sunglasses, and bought me the coolest pair in the shop.

'You've got to look right,' he said, 'if you're travelling with me.'

It was a joke, of course, but the kind of joke that makes you feel really good.

On the flight into Somalia, Suliman made Amina and Khadija sit together, so that I could have the place beside him, next to the window. We set out very early in the morning and for most of the journey it was too dark to see anything. But as the sun came up, Suliman touched my arm and leaned across my seat, pointing out of the window.

'Look!' he said.

There below us was the line of the Somali coast, slicing across the blue spread of the sea. As the plane began its descent, I pressed my face to the window and stared at the spread of cliffs and hills and ravines unfolding in front of my eyes.

It was my first sight of the country where I belonged.

Khadija

As soon as I stepped out of the aeroplane, I knew I was home. The sun was bright on my face and the air had the clean, familiar smell of the desert. When my feet touched the ground at the bottom of the steps, I felt like crying. While I was in England, in the cold, grey light and the endless dripping rain, I'd tried not to think about how much I missed Somalia. Now all that burst up inside me as I walked across the runway.

But home is more than a place. It's family too. And no one from my family was there to welcome me. It would only have taken one email to bring them all to the airport, but Suliman had forbidden me to tell them I was coming. He said it was too dangerous.

'You never know who might see an email. We can't afford to let the kidnappers know you're here. They might decide you're more valuable than Mahmoud and snatch you instead.'

'At least Mahmoud would be free,' I'd said.

Suliman had just looked scornful. 'You think they'd let him go alive? Don't be stupid, Khadija. If you want to rescue him, this has to be a secret visit.'

I still wasn't sure I understood why, but the first thing he'd said went on ringing in my ears. *You never know who might see an email.* If someone had seen my email to Mahmoud, telling him about Sandy, then the kidnap was all my fault.

But *had* anyone seen it? How was that possible?

Suliman was right about one thing. I wasn't going to risk making more trouble for Mahmoud. So I went into Somalia as Khadija Ahmed Mussa, travelling with my brother Abdirahman Ahmed Mussa and two friends of our family.

I didn't have to worry about being recognized by accident. Ever since we arrived in Dubai, I'd been hidden behind my black veil, wearing the clothes that turned me into Qarsoon. No one saw my face as I stood in the airport with Abdi and Amina, watching Suliman pay our entry money.

He collected our luggage and then haggled for a car to take us into Galkayo. I didn't want to be shut up in a town. I wanted to run and run under the wide sky, breathing the clean air and feeling the hot sand under my feet. But that wasn't part of Suliman's plan.

Amina and Abdi and I were squashed into the back of an old, battered car, with the windows tightly closed and bags on our knees. I could hardly breathe as we lurched out of the airport and along the road into the town centre.

All the way, Abdi was looking out of the window, with his nose pressed up against the glass. He shouted out at everything he saw, even ordinary sights like camels and goats and the pictures painted on the shops. When we passed an ammunition stall at the side of the road, he was so excited that he wanted Suliman to stop the car.

But we didn't stop until we came to a house in the middle of the town. Suliman ordered the driver to park close to the door and shooed us inside the house, before people could gather round to look.

There was a woman in the house, making tea and *lahooh*. She was old and heavy and she fumbled sometimes, as though she could hardly see. Suliman greeted her like a relative and she mumbled a reply too softly to hear. Then we all sat down and watched her fill cups for us to drink.

'What's happening?' I whispered to Amina. 'Why are we here?'

She shrugged and shook her head.

Abdi was the one with all the answers. 'We have to stay here until Sandy arrives,' he said importantly.

'Then we'll go out of town, to the village where we're doing the show. Suliman's got it all arranged.'

'What about Mahmoud?' I said. 'We could be trying to find him, instead of sitting around here.'

'Don't try and change things now!' Abdi said fiercely. 'Suliman knows what he's doing. Leave it to him—and don't interfere.'

I nearly shouted back, but Amina put a hand on my arm. 'Let them work it out,' she said quietly. 'It's better that way.'

I didn't understand how she could let herself be ordered around like that. She was a clever woman. 'Abdi doesn't know anything,' I said. 'He's only a boy—and he's never been here before.'

'But he's working with Suliman,' said Amina. As though that settled everything.

We stayed in that dark little house for two whole days, with men coming in and out all the time to talk to Suliman. The silent woman cooked for everyone, making tea and pancakes and watery goat stew. Her name was Haleema, but Suliman never told us who she was or why she was living on her own, without a husband or any children.

Amina offered to help her, of course, but she'd never cooked on anything except an English stove.

When I tried to show her the Somali way, Suliman told me not to interfere. And he made me keep my face covered, even in the house.

He made us stay inside too. That was very hard on Abdi, because it was his first time in Somalia and he was longing go out and explore. But Suliman was very firm.

'No one goes out except me,' he said. 'I've got work to do and I don't want to waste my time worrying about you. You're staying with Haleema until we hear from Sandy.'

That happened on the third day, very early in the morning. The phone call woke everyone up and I heard Haleema complaining under her breath as Suliman went outside to talk. She heaved herself on to her feet and stirred up the fire.

Suliman was only outside for two or three minutes. Then he came inside and started giving orders. 'Sandy Dexter's on the plane from Dubai—with her whole crew. She's expecting to see us at the airport when she lands, so pack everything up, as fast as you can. My cousin Ied's coming to take us in his car.'

Abdi yawned and rubbed his eyes and Amina began hunting round for her morning vitamin tablets. They both took a long time to start the day properly. Before they were on their feet, my bag was half packed, and I would have packed theirs too, if I'd dared. Why couldn't they hurry?

I wanted to be in the car and on the way to the airport. Once Sandy was there, I could start working at last. That was what I'd come for.

To earn the money that would save Mahmoud's life.

Freya

Our journey to Somalia was utterly, *utterly* different.

Abdi and Khadija slipped out of England with no fuss at all. Like an ordinary family going home to Somalia for a visit. But we were the biggest story in the fashion world.

Two days before we left, Sandy and Marco leaked Dad's picture of Khadija on the balcony. And they laid a trail of rumours that the tabloids snapped up.

Secret face of super-Q! said the headlines. *What has she got to hide?*

Wild stories flew round London, growing crazier every time someone passed on the gossip.

Qarsoon hid her face because it was scarred from an acid attack.

No, she was a celebrity who wanted to try modelling without damaging her other career. (*You wouldn't believe who she really is . . .*)

Rubbish! She was actually a man—with a thick black beard to prove it.

By the time we left London—the day before Fashion Week started—there were half a dozen photographers camped outside Sandy's flat. They trailed us to the airport and surrounded us when we got out of the car.

Sandy made sure there were a few red herrings, just to keep them thinking. The Tony Morales picture showed a glimpse of Khadija's cheap trainers and she bought an identical pair for one of the new models she was taking.

Poor girl! You should have seen her face when Sandy gave her the shoes. But she couldn't refuse to wear them. Sandy's show was going to be her big break.

She wasn't the only one to suffer. Another girl got a shoddy denim backpack—just like Khadija's. And someone else had to imitate the way Khadija stood in Dad's picture. None of them liked it, but they all did what they were told—and the photographers noticed everything, muttering to each other as they tried to guess which was the 'real Qarsoon'.

Sandy was stuck away in the VIP lounge, of course, but the girls had to queue at the ordinary check-in. Once or twice she bobbed out to talk to them—just to make sure the photographers didn't miss anything.

And every time she appeared, she was surrounded by flashing cameras and shouted questions.

'Which one is it?'

'Come on, Sandy. Give us a break!'

It was quieter up in the VIP lounge—but not more peaceful. Dad was unbelievably angry that Sandy was taking me. Whenever she appeared, he tried to make her change her mind.

'It's *irresponsible,*' he kept saying. 'You can't bring Freya just because she wants to come. She's not old enough to make a decision like that.'

Sandy didn't tell him I was blackmailing her. She just looked vague and waved her hands about. 'Qarsoon needs a dresser,' she said. 'Someone I can really trust. And I'm not letting any more people into the secret—so it *has* to be Freya.'

She said it so often it almost sounded convincing.

By the time we reached Dubai, Dad wasn't speaking to either of us. I left him to sulk and went off to do a bit of research on the internet. There was so much stuff about Qarsoon that I couldn't read it all. I flicked through the news pages and then glanced at some of the freaky fringe sites.

I was just reading a really juicy piece of conspiracy theory (*Why do they hide her face? Because it's not JUST HERS!! She's the first human clone—and she's off to her unveiling in the continent where humanity began. WE*

MUST END THIS MADNESS NOW!!!!) when some-one leaned over my shoulder and a familiar, creepy voice spoke into my ear.

'Come on, Freya, give me a clue. It's got to be my story.'

You don't want to know what it's like feeling Tony Morales's breath on the back of your neck. I was out of that chair so fast I nearly left my shoes behind. Not that he cared, of course. He just laughed at the look on my face.

'Don't hold out on me, Freya. I'm not asking you to blow the whole secret. I just need to know which flight you're catching into Somalia.'

'One without you on it,' I said. Already walking away.

When I told Sandy what he was planning, she clapped her hands together. 'Fantastic! We must make sure he comes. Tony's always good for publicity. If he gets a really good picture, we might even make the front pages. But he'll be suspicious unless he has to work for the information. Why don't you take Zoë for a coffee and let him overhear a few things?'

Zoë was the student she'd recruited to co-ordinate all the make-up. She was large and cheerful and very talkative. When I went to find her, in the departure lounge, she was delighted at the idea of doing a bit of under-cover work.

We bought a couple of lattes and I let her rattle on about how she could make my eyes look bigger and improve my skin. All the time, I kept an eye on the mirror behind the bar and when I saw Tony Morales sneaking into a chair behind us I glanced at my watch.

'Is our flight boarding yet?' I said, in a clumsy whisper.

Zoë jumped up and went to look at the screen. 'What's the number again?' she called back at me.

I scowled impatiently as I went to join her. 'There aren't a million flights to Galkayo. Look—it's that one. And there's nothing happening yet.'

Zoë glanced over my shoulder. 'Good work,' she muttered under her breath. 'He's gone scuttling off to try and pick up a seat. Let's hope there's one left.'

'Oh, there will be,' I said. 'Sandy never leaves anything to chance.'

And sure enough, when we boarded the little plane there he was, a couple of rows behind us.

We landed in Galkayo very early in the morning and I stumbled sleepily off the plane. Even though it was early, I could feel the heat coming up off the tarmac. I didn't want to think what it would be like by the middle of the day.

259

As I came down the steps, I heard Dad catch his breath behind me. When we reached the bottom, he put an arm round my shoulders.

'Can you smell that?' he said.

I sniffed obediently. And there was certainly something. A kind of zing in the air. 'What is it?' I said.

'It's Africa. I didn't realize how much I'd missed it.' Dad gave me a rueful smile. 'I've always wanted to bring you here, you know.'

I pulled a face. 'You could have fooled me.'

'No, I mean it. It's just—' He shrugged. 'I'd rather have waited until things got better.'

'Maybe they *are* better,' I said. 'You never know.'

We walked across the runway side by side, with the models stumbling along behind us in their silly high heels. As we reached the arrival hall, Dad hung back, waiting for Sandy.

'Is anyone meeting us?' he said when she caught up. 'What did you arrange?'

'Suliman should be here,' Sandy said. 'With cars to take us all into the desert.'

Dad looked startled. 'What—straight away?'

'Of course,' Sandy said firmly. 'We've got three days to set the whole thing up and then we're on stream live, to the world. There's no time to hang around.'

And she led the way into the arrival hall.

Just when it was beginning to seem as though nothing would happen, ever again, when Mahmoud had been shut up with Sanyare for three days in a row, the door flew open suddenly and in came the man called Yusuf, with Rashid behind him. They were gesturing with their guns.

Yusuf had looked lazy and relaxed when he was sprawled in front of the television, but there was nothing lazy about him now. He was obviously the one in charge.

'On your feet!' he said. 'You're going to have your picture taken.'

Rashid grinned and slapped Mahmoud on the back. 'You're going to be a celebrity.'

Yusuf had a newspaper tucked under his arm. He threw it across the room at head height, without any warning, aiming at Mahmoud's face. Automatically, Mahmoud's arm shot out and he caught it before it could hit him.

'Fresh news,' Rashid said, nodding down at the headline. He sniggered. 'You mustn't be out of date.'

The words shouted up at Mahmoud. SOMALI PIRATES CAPTURE THIRD TANKER. What did Rashid mean? Were they going to sell him to the pirates?

'Don't worry,' Sanyare said softly. 'It's just to show your family that you're alive today.'

Yusuf pushed Mahmoud back against the wall and Rashid lined up the camera.

'OK,' he said. 'Ready to smile?'

It was meant as a jeering joke, but Mahmoud smiled anyway, nervously parting his lips. Rashid was already taking the picture and he shouted angrily.

'Are you an idiot? Do you want your sister to think you're happy here? Don't you know that we'll kill you if she refuses to pay the money?'

Mahmoud knew the shouting was meant to frighten him. They wanted the photograph to show a pathetic, trembling boy. But he wasn't going to let anyone see him like that and he forced himself to keep on smiling. His muscles grew tighter and tighter until they ached with the strain, but he dared not let them relax. The smile was the only thing that could save him from crying.

When Rashid had taken half a dozen photos, Yusuf went across to look at them. What he saw made him laugh.

'No need to take any more,' he said. 'Those will do what we want.'

He snatched the paper away from Mahmoud and he and Rashid went away, banging the door behind them. Mahmoud was left alone with Sanyare again.

And he let himself stop smiling at last.

Abdi

Suliman had arranged a whole fleet of cars and trucks to meet Sandy at the airport. Three or four were full of girls—including the English models and Zoë the make-up girl. Then there was one for Amina, Khadija, and me and another for Freya and David.

Sandy insisted on going in the truck with the clothes—ten huge, flat suitcases full of them. She didn't take her eyes off the men who were loading them into the truck and when they balanced the last one on top she made them rope it down tightly.

'If anything happens to *these*,' she said fiercely, 'everything else is off. We'll just pack up and go home and no one will earn any money.' And she watched as the message was passed along the line, from one security guard to another.

The guards were the reason we needed so much transport. There were twenty of them—tall men, with guns slung over their shoulders. The knives on their belts reminded me of my father's dagger—blades that meant business, in well-worn leather cases. They stood around chatting to Suliman, watching everything with interest and chewing the green qat leaves he gave them.

'Do we really *need* all these people?' Sandy muttered, coming up behind him.

Suliman shrugged. 'If we take them, then probably—no, they won't be needed. But if we don't take them—' He frowned and shook his head. 'You've got a lot to protect. It's better to be safe, I think. But it's your decision, of course.'

The models were whispering and fluttering about, staring anxiously at the guards from under their eyelashes. 'I didn't know it was going to be like this,' I heard one of them mutter.

Suliman looked at Sandy and tapped his watch. 'We have a long drive ahead of us. If you want to change the arrangements, you have to do it now.'

David appeared suddenly beside Sandy. 'She doesn't want to change anything,' he said abruptly. 'This is good.'

Sandy blinked and looked up at him. Then she nodded. It was the first time I'd seen her give in to him.

'Let's go,' Suliman said. He turned and signalled to the guards, and they all started piling into the trucks.

Freya was standing with her back to the rest of us,

looking out at the bare, rocky ground beyond the airport. When David touched her shoulder, she jumped and turned round.

'We're following the truck in front,' David said briskly. 'Come on, Freya. We need to get this journey over before the sun goes down.' He opened the door of their car and hustled her in.

I was in the car behind, with Amina and Khadija. Two security guards jumped into the front and I thought we'd be off straight away. But nothing happened as fast as that. We were stuck in the hot, stuffy car for another quarter of an hour before the engine finally fired up and we swung out on to the road.

We were in the middle of a long procession of vehicles heading out into—nowhere. Galkayo was left behind and we were driving over dry, rocky ground with nothing growing on it except a few dry, thorny bushes. The air was hot and heavy and we travelled in a cloud of dust thrown up by the vehicles in front. When I looked through the rear window, I could see it hanging above the ground in a long trail behind us.

It was like that for the next ten hours. We went on and on and on, occasionally passing through villages that were just clumps of little houses roofed with corrugated iron. There were very few other vehicles on the road. Just a few children driving scrawny goats, and some women loaded down with heavy bundles.

I kept struggling to connect. *This is your country,* I kept telling myself. *This is where you belong.* But I didn't even know what that meant.

In Battle Hill, when the old people talked about Somalia they went on about the big skies and the huge, empty spaces—as if emptiness was something to be proud of. I just didn't get it. When we drove away from Galkayo, I felt as though we were dropping out of the world.

What was it like living here all the time? Looking after goats like those boys we'd passed on the road? It was impossible to imagine. What did they do for music? Where did they meet their friends?

If I'd been sitting next to Khadija, I might have asked some questions, but Amina was between us, leaning forward to stare through the windscreen, between the shoulders of the guards. It was a while before I realized that she'd never been here either. It was all as new to her as it was to me.

The village where we finally stopped was bigger than the others we'd passed. There were thirty or forty buildings at least. Some of them were permanent, built out of bricks and corrugated iron, and some were temporary structures, made of bent branches and woven mats. Lurching poles carried electric wires in from the horizon and there were a couple of small shops with pictures painted all over their front walls.

We didn't get much idea of what the village was normally like. As our vehicles drove in, pulling up one behind the other, people stopped whatever they were doing and crowded around us.

Suliman was travelling with Sandy, in the truck. When he jumped down, he was surrounded by a crowd of men, all eager to introduce themselves. As I started to understand what they were saying, I realized that most of them didn't live in the village at all. These were the people Suliman had booked for the show.

As soon as I got out of the car Sandy climbed out of the truck and ran across to me.

'Stay close to your sister. I don't want anyone trying to sneak a look at her face.'

Did she seriously think anyone there was interested in Khadija? I thought she was being paranoid—but she was in charge. I nodded obediently and she patted my arm and ran off to join Suliman.

Amina and Khadija were standing on the edge of the crowd, listening to the women trying to talk to Zoë.

'Who's come to work with me?' Zoë was asking. 'I'm the make-up artist.'

267

She waved her arms about, drawing invisible lines in the air and the women laughed and nudged each other. Then she opened her make-up box and they began examining the cosmetics critically, discussing the colours and trying them out on their hands.

Some of them had henna patterns on the palms of their hands and when Zoë saw them, she squealed with delight, like a six year old. 'Hey, Sandy! Look at these! Could we use them in the show?'

Sandy swooped across, leaning into the circle to look at the women's hands. Her face lit up like Zoë's. 'Wow! I've seen them before, but never this beautiful. Who does them? How can we ask?'

She looked round for someone to translate and Khadija was there at once, talking in English and Somali alternately. She stood out dramatically in her black clothes, surrounded by the women in their long bright dresses and their big headscarves.

When she explained what Zoë had said, they laughed and waved their hands in the air, and there was a babble of female chatter in two languages at once. Not a good place for me to be. I backed away and went to look for Suliman.

He and David were with the men. They were introducing themselves, and there was a lot of polite talk going on. I edged closer, hoping they would include me, but before they'd even noticed, Freya suddenly popped up beside me. Her face was very pink under her big sun hat and she looked hot and uncomfortable. But it wasn't only the heat that was making her pink.

'Look over there!' she said crossly, pointing past the houses.

A battered Discovery was driving into the village. It was carrying a couple of guards and a short, plump man with a blob of sunscreen on his nose.

'Who's he?' I said. 'Another of Sandy's people?'

Freya pulled a face. 'You've got to be joking. That's Tony Morales. He's on a personal mission to photograph the face behind Qarsoon's veil. If we don't watch him, he'll probably walk straight up to her and rip it off.'

Oh no he won't! I thought. That would be a terrible insult—especially here. Khadija might not be my real sister, but it was up to me to protect her from things like that.

'Someone needs to warn her,' I said. I meant to do it myself, but Freya was too quick for me.

'I'll go,' she said. And was off before I could say anything, almost running in spite of the heat.

Khadija

When Freya came running up, the women were just starting to talk to me.

Sandy didn't understand how difficult it was coming into a Somali village and being forbidden to tell my name. Of course the women were suspicious. They wanted to know my family and where I belonged and, when they found out I wasn't going to say, I knew what they were thinking. Someone who won't tell those things surely has a secret to hide.

But if I had been allowed to tell them, which name would I have used? Khadija Ahmed Mussa? Geri? Or my real name, which would give away everything? Maybe it was simpler just to say, *I am Qarsoon.*

I tried to explain, in between translating for Sandy and Zoë, and the women were just beginning to be friendly when Freya came racing over to us, waving her arms.

'That one won't last long if she keeps running around,' one of the Somali women muttered. Her

270

name was Nhur and she'd hardly spoken until then. Now she watched Freya scuttling towards us and the other women frowned and nodded. It was heavy, oppressive weather.

Freya's face was certainly very red, but she hardly seemed to notice how hot she was. As soon as she was near enough, she began to talk frantically, almost throwing herself at Sandy.

'It's Tony Morales. Look—he's just driven in! We need to be careful—'

Sandy caught hold of her shoulders and held her still. 'That's *good*,' she said firmly. 'He's going to give us great publicity.'

Freya was still agitated. 'But if he tries to pull off the veil—'

'He wouldn't dare,' Sandy said. 'He may be determined, but he's not a complete fool. Still, it might be a good idea to warn people about him.' She turned to me. 'Can you tell them?'

One or two of the women had picked it up already and they were passing it on to the others, looking puzzled and wary. When I started talking again, there were more sympathetic looks than before.

'The man who's just come wants to photograph my face,' I said. 'I can't let him do that. Is there anywhere I can hide away from him?'

There was some more muttering and then Nhur

gave me a big smile. 'You can go into my house whenever you like. And your friend too. Maybe we should
go there now. I think she needs to get out of the sun.'

Some of the other women nodded approvingly and
I caught hold of Freya's hand. 'Nhur's offering a place
where I can hide. Shall we go and look?'

It was a small, single-roomed house, right on the
edge of the village. It was hot and close inside, but
at least we were out of the blazing sun. Freya sighed
and took off her hat.

'Thank goodness for that! I hate this wretched
thing. I know I have to wear it, but it makes my head
so *wet*.' She ran her fingers through her hair and little
damp curls sprang up all round her face.

Nhur flicked her fingers scornfully at the sunhat.
'No good,' she said, in English. Then she shook her
head at Freya's trousers, with their narrow legs and
their tight waistband, and she pulled a funny face.
'Hot, hot, *hot*.'

'I know,' Freya said fretfully. 'But I have to cover
myself up. Otherwise I burn bright scarlet.'

Nhur didn't understand all that, but she knew
what Freya was saying. She gave her a long, thoughtful look and then raised her hand. 'Wait. I will come
back.'

As she went out of the house I heard the other
women calling to her. 'What are you doing, Nhur?

Come and show Zoë your beautiful henna patterns.' I didn't hear Nhur's reply, but a couple of minutes later she was back, with her hands full of bright cloth.

'This is better,' she said to Freya.

I saw at once what it was and I could tell—from the pattern, from the quality of the cloth, from the careful way it was folded—that these were someone's best things, kept for special days.

Freya just stared at them. 'What does she want?' she muttered. 'What am I supposed to do?'

'She's lending you some better clothes,' I said. 'It's a very kind action. You must put them on.'

'But—how?'

It was the first time I'd ever seen Freya looking uncertain. She reached out and touched the cloth as Nhur unfolded it.

'We'll help you,' I said. 'Take off all those hot, tight things you're wearing.'

It took me a little while to persuade her, but in the end she did. And then we had to dress her, the way you dress a child. She stood still as we pulled on the dress and pushed her arms into the sleeves. The awkward moment was when Nhur picked up the big headscarf, ready to drape it around her head.

'She wants me to wear *that*?' Freya said. And she took a step backwards.

Nhur frowned. 'She must cover her head,' she said

273

in Somali. 'Doesn't she understand that the sun can make her ill?'

'Yes she does,' I said. 'But she has some stupid, superstitious ideas. Wait a moment.' I changed to English, shaking my head at Freya. 'Look, I know what you're thinking—but it's different in Somalia. The scarf is the best thing to wear on your head. Please try it.'

Freya looked warily at it. 'I don't—'

'*Please*,' I said. I couldn't bear to think of her wearing that horrible, sweaty hat.

She put her hand out and felt the material. 'All right,' she said at last. 'But you'll have to show me how to put it on.'

I draped it round her head and over her shoulders, showing her where to put the pins if she needed them. Then I stepped back, pulling the dress straight. 'Now try walking,' I said.

The house was so small that there was only room for a few steps, but I saw Freya's face change as she felt the draught from the long skirt moving round her legs. Nhur saw it too, and she smiled.

'Now I shall make tea,' she said.

Freya

Nhur had obviously decided I was a total
fool. When she gave me the tea, she put
a hand across the top of the cup and said,
'Hot. Very hot.'

But I couldn't be annoyed. She was so kind and
gentle. And, let's face it, I'd been pretty incompetent
so far. I just can't cope in hot climates. You've only got
to look at me to realize that.

No use griping about it though. There I was, in
Somalia, and it was all my own fault. *So put up with it,
Freya, and do the best you can.* I sat on the floor between
Nhur and Khadija (I couldn't even squat properly) sip-
ping the tea and feeling utterly foreign and strange.

Khadija leaned towards me, and murmured in
English, 'Would you like to hear a story? One of the
women told me that Nhur's the best storyteller in the
whole village.' She said it as though she was offering
me a treat.

I wanted to say yes—but it all seemed too

complicated. 'You'd have to translate the whole thing for me.'

'I don't mind.' Khadija touched my shoulder lightly. 'I want you to hear one of our stories.' She nodded to Nhur and said something in a soft voice.

Nhur nodded back and closed her eyes for a second. When everything was quiet, she began to speak, pausing after each sentence to let Khadija translate. There was no fuss. Just the two voices, taking turns.

'Once, there was a man who had three wives. They were all very jealous women and they kept nagging at their husband to say which of them he loved the most . . . '

Stories get under your skin, don't they? I cupped my hands round the tea and bent my head, so that my face was hidden in the shadows.

'The man tried to put them off, but they kept on and on with their nagging. "Which of us do you love the most?"'

I could hear Suliman talking to some men outside. There was a lot of rough laughter and I guessed they were teasing him. But that seemed a long way off. Almost part of another world.

'One day, the poor husband couldn't bear it any more. So he called his wives together and said, "Very well, I will do what you ask. I will tell my favourite wife that I love her most." But first—'

I was holding my breath, waiting for the next line of the story. But before Nhur could speak, a

276

sharp sound cut through the noise outside, silencing everything else.

A gunshot.

The next moment, we heard the roar and rattle of a jeep being driven very fast into the centre of the village. And now there were different voices talking. Shouting aggressively.

Nhur and Khadija jumped up at once. It took me a few extra seconds, because my legs were tangled in my long skirt. By the time I reached the doorway, the other two were outside, peering round the corner of the building in front.

I ran to catch up and I would have gone a bit further, but Nhur caught at my arm, holding me back. 'No,' she whispered. '*No.*'

The jeep had pulled up in the open space ahead of us and the men inside were shouting half in English and half in Somali. I hardly understood anything, but one phrase came across clearly.

' . . . ten thousand dollars . . . '

They must have said it three or four times, flinging the words out defiantly. Then the engine revved up again and the jeep was off. When we stepped clear of the building we could see it bouncing down the track in a haze of dust.

Everyone was stunned and still—except Tony Morales. As soon as the men started driving away

277

he'd jumped clear of the crowd and now he was busy photographing everything in sight. The dusty, disappearing jeep. The shocked faces of the girls from England.

And the photograph lying on the ground, where the men from the jeep had thrown it.

It took me a couple of seconds to realize that no one had actually been shot. By that time, Khadija was running through the crowd to pick up the photograph. She reached it half a step ahead of Sandy and snatched it off the ground with both hands.

'What is it?' Sandy said. 'What do those men want?'

'Pretty obvious, isn't it?' That was Tony Morales, pushing his nose in as usual. 'They want ten thousand dollars. It's a ransom thing.'

Now everyone was pushing closer to see what the men had left. I squeezed between Zoë and Suliman, edging my way forward until I reached Khadija. Her hands were shaking as she held the picture out.

As soon as I saw it, I knew Tony Morales was right about the ransom. The boy in the photo was holding up a copy of that day's newspaper, in the classic, clichéd way, to show he was still alive. Or, at least, he *had* been alive a few hours ago.

He was about twelve or thirteen and he was staring out at the camera with his face stretched into a fake, defiant smile. A very frightened boy, struggling to look brave. It was horrible. Heart-breaking.

'Who is it?' Sandy said sharply. 'What makes them think we'll pay ten thousand dollars for a complete stranger?'

I thought Khadija was going to say something. But before she could speak, Suliman looked over her shoulder and sighed, very loudly.

'This boy isn't a stranger to me,' he said. 'He's one of my relations.'

'And they think you'll pay ten thousand dollars for him?' Sandy said.

Suliman shrugged and looked down. 'They know I haven't got ten thousand dollars. But maybe they think that you—?'

He stopped and looked at her, leaving the question hanging in the air.

When the men came back in the jeep, their mouths were full of qat and they were whooping and slapping each other on the back. Mahmoud could hear the noise from inside the little room where he and Sanyare were sitting.

'They're happy,' Sanyare said, in a dry voice. 'I think it was a good day.'

It was already dark. When Sanyare opened the door, the jeep's headlights shone straight in from outside, right across the main room of the house. Mahmoud stood up, shielding his eyes with one arm.

The men whooped louder when they saw him. 'OK, Mahmoud!' Rashid shouted. 'Are you ready to make us rich?'

Something had happened. They were behaving as though they could smell the money now, as though it was almost in their hands. Although he knew it was wrong, Mahmoud felt his heart lift and he laughed, before he could stop himself.

What happened then was very quick. Yusuf strode across the room, laughing back at him. And, as he laughed, he swung his AK47. The handle of the gun came up and hit Mahmoud on the mouth, square on his front teeth. Very hard.

Mahmoud cried out and clapped a hand over his face. When he pulled the hand away again, two of his front teeth were lying in the palm, cracked and smeared with blood. The laughter choked in his throat as he looked down at them.

Sanyare made a growling noise, as if he was going to protest. But he didn't. Yusuf met his eyes aggressively and took a step forwards and Sanyare looked away from Mahmoud and dropped his head. With another laugh, Yusuf jabbed his gun into Mahmoud's ribs.

'Smile,' he said genially. 'Go on. Let us see you.'

Mahmoud looked down at the gun barrel and wished he was brave enough to spit on it. Slowly, uncertainly, he opened his mouth in a false, blood-stained grin.

'Good,' Yusuf said. 'Very good.' He waved a hand at Rashid and suddenly the camera was there again, and a flash went off in Mahmoud's eyes.

When Yusuf saw the picture, he smiled and nodded. 'That's what we need for the next step,' he said cheerfully. 'They'll listen to us now.'

Afterwards, Sanyare took Mahmoud away to the little room and bathed his face, to wash away the blood. His fingers were gentle and careful.

'Does it hurt?' he said.

'No,' Mahmoud answered, lying. His mouth was sore and swollen and his breath came strangely through the gap in his teeth.

'Maybe you should take something,' Sanyare said, 'in case there is pain later.'

He went away and found a small white tablet and some water. When he brought them back, Mahmoud looked at the tablet, thinking that he didn't know what it was. Then he swallowed it anyway. Sanyare held a cloth under his chin while he drank, to catch the water that ran out of his mouth.

'What will Yusuf do with the photo?' Mahmoud said.

Sanyare looked away from him. 'He'll use it to make your family unhappy. And when they're unhappy enough, they will pay to save the rest of your teeth.'

Mahmoud tried to imagine Geri looking at the photograph. But he couldn't. Whenever he pictured her in his head she was always smiling. And he knew she wouldn't smile when she saw his mouth full of blood.

'My family won't pay you!' he said fiercely. His lips were so swollen that it hurt them to make the words, but he forced himself to speak. 'It's not right to give in to evil men.'

Sanyare looked at him sadly and shook his head. They both knew that what was right and what happened were two different things.

Abdi

The second photograph arrived the next morning—but not in the same explosive way. If the kidnappers had tried that again, there would have been a full-scale battle.

Sandy was white hot with anger at how our security guards had been caught out. While the rest of us were still looking at the photograph, I heard her ranting at David.

'I'm paying astronomical amounts of money—and for what? Any thug can drive straight into the village without being challenged. They could have shot us all!'

David seemed to be trying to calm her down. ' . . . only firing into the air,' I heard him say quietly. 'If they'd started serious shooting, our guards would have—'

But Sandy wasn't interested in what our guards would have done. She sent David off to talk to them and then she made a speech, standing on a rock so that everyone could see her.

'Suliman's young cousin has been kidnapped. But we don't know where he is, or what the kidnappers want us to do next. All we know is that they're asking for a lot of money. Until we hear some more, we'll get on with trying to earn that money, and I'll make sure our guards are ready if the kidnappers come back!'

Her face was fierce and sharp. As Suliman began to translate what she'd said, she looked round at the open space where we were standing, with her eyes narrowed, as though she was making calculations. The moment the translation was finished, she jumped off her rock and began talking to Suliman in a fast, low voice, beckoning left and right to get people to join them. By the time it was dark, she'd worked out a detailed plan about how the show was going to be set up.

'We're starting first thing in the morning,' she said, as we went off to separate houses to try and sleep.

I hadn't really thought about the show itself. Why would I? It was only a line of girls walking up and down in weird, expensive clothes. What was there to arrange, apart from the computer stuff?

As soon as the sun rose next morning, I started finding out how wrong I was.

It was like putting on some huge drama. OK, it was only going to last twenty minutes, but Sandy wanted a proper catwalk built out of wood. She insisted on having the make-up practised until it was perfect and everything had to be done in time to allow for rehearsals.

'The timing's crucial,' she kept saying. 'Those people in London will only be watching a screen. If the show is too long, or if it starts dragging, they'll be off without waiting for the end.'

Within a few minutes, she had people scurrying everywhere. Amina was pulled in to translate for the carpenters building the catwalk and Suliman went off to set up the web link with some computer technicians from Eyl. I wanted to go too, but Sandy wouldn't let me.

'Zoë has to have an interpreter,' she said. 'And you're the only one left.'

My face must have shown how I felt. 'Can't Khadija—?'

Sandy corrected me sharply. 'Qarsoon! And no, she can't. She's the key to the whole show and I don't want her distracted.'

If you only knew what's really distracting her, I thought, but I didn't dare to say a word about Mahmoud. I just trailed across to the table where Zoë was setting out her equipment.

She waved a hand when she saw me coming. 'Hey, Grumpy! You don't look too keen on helping here. Don't you realize it's a great art form? You ought to have a go yourself.'

The women didn't know what she'd said, but they understood the expression on my face. Before I'd said a word, they were all laughing at me.

'You want your face painted?'

'Come here and I'll make you beautiful!'

I wanted to zap back at them with something funny and smart, the way I would have done with the girls at school. But they were speaking too fast and I didn't catch half of what they were saying. All I could do was laugh back and pretend not to care.

Zoë slapped her hand on to the table to get their attention back. 'OK, folks, let's get down to work. The look for this show is all about *eyes*.' She glanced at me, to make sure I'd got that. 'It's going to be the same for every model, so I'll demonstrate on Emily and then you can all have a go. OK?'

I translated as well as I could, trying not to notice how the women smiled whenever I made a mistake. Then I took a step back.

Zoë shook her head at me. 'You haven't finished yet. I'm going to talk them through it while I demonstrate.'

That was a nightmare. She began by telling them

about everything on the table. How was I supposed to know the Somali for 'eye-liner' or 'false eyelashes'? I had to make up the names—and then remember what I'd said. And the more I tangled things up the more the women laughed at me.

Then Zoë started demonstrating what she actually wanted them to do, and it wasn't like anything you'd ever see in real life. Emily looked very striking when the make-up was on—but I'd run a mile from a girl with royal blue eyelashes and gold triangles over her eyes.

After that, the translation was even more hectic. Once the women started practising on the other models, they had endless questions to ask. I found myself running up and down the line, peering at what they were doing to try and understand what I had to say.

After an hour or so, Sandy came over to check how things were going. She was right beside me, examining the colour of a model's eyebrows, when the girl suddenly frowned and looked past her.

'Who's that?' she said nervously. 'It's not—?'

Everyone stopped and turned round, and someone gasped. The jeep that had brought the kidnappers yesterday was just coming into view on the horizon, bouncing down the road towards us.

Suddenly everything was dead quiet, except for the small, metallic noises of guns being taken out and made ready. The security guards always carried theirs, but now every one of the Somali men seemed to have a gun in his hand. And even Tony, the snoopy photographer, turned out to have a revolver in his bag. Suliman reached under his jacket and took something out of a shoulder holster, and I heard Amina catch her breath when she saw it.

But the jeep didn't come within range of anyone's gun. It stopped when it was still a long way out of the village and someone climbed out and began to walk towards us. Someone small and stooped and very, very slow.

As the figure dragged itself closer, we could see that it was an old woman leaning heavily on a stick. A very, *very* old woman.

'Is it a trick?' Zoë muttered under her breath.

No one answered. The Somali women were watching carefully and I could hear the models breathing fast and hard. We all stared at the old woman as she came closer, step by painful step.

'We can't just stand here like dummies,' Sandy said impatiently. 'We have to know what this is all about.'

She glanced round for Suliman, but he was on the other side of the catwalk, muttering to David. Sandy hesitated for a moment and then she gave her head a little shake and looked back at me.

'Come on,' she said briskly, and she set off, without

waiting for me to answer. Just assuming I would follow her.

And what else could I do? She had to have *someone*
to tell her what the old woman said.

As we walked out of the village, Sandy spread
her hands wide, holding them away from her body
to show that she wasn't carrying a weapon. I found
myself doing the same, almost without thinking.
That might sound like play-acting, but believe me it
felt deathly real. The men who were still in the jeep
were pointing their guns at us, and by the time we
met the old woman we were going to be well within
range.

When she saw us coming, the old woman stopped,
resting on her stick. As we got closer, I could see the
wrinkles on her face and the sharp brightness of her
eyes. She watched us steadily until we came to a stop,
about a metre away from her.

Then she said, 'Assalaamu alaykum.'

'Alaykum assalaam,' I said and Sandy copied me,
laying a hand against her chest and bowing politely.

The old woman reached into the folds of her scarf
and took out an envelope. 'Sandy Dexter?' she said.
Her accent was strange, but the words were very
clear.

Sandy bent her head and reached out to take the
envelope. As soon as it was in her hand, the old

woman turned away and began to shuffle back to the jeep.

'Let's get out of here,' I said. I turned round and started walking, but Sandy didn't follow me. When I looked back, I saw her standing very still, looking at what she'd taken out of the envelope.

I went back to fetch her. 'Come on,' I said. 'It's not safe here. That can wait until we get back to the village.'

She didn't even move. But she held out the photograph she was holding, so that I could see. It was the same boy as before—Khadija's brother Mahmoud— but this time both his top front teeth were missing and his mouth was bleeding in three different places. He looked shocked and terrified.

The photograph was clipped to a piece of paper with four words scrawled across it. TEN THOUSAND DOLLARS TOMORROW.

'What am I going to do?' Sandy said softly.

She wasn't really talking to me, but I answered anyway. 'Couldn't they have faked it?'

'Only the teeth,' Sandy said drily. 'Not the look in his eyes.' She went on staring at the picture, as if I wasn't there. After a moment, she murmured, 'You know the worst thing about this? I could pay that money tomorrow. It wouldn't even cause me a lot of pain. But if I do—what happens to the next boy they kidnap? And the next? Someone has to make a stand.'

She gave a little, unhappy laugh and then started back towards the village. I stood and stared for a moment—until the jeep hooted suddenly and sent me scurrying after her. With the kidnappers jeering as I ran.

Khadija

Freya and I were in Nhur's house again, hiding away from Tony Morales. It was the silence that brought us out. One moment there was a loud noise of people chattering and the carpenters sawing and hammering. The next moment—nothing. When I got to my feet, Freya looked up at me nervously.

'We ought to be careful. It might be those men again.'

'That's why I'm going,' I said. 'If it is, I have to know.'

She caught at the bottom of my skirt, to hold me back. 'Well, you're not going on your own. Wait for me.' She scrambled up awkwardly and gave her scarf an impatient tug to pull it over her head. 'We're in this together.'

By the time we reached the middle of the village, Sandy and Abdi were already heading towards the jeep. When Freya saw them, she caught her breath and began to run forward.

But her father was watching out for her. Before she'd taken two steps, he was there beside her, catching hold of her arm. 'Don't do anything,' he said in a low voice. 'If we spook them, they might start firing.'

'How could you let her go?' Freya said bitterly. 'What were you *thinking*?'

Her father pulled a face. 'I didn't see what she was up to—until too late. At least she had the sense to take Abdi with her.'

I could see him beside her, walking very straight and tall, and I felt proud and afraid at the same time. As if he really was my brother.

But I wasn't as afraid for him as I was for Mahmoud. I held my breath all the time Sandy and Abdi were with the old woman. And the moment she was back in the jeep and it began driving away I started running as fast as I could.

We were all running—Freya and her father and me—but I was in front, ahead of the other two. I was desperate to know what had happened out there.

'What did they want?' I called, as soon as I was near enough. 'Is there another message?'

'It's another ransom demand,' Sandy said. Her voice was cold and stiff. 'They're saying they want the money tomorrow, but there aren't any instructions about how to pay. Or where.' She folded up the message and pushed it into her pocket. 'We'll just have to wait for the next thing. And carry on with the show.'

'Are you *sure*?' said Freya's father. 'Have you thought—?'

Sandy lifted her head higher. 'We're carrying on,' she said firmly. 'They might not even come back until the show's over.'

'Don't be silly,' Freya said. 'They're bound to use the show to pressure you. They must know why we're here.'

'I'd just like to know who told them,' Sandy snapped. She marched on towards the village, without waiting for the rest of us, and Freya and her father followed.

I looked at Abdi. 'No more news about Mahmoud?' I said.

He hesitated for a moment and then shook his head. 'Just a demand for the money. But Sandy told me—' He stopped.

'Go on,' I said impatiently. 'What did she tell you?'

He held back for a second and then said it all in a rush. 'She can pay the money if she wants to. She has so much money it wouldn't be hard for her. But she's not sure it's the right thing to do.'

'Not right? To save Mahmoud's life?' I turned round then, on the brink of running after her to argue.

'No!' Abdi said fiercely. 'If you talk to her, she'll see how much you care. And she might guess that the kidnappers know who you are. We have to trust Suliman and let him handle her.'

Then he went away too, back to Zoë and the make-up, and Zoë waved at me, calling me over there as well. I sat down on one of her chairs and tried not to think about Mahmoud.

'I need to practise on your eyes,' Zoë said. 'It's going to be a bit tricky with your veil, but I can't persuade Sandy to let me take it off.'

What did I care? I felt as though I was in the kind of dream where real things are unimportant and tiny details shake the earth. My brother had been captured by violent, ruthless men, but no one seemed to care whether he lived or died. The only thing that mattered was how my eyes were painted. The women clustered round to see what Zoë was going to do and I sat like a statue while she explained what she was doing—with Abdi translating what she said into awkward, stumbling Somali.

'Basically this is the same eye make-up as we've done for everyone else . . . I have to be careful, because of the veil. And I need to exaggerate the look, to make sure it comes across . . . especially the gold . . . '

So much money being spent on such trivial,

frivolous things. What did these people think they were doing?

'... I'm putting the gold on as thickly as I can.' Zoë leaned forward with her little brush. 'We just need a bit more gold here ... and here ...'

They didn't care about anything except the gold.

Freya

Sandy didn't let up on anything, all day. In the end, we had to give up because it was too dark to work, and by that time everyone was exhausted. There was a meal of rice and spicy stew and we swallowed it down, without bothering to talk very much, and then headed off to our sleeping places.

But it wasn't easy to sleep. The night was hot and heavy and the floor was hard. Khadija and I lay side by side in the dark, next to Nhur and Amina, so close that we couldn't turn over without disturbing each other. Khadija lay very still and quiet, but every time I woke up I knew she was awake too.

Somewhere in the middle of the night I gave up pretending to sleep. I rolled over, so that my mouth was next to Khadija's ear, and muttered, 'Do you want to go outside for a bit?'

She nodded and sat up, reaching for her veil.

'Who's going to see you?' I whispered.

She left the veil where it was and we slipped out through the door and round to the back of the house. It was very quiet there, and we were hidden from the rest of the village.

I was expecting a sensational display of stars—the kind of thing people rave about in travel books—but the sky was overcast and it was so dark that I couldn't even see Khadija's face as she leaned back against the wall.

'Are you worried about the show?' I said.

'What?' She sounded puzzled, as if that hadn't even occurred to her. 'Why would I worry about walking up and down?'

'What about the boy who's been kidnapped?' I said. 'Your father's cousin. Is he someone you know?'

There was a long pause. Then she said, 'Yes, I know him. I know him very well.'

Her voice was shaking and I felt bad about asking the question—until I remembered how Ben's voice had shaken that day at school, when he said *Alice*. When he was desperate to talk about her.

'Look,' I said carefully, 'you don't have to say anything. But if you do, I won't tell anyone. I promise.'

For a minute, or maybe more, there was no sound at all. Only the quiet noises of people turning in their sleep. I began to think that I'd said the wrong thing. After all, why should she trust me?

But she did. All at once she started speaking. Her voice was so soft that I had to lean closer to catch the words.

'He isn't my father's cousin. He's my brother.'

I thought I must have heard wrong. 'The boy they've kidnapped is your *brother*?'

'My only brother. The son of my father and mother.' I could see her profile now, a dark shape against the sky. 'My parents have no money to buy him back— not since they sent me to England. Mahmoud has no hope except me.'

There was a whole story there that I didn't understand and my head buzzed with questions. But when someone's telling you things as big as that, you don't ask anything. All you can do is wait. And listen.

It was a long time before she spoke again. When she did, her voice was as harsh as sandpaper, as if she had to scrape the words out of herself.

'Somehow, those men found out I was going to work for Sandy. That's why they kidnapped Mahmoud. Suliman says I mustn't tell her, because she'll be angry—but how could she be so hard-hearted? If she knew he was my brother, wouldn't she understand—and help me?'

I knew what it was like to have all your hopes hanging on Sandy. On what she *might* do. If she felt like it. I wanted to say something comforting, but there was only one thing I knew for certain.

'Sandy won't think about *anything* now until the show is over. She's totally focused on that. If it goes well then—yes, she might do something for you. She can be very generous sometimes.'

'But that might be too late,' Khadija said. 'I have to decide what to do—and suppose I make the wrong choice?'

What answer could I give? We didn't talk any more after that. Just stood side by side watching the sky grow pale. When there was enough light for us to see each other properly, Khadija stood up straight and lifted her head.

'Time to hide my face,' she said. And she went back into the house.

Within half an hour, Sandy was up and rousing everyone else.

'Only five hours left before we go live,' she called, going from house to house. 'Get out here as fast as you can. We need to check everything—and rehearse.'

Complete rehearsal is pretty much a luxury for an ordinary fashion show, but this wasn't ordinary. Within an hour, everyone was in place and the models

300

were parading up and down, covered in sunscreen and trying to look cool.

The catwalk began on the edge of the village and ran right into the centre, where there was a small, square stage for the models to turn. Dad had set up the camera just beyond that, so that nothing was in shot except the catwalk itself and the open country beyond it. As the models walked towards the camera, their clothes stood out against a backdrop of bare, reddish ground with the wide sky above it. That was what the people in London would see. A clean, uncluttered picture of space and air.

The rest of the place was—chaos. Everything that would normally be hidden away backstage was in full public view. Cosmetics. Shoes. Brushes and combs. Tins full of clips and pins and needles, and all kinds of thread for emergency repairs.

The clothes were hanging on rails out in the open, each set complete with all its accessories. There was a photo clipped to every hanger to show how the complete outfit should look and Amina was busy working through them all, showing the dressers what they needed to do. Emphasizing how quickly they had to work.

Suddenly she turned round, frowning. 'Which houses are you using as dressing rooms?'

Sandy was busy checking the rails and Amina's

words took a few seconds to register. When they did, she looked up absently. 'What do you mean *dressing rooms*?'

A catwalk show is about smooth running and lightning-quick changes. As soon as the models come off the catwalk, the dressers are on to them, peeling off one set of clothes and slipping on another. There are always dozens of people milling around, but nobody worries about that. This time, the backstage area was outside—and Sandy had just assumed that everyone except Khadija would change there.

When she turned round and saw the shock on Amina's face, she reacted very quickly.

'Screening!' she called out crisply. 'Suliman—get the men to screen off a space. As near the catwalk as possible, but out of view of the camera.'

I couldn't see how there was anything in the village to use as screens, but I was wrong. In the middle of everything else that was going on, the carpenters started dismantling the houses on the edge of the village. They were made of branches and mats and the men carried those materials into the central area and began constructing a roofless dressing room.

And, as if all that wasn't enough to drive anyone insane, Tony Morales was leaping around everywhere, taking photographs. I kept thinking people would fall over him, but he was amazingly nimble.

I spent most of the morning keeping Khadija out of his way.

It wasn't an easy morning for her. She only had two sets of clothes to wear—one to open the show and the other to close it—and that left her with far too much time to stand around worrying. There was no point in that, so I hauled her off to see Dad.

He was on the satphone, talking to Marco in London. All the equipment for the web link had been hired and shipped out with us and of course none of it worked straight away. It never does. But they'd just made contact and there were four men at our end running round with cameras and cables, watching the results on several different monitors.

'Look, Marco,' Dad was saying—in that very patient voice he uses when anyone else would be yelling— 'just tell me what you can see.'

From four thousand miles away, Marco bellowed back at him. Even Khadija and I could hear what he said.

'This is craziness! This whole business is craziness! I told Sandy that, from the moment she suggested the idea. Do you think she's losing her edge? She can't seriously expect—'

'Isn't it going to work?' Khadija muttered in my ear.

'Don't worry about Marco,' I muttered back. 'It's just noise.' He might be yelling, but he wouldn't be ignoring Dad's instructions. I knew his eyes would be fixed on the screen at his end, just as Dad's were fixed on the monitor at ours.

The proof of that came half a second later. Marco was in mid-rant when he suddenly stopped shouting. 'Aaah!' he said, in a satisfied voice. And then, 'My God, David, is it really that basic where you are?'

'Of course not,' Dad said sarcastically. 'This is a Somali Heritage Theme Park.' Then he laughed. 'Don't you think it's a great backdrop?'

'Not bad.' I could almost see Marco nodding. 'Not bad at all. I've got it up on the big screen now, and she looks sensational.'

Khadija and I turned round to face the monitors. And there was Emily Bate (yes, *that* Emily Bate—it was her very first show) coming down the catwalk in a sharp little pinstripe suit with wide shoulders and a leather mini-veil that matched her briefcase. Marco was right. She did look sensational.

'Isn't that great?' I muttered to Khadija.

When she didn't answer, I glanced up at her. She was staring at the monitors, with her eyes flicking from one to another. And she looked—sick.

'What's the matter?' I said.

304

She answered without looking at me. 'I was think-ing how easy it is to have the same picture on more than one screen. If they can do that here, maybe other people can do it too. Maybe . . . in an internet café?'

'It must be possible,' I said. 'But why would any-one bother?'

She didn't say anything. Just went on staring and staring at Emily Bate prancing down the catwalk.

They woke Mahmoud early and gave him rice and bananas to eat. Then they tied his ankles and his wrists together and threw him into a truck, with Sanyare beside him to keep him from making trouble.

'Where are we going?' Mahmoud said. 'What's happening?'

But Sanyare wouldn't tell him anything. He just smiled and spread his hands. 'Don't be afraid,' he said. 'You have a good sister. She won't let you down.'

Did that mean Geri had found the money to set him free? The idea of that made Mahmoud feel angry and afraid. He couldn't think of any honest way she could have gained so much money.

'Hey,' Sanyare said. 'Don't worry.' He slung his gun over his shoulder and leaned back against the side of the truck, closing his eyes against the sun. 'We're not bad men. We're just doing what we can to make a living. Getting some money back into Somalia.'

'It's not honest money,' Mahmoud muttered, half under his breath.

Sanyare smiled, without opening his eyes. 'You'll understand all these things one day. But for now, all you have to do is obey Yusuf's orders. If you do that, I won't let anyone hurt you.'

Mahmoud wanted to believe in the smile and the easy way that Sanyare spoke to him, as though the two of them were on the same side against the world. But he knew it wasn't true. He could see the narrow gleam that meant Sanyare's eyes weren't totally closed. He was being watched, in case he made a wrong move.

Well, he could do that too.

He copied Sanyare, pretending to sleep as the truck bumped down the rough road, heading into the desert. But he was watching. From under his eyelids he watched the gun, planning how to snatch it away if the right moment came. One of his uncles had an AK47 like that, and he knew exactly how to use it and what the trigger would feel like under his finger.

All he had to do was be ready . . .

Abdi

That morning, the village came alive. When we arrived, I thought I'd come to the dead end of the world, but now the whole place was transformed, buzzing with life and purpose.

Sandy had the power to make her ideas real— because she could pay for what she wanted. What was it she'd said when she saw that photo of Mahmoud? *I could pay ten thousand dollars . . . it wouldn't cause me a lot of pain.*

I thought of the odd little conversation I'd had with Suliman the day before. When Sandy and I came back to the village, he'd waited a little while and then beckoned me over, with a quick flick of his fingers.

'Well?' he'd muttered as I came up beside him. 'Is she going to produce the money?'

'You mean—Sandy?' I said warily.

Suliman raised his eyebrows. 'Who else? What did that old woman give her?'

'It was another picture of Khadija's brother,' I said. 'They've been beating him up.'

'Hurting him?' Suliman sounded surprised.

'They've knocked out his front teeth,' I said. 'And split his lips.'

'So—nothing really serious,' Suliman said.

He sounded very casual and I had a sudden sharp memory of Khadija's voice. *Abdi—there's a gun under Suliman's seat.* For the first time, I wondered if he'd ever used it.

He was still asking questions. 'Well? What did Sandy say about the picture?'

I shrugged. 'She said she could find the ten thousand dollars—but she doesn't think it's right to pay kidnappers.'

'Did she now?' Suliman looked thoughtful. 'She said she could pay?'

I thought he was going to ask something else, but he changed his mind and walked off.

Standing in the middle of the village next morning, I could hardly believe Sandy had seen that photograph. She was totally focused on her show. With only an hour to go, she was still making little alterations to the clothes and changing her mind about the running order.

309

Then, suddenly, there was no more time to prepare. She whirled round and started shouting.

'Twenty minutes! We're going live in twenty minutes! I want you all in your places—and *concentrating*. We only get one chance at this. If we blow it, no one in London is going to hang around to give us another go.'

Immediately, everyone started moving. The models came out of the shade of the dressing area and lined up beside the catwalk, with their dressers fluttering round them. Amina called Marco on the satphone. The men on the web link checked everything for the thirtieth time. And Tony the photographer danced about, sneaking shots of everything that was going on.

With ten minutes to go, Khadija came forward, to take her place at the front of the line. I'd been expecting something spectacular, but she looked really dull, dressed in black from head to foot—like the stuff she'd been wearing ever since we left home, only in a different material. It wasn't ugly or immodest or anything like that. It was just . . . a waste. Why had Sandy gone to all that trouble to get Khadija on the catwalk if that was all she was going to give her?

It didn't put off Tony Morales, though. He gave a kind of yodel and pranced up to her. 'Just stand for a moment, Qarsoon. I must have a shot of this. And one like this . . . and this . . . '

I thought he would make Khadija nervous, but she behaved as if she'd spent her whole life working with internationally famous photographers. She stood where he asked her, calmly turning her head left and right as he darted around. And Freya hovered a few inches away, ready to leap forward if Tony did anything stupid like trying to grab Khadija's veil.

'Five minutes!' Sandy called. 'Let's have silence now. Amina, get ready to turn on the music—three, two, one—*now!*'

The real music was being played in London, but Amina had all the tracks on an iPod, to keep the models walking in time. As Sandy said *now* a thin thread of notes began winding its way out of the speakers and across the village. For a second, there was no other sound.

And then, from the distance, came the noise of the kidnappers' jeep, driving very fast, straight towards us.

Khadija

We all turned to look—straight down the catwalk and into the open desert behind. How could we help it? The show was just about to start, but surely it couldn't begin while Mahmoud's life was balanced on the edge of a dagger? If the men didn't get the money they wanted this time, they were certain to kill him.

It couldn't be an accident that they were coming now. *Someone* must have told them when the show was starting. Maybe they thought Sandy would pay up without arguing, to get them out of the way before it began.

If they did, they were making a huge mistake. As soon as she saw the jeep, Sandy leapt on to the catwalk and shrieked at the security guards.

'Get moving! I'm paying you to keep this show safe, so get out there and earn your money! I don't care how you do it, but keep that jeep away until the show's finished!'

Suliman and Amina both started translating, but that wasn't necessary. The guards had already grabbed their guns and piled into the trucks. Before Sandy even finished yelling, they were roaring out of the village, towards the kidnappers.

'They'll be in the picture,' Freya's father said, looking into the camera. 'I can't cut them out.'

'Too bad,' Sandy snapped. She jumped off the catwalk and went to take a look. 'Just pull the shot in as tight as you can and carry on. She turned and shouted at everyone else. 'Two minutes to go! Forget the James Bond stuff. All you need to worry about is showing off the clothes. Make sure you're ready.'

The air was so heavy that my dress felt suffocating. From where I stood, I could see the jeep coming closer and the trucks racing out to meet it. In the trucks were guns pointing towards Mahmoud. *I can't go up there and show off clothes,* I thought. *Not now.*

' . . . thirty seconds . . . twenty . . . ten . . . '

I can't—

'Now!'

Sandy put a hand on my back and pushed and I couldn't resist her, because she was Mahmoud's only hope. Suddenly I was stepping on to the catwalk, with my head held high and my feet stepping left, right, left, right, left. It was like walking on knives. Now my back was to the jeep and I couldn't see anything that was happening. All I could do was walk the way Sandy had told me to, getting faster as I went, so that when I came to the square stage at the end I was ready to—

SWIRL!

I don't know if they gasped in London, but everyone in that village cried out as my dress flared open diagonally, flashing bright scarlet. Even the veil opened up, transformed to the colour of fresh, flowing blood.

I spun once, twice, three times. Then I stopped, and the brightness disappeared. Everything was black again as I strode back down the catwalk, forcing myself not to look up at the jeep. Not yet. I had to do everything perfectly. Exactly the way Sandy wanted.

As I walked, I was undoing the hidden fastenings at the front of my dress. One with each step I took, the way I'd practised. As I reached the end of the catwalk, I slipped the dress off my shoulders and stepped out of it, pulling the veil away and turning to show—

—another dress. And another veil. Made of reddish-brown material that merged with the desert behind me.

I stood for a moment, turning once to show off my camouflage. *Qarsoon the Invisible. The girl you never see.* Then I picked up the black clothes and stepped off the catwalk, passing Emily on her way up.

314

And even then there was no time to stop and stare at the jeep. Once I was out of the camera's eye, I had to pick up my skirts and run to Nhur's house with Freya, to change into my other set of clothes.

'Hurry! Please hurry!' I hissed at her. 'I need to go outside and see what's happening.'

Freya

What was Sandy doing? How could she let the show carry on? It was monstrous— *outrageous*—for girls to be parading up and down out there when someone's life was at risk. But Sandy was *making* it happen, by simple, fierce willpower. I could almost hear what she was telling herself.

We only need another eighteen minutes to finish the show . . .

. . . only another seventeen minutes . . .

. . . only . . .

What could the people in London be thinking? They must be able to see the kidnappers too. I pictured Merry, sitting in a row with all the other fashionistas. Wasn't she horrified, like me?

'You don't have to carry on with this!' I said to Khadija. 'Just go out there and tell Sandy you're stopping.'

Khadija shook her head fiercely. 'How would that

save Mahmoud? I *have* to do this. Please help me, Freya.'

I didn't understand, but if that was what she wanted I wasn't going to let her down. As fast as I could, I took off her 'invisible' dress and its sleek, tapering veil. Then I slipped the other dress off its hanger and she stepped into it and stood straight and tall while I fastened the buttons.

She didn't hustle me, not even when my fingers fumbled halfway up, because I'd missed a button-hole. She just waited patiently while I went back and did the whole lot all over again.

When I'd finished, I handed the veil to her, so she could fix it herself. I'd practised five or six times, but my hands were sweating in the heat and I couldn't be sure of getting it right first go. I knew Khadija could do it faster.

We were meant to wait inside the house until Sandy gave us the signal to come out. But there was no way that was going to happen. The moment the veil was in place, we both headed for the door, without even needing to discuss it.

We'd only been inside for three or four minutes, but even in that short time everything had changed.

The jeep had stopped a hundred metres away from the village and three of the kidnappers were lined up beside it, surrounded by our security guards. It didn't look as though anyone could get through.

But two of the kidnappers were walking straight at the guards. Two tall men with *kefiyahs* wound round their faces. Even at a distance, I could see that one of them was carrying a gun and I thought, *Why don't the guards shoot? Why are they just letting them through?*

Then I saw why.

Walking with the two men—jammed close in front of them—was a boy about twelve years old. They were using him as a shield. The guards hesitated and then parted, to let them through.

The boy's face wasn't covered. As he came closer, I could see his big, frightened eyes and the splits in his swollen lips. Khadija saw them too and she caught her breath, with a small, strange sound, as though someone had hit her. The she started running forward.

But Dad had spotted her. He left the camera to take care of itself and raced round the end of the catwalk to grab her and hold her back.

'Don't do anything!' he said frantically. 'They're bound to be edgy. If you run out suddenly, anything could happen. Just remember that no one wants to kill the boy. They want to trade him.'

Khadija moaned and pressed her hands over her mouth.

And in the middle of all this, Sandy was up at the

far end of the catwalk, grimly pushing each model up the steps as her turn came round. Afterwards, Merry told me what it was like to sit in London and watch it happening.

We thought it was part of the show at first. One of Sandy's clever ideas, to make a point. But as soon as we saw the boy, we knew it had to be real. Even Sandy wouldn't fake something like that.

It dominated the whole of the rest of the week. Spoilt it, really. Wherever I was, I kept thinking about that boy. And the look on his face.

There were guns all around. Guns in the jeep that brought him there. Guns in the trucks that came out to block their way. And Sanyare's gun, digging into his back as he walked towards the village.

The air was stifling, and he was jammed between Sanyare and Yusuf, so close that he could smell Yusuf's breath. He could feel the stiff shape of the leather sheath that Sanyare kept strapped to his belt, to hold his dagger. There didn't seem to be any way of escaping.

They were walking towards a crowd of people, mostly women and girls. Mahmoud kept scanning their faces, because surely Geri was one of them. Why else was he being taken into the village? She had to be there.

But he couldn't see her. Not one of the faces was hers. And if she wasn't there, who else would pay for his life? He could feel the ugly taste of fear in his mouth. Fear and despair.

He refused to give in to it. Somehow, somewhere, there had to be a chance to get free. As long as he kept watching for it. As long as he was ready . . .

Abdi

They were ordinary men, in jeans and T-shirts. The kind of people you might have met anywhere in the world—except for the cloths over their faces. When they came to the end of the catwalk, they jumped on to it, hauling Mahmoud up with them.

The model who was walking towards them gave a frightened little squeal and jumped off at the side, leaving the whole length clear. Slowly, the men paraded down the catwalk, looking down on us as we stood staring up at them.

Some of our guards were following them now, at a distance, but there was nothing they could do to rescue Mahmoud. One of the men was gripping him tightly, by the arm, and the other was holding a gun pressed into his back.

When they reached the square at the end of the catwalk, they moved apart, to stand side by side, showing off their power to the people below them. The long barrel of the gun swivelled round, pointing into the crowd, and the man holding Mahmoud's wrist jerked it up in the air. No need for any words. That gesture said it all. *Look who I've got!*

I looked at Mahmoud. We all looked. But I saw something different too. The man nearest me—the one with the gun—had a battered leather sheath hanging from his belt. And down one side of it was a deep, jagged scratch.

I knew the shape of the scratch as well as I knew my own hand—and I knew what was inside the sheath, too. It was a short, thick dagger, perfectly weighted and deadly sharp, with a tiny nick halfway along the blade.

My father's knife.

How had the kidnapper got hold of that? There was only one possible way I could think of.

I was looking at the man who'd murdered my father.

For a second it was like being strangled. All the breath was squeezed out of my body by a great wave of rage—and shame. My father's killer was in front of me, taunting me with a gun while his companion's voice boomed over the village:

'Here's the boy! We've kept our side of the bargain. Where's the money to buy him back?'

'What's he saying?' Sandy called, and Suliman

started translating, but I didn't hear what he said. I couldn't even hear the whispers of the people around me. There was only one thing in my head, only one thing that mattered.

I couldn't stand by like a coward, with my father's killer sneering down at me. It was my duty—my *responsibility*—to make sure people respected my family. I couldn't avenge my father now—not without a weapon—but at least I could uncover the murderer's face. If I knew what he looked like, I could come back and track him down later on. Even if it took me years.

The shouting stopped and the two kidnappers looked round, waiting for an answer. Sandy was the only person who could give it and when she stepped forward, she was shaking with anger.

'I'm not giving in to a crowd of bullies!' she shouted. 'Let the boy go! This minute!'

The two men looked at each other—and I knew that was my moment. The only moment. Whatever happened next—whether they started firing or disappeared back to the jeep—my opportunity would have gone. The only chance I had was that instant, when everyone was staring at Sandy.

Now!

I jumped on to the stage and my hands reached for the cloth that covered the murderer's face. As my fingers closed round it, I realized that he might turn and fire. He might even kill me. But it was too late to worry about that. I gripped the headcloth hard and pulled it away. The man whipped round, pointing his gun at my chest and I knew I was going to die. I knew he was going to shoot—

But he didn't. When he saw me, the gun barrel dropped and his eyes opened wide. We stared at each other.

The other kidnapper turned, to see what was going on. As he did so, Tony the photographer stepped out of the crowd, with his camera held high and a flash gun in the other hand. He was right up close to the stage when the flash went off.

That flash gave Mahmoud his chance. As Tony took the picture, he wrenched his hand free and spun away from the man who was holding him. And as he spun, his other arm went out and grabbed at the gun, twisting it out of the murderer's fingers.

Suddenly everything was completely different. Mahmoud was backing away down the catwalk, with the gun trained on the two men who'd brought him there. He was yelling in Somali, at the top of his voice.

And I was still standing there with the headcloth in my hand, staring at the face I'd uncovered.

My father's face.

Khadija

Mahmoud was so brave, so clever—I could hardly believe it!

Everyone else was standing around helplessly—all those rich people who'd come into the village and started giving orders. They had no idea what to do and they were terrified. Probably most of them had never even seen a gun before. The only one who dared to speak was Sandy, and what she said just made things worse. I thought the kidnappers were going to start shooting everyone.

But Mahmoud saved us all.

He saw the moment and seized hold of the kidnapper's gun, stepping back to take control of the situation. And he knew how to use what he'd taken. When one of the men took a step forward, Mahmoud moved the gun sharply and shot him in the foot. There was a yelp of pain and then—no one else argued with him.

I was watching it all from behind, because I was up

at the far end of the catwalk, ready to close the show. I couldn't see Mahmoud's face, but I saw his straight back and the confident way he held his head. Everyone was looking up at him.

That was what I thought. But then I took a step sideways and I saw Abdi and the second kidnapper. They were staring at each other as though Mahmoud and the gun and the rest of the village meant nothing at all.

Mahmoud jerked the gun, signalling roughly to the men. 'Get down!' he shouted. 'Get down off the stage and go back to your jeep. Before I shoot!'

If they'd both been fit, and acted together, maybe the men could have rushed him then, and wrenched the gun away. But only one of them was even watching Mahmoud, and he had a wounded foot. He hesitated for a second and then sat on the end of the catwalk and let himself down, very carefully, on to the ground.

'Come on, Sanyare!' he called over his shoulder. His voice was scornful and angry. 'Or do you want to stay there—and get what you deserve?' When the other man didn't react to the insult, he called him again. 'Come on, Ahmed!'

As soon as I heard the man's real name, I understood. He was Abdi's father. That was why the two of them were staring at each other like that. Once I realized that, it seemed obvious, not just from the man's face but in the way he stood and moved.

For another long moment he stared at Abdi, as if he was waiting for something. But Abdi didn't say a word. So finally his father jumped off the stage and joined the other kidnapper, putting an arm round his back to support him as they walked out of the village.

From behind, he looked even more like Abdi. The way Abdi would look when he was a man, if he ended up disappointed and defeated.

And Abdi was like him. As he stood watching the kidnappers trail past the catwalk, I knew exactly how his father must have looked when he was a young man, understanding for the first time how hard life is. When you lose your father, you say goodbye to a part of yourself.

The two men headed out into the bare, empty land beyond the village, walking past me as if I were invisible. Mahmoud swung round, following them with the barrel of the gun. I left him to concentrate until they were right out of the village, safely in range of the security guards.

Then I jumped on to the catwalk. He turned towards me and when I saw what those men had done to his face I wanted to snatch the gun and run after them. Instead, I waved my arms and shouted his name.

'Mahmoud!'

For a moment he looked puzzled—until I realized why and ripped off my stupid golden veil. When he saw my face, he shouted with delight.

'Geri!'

As I started towards him, the heaviness in the air finally lifted and it began to rain. I went down the catwalk with my arms out and water drenching my shoulders and running down my dress.

Freya

It was more beautiful than you can possibly imagine. Khadija ran down the catwalk laughing, with her arms held out to Mahmoud. And the rain—the lovely, clean, reviving rain—fell out of the sky and flooded over her dress, pouring in long streams down the whole length of the skirt.

All the clothes on the rails were ruined, but no one gave them a thought. Not even Sandy. She was jumping up and down with relief and delight, with her hair sticking up and a huge grin on her face.

And, unbelievably, the camera was still running and the web link was open. All those people staring at the screen in London saw Khadija coming towards them like a pillar of light, with her face uncovered and tiny droplets of water flashing and glittering from every golden centimetre of her dress.

People still talk about it. That was the moment that made the whole show a triumph.

That evening, when the rain stopped, the guards built a fire in the centre of the village and we all sat round it to eat together.

It should have been a celebration. A wonderful end to everything. We'd already heard from Marco that the show was a huge success, and Merry had wangled her way on to the satphone as well, offering Khadija a contract to think over—the kind of contract most models can only dream about.

But something wasn't right. I knew that when I saw Abdi's face and the way he and Khadija avoided Suliman. They sat on the far side of the circle, with Mahmoud between them, and Abdi looked grim and unhappy.

It was Tony Morales who brought everything to a head. When the meal was over, he produced his camera, flicking through the photographs to show Sandy and Dad. He had almost finished when he grinned and raised his voice.

'The clothes look great, but—I'm sorry, Sandy—*these* are the pictures that are going to earn the real money. Mahmoud and the villains who kidnapped him!'

From the other side of the circle, Abdi's voice came suddenly. 'Those aren't the only villains! The worst villain is sitting here with us!'

He jumped up and ran round the fire to where I was sitting with Sandy and Dad. Suliman was next to Sandy, and Abdi pointed a finger at him, yelling wildly.

'*That's* the man who planned the kidnap. He's not my father—or Khadija's father! But he knew about Khadija's real family and he snooped on her when she was using the internet in his café. It must have been him. No one else had all the information.'

Everything stopped and, all round the fire, faces turned to look at Suliman. Khadija stood up and came across the circle very quickly, with Mahmoud behind her.

'That's right,' she said to Suliman. 'You watched me visit Sandy's website, didn't you? And you read my email to Mahmoud. Then you arranged the kidnap—and gave Abdi's phone back, so the kidnappers could call him!'

Suliman opened his eyes very wide. 'What is all this? Why are you slandering me, after all I've done to help you?' He turned to Sandy. 'I did pretend to be their father—so that you could have Khadija for your show. But the kidnap was nothing to do with me. You can see the guilty man, in Tony's photographs.'

I saw Sandy frown as she looked from Suliman to Abdi and back again. Trying to make sense of it all.

Suliman gave her a winning smile. 'Don't judge Abdi too harshly. He's upset because one of those kidnappers is his real father. A small-time crook.'

'He's not a crook!' Abdi said fiercely.

Suliman raised his eyebrows. 'No? Why do you think your mother told you he was dead? He took the money you saved to bring him to England and bought a share in a pirate ship—which sank before it could capture anything. You have to face it, Abdi. He's no good.'

Abdi's face crumpled and he turned his head away. It all sounded horribly plausible. I glanced at Dad, to see what he was thinking.

He was watching Abdi with a kind of terrible pity. 'You can't just make accusations like that,' he said gently. 'Not without evidence.'

'*Suliman's* the one making accusations!' Abdi shouted. 'He's saying wicked things about my father. How can he talk about his friend like that? They've been together ever since they were boys. My father used to talk about it. Sanyare and Sanweyne, the cleverest boys in the school.'

Mahmoud suddenly sat up very straight. Then he leaned forward and said something to Khadija, pointing at Suliman.

I didn't understand, but whatever it was it made a great stillness round the fire. All the Somalis were staring at Suliman now, and Amina tensed suddenly, sitting very straight.

'What is it?' Sandy said. 'What did he say?'

'He's lying,' Suliman muttered angrily. 'Or trauma-tized, maybe. He's lost touch with reality anyway.'

Sandy's eyes narrowed. 'What did he say?' she asked again. Very quietly and coldly.

No one answered for a moment. And then—amazingly—Amina stood up. '*I'll* tell you,' she said. Her voice was even colder than Sandy's. Naked ice. 'Mahmoud heard the kidnappers phoning a man called Sanweyne, a man they said was in England. And I believe him—because I heard the other end of that phone call. I heard my husband talking to a man he called Sanyare.'

Suliman was gaping at her. Looking as though she'd punched him. 'You're my *wife*. How can you—?'

'I know what you are,' Amina said. 'And I'm tired of telling myself to ignore it. When I saw how they'd hurt that boy's face, I made myself a promise. *If that has anything to do with Suliman, then everything's over.*'

'What can you do?' Suliman said scornfully.

Amina lifted her head. 'Nothing here, maybe. But don't try coming back to England, Suliman Osman Hersi. You've deceived me—and deceived your father and mother too. You won't like the way people treat you, when they know everything you've done.'

333

'You wouldn't dare,' Suliman said easily. 'The shame—'

'I am already ashamed,' Amina said. 'I'm going now. Don't follow me.' She turned round and went away from the fire, disappearing into the house where she slept at night.

We couldn't really go on celebrating after that. People started drifting away, leaving Suliman on his own by the fire. I don't know what happened to him. By next morning he'd disappeared, with one of the trucks, and he never turned up again.

When Abdi walked away, I almost went after him. I wanted to tell him that I understood—a little bit—what it's like finding out that your father's a traitor. But Dad was too quick for me. As Abdi went past him, he stood up and fell into step with him.

'Fancy a bit of a walk?' he said softly.

For a second, I thought Abdi was going to ignore him. Then he changed his mind. He glanced up at Dad and gave a quick little nod and the two of them went off into the darkness side by side.

I hung around for a while, but they didn't come back. Whatever they were talking about, it seemed to be taking a long time. In the end, I was too tired to wait any longer, and I went back to Nhur's house with Khadija.

As we settled down to sleep, I said softly, 'Did Abdi really think his father was dead?'

'That's what they told him,' Khadija said. 'When he jumped on to the catwalk today, he thought he was facing his father's murderer. He was very brave.'

So was it better or worse to discover that his father was alive?

'Poor Abdi,' I said. 'He must feel as though he's lost everything.'

Khadija reached out and gave my hand a little squeeze. 'You're a kind girl, Freya. You care about people.'

'I just like them to be all right,' I said. 'It must have been so hard for Abdi, when he pulled off that mask—'

'He could have chosen to go with his father,' Khadija said quietly. 'Have you thought of that? He could have stayed in Somalia for ever. But he didn't.'

He knows where he belongs, I thought. For a second, I almost envied him.

It rained again, almost all the next day, but somehow we managed to pack up the equipment and pay off all the local staff, except the security guards. By the time the rain stopped, the village was quiet and half empty.

335

Around midday, Khadija and Mahmoud took off in a jeep full of villagers, heading for the camp where their parents were living. Khadija was desperate to see them before she had to fly back.

That left Abdi and me to help with clearing the village. We worked side by side for most of the day, but we hardly said a word to each other—until, suddenly, we found ourselves with nothing more to do.

Abdi heaved the last box into the last truck and then muttered at me, without turning round. 'Is your dad a proper photographer? Like Tony Morales?'

'He's much better than Tony Morales!' I said hotly. 'Why?'

Abdi shrugged and then turned round, doing a feeble imitation of someone who didn't really care. 'He said he'd teach me to do it.'

'You want to be a photographer?' I said. 'What for?'

'So I can make people see things my way!' Abdi lifted his head fiercely. 'Everyone's going to remember those photos Tony Morales took, aren't they? Somalis with guns, in the desert. But they don't tell the whole story. They're not the *truth*. Now if I'd had a camera—'

His face was alight now. Almost like Sandy's, when she was really worked up. I wondered for a second whether Dad had been like that once, before he stopped taking pictures that really mattered.

In the evening, I went for a walk in the dark, with Sandy and Dad. They were walking side by side, looking up at the stars, and I felt as though I was tagging along behind. Then Dad put an arm round Sandy's shoulders, pulling her close to point out the constellations.

'You two are crazy,' I said. 'Why don't you give up all that rubbish about being separated? You make me feel like a gooseberry.'

It was meant as a joke, but my voice cracked and suddenly it didn't sound funny any more. Sandy twisted out of Dad's arm and turned towards me.

'It's not like that, Freya. Really it's not.'

'That's right,' Dad said. Very earnestly. I knew he was remembering what I'd overheard—*do you really think I'm going to choose Freya instead of you?*—and for one horrific second I thought he was going to apologize.

But he's got too much sense for that. Instead, he reached out and caught hold of my wrist, pulling me towards them.

'Let me tell you a story,' he said. 'It's an old Somali story. I've heard it all over the place.'

337

He paused for a moment, until we could all hear the silence, and then he started, very softly.

'Once upon a time, there was a man who had three wives. They were all strong and beautiful—but they were all very, very jealous. Day after day, they argued about who was his favourite, and they kept nagging him to tell them: *Which of us do you love the most?*'

My heart tightened in my chest. I wanted to end the story there, but I couldn't speak.

'The man tried to ignore the question,' Dad went on, 'but his wives became more and more insistent— and more and more unhappy. At last, he called them together and said, "Very well, I shall do as you ask. But first you must all close your eyes."'

Slowly and deliberately, Dad stopped talking and shut his own eyes. Sandy frowned at him for a second and then her eyes closed as well.

Sandy and Dad. Dad and Sandy. I looked at them both and thought *I don't have to do this.* Then I copied them and shut my eyes too.

'When all the wives had closed their eyes,' Dad murmured, 'the man said, "Now I shall touch the one I love the best." And he reached out—'

There was a split second when nothing happened. It was all I could do to breathe. Then I felt the touch of Dad's hand, familiar and unmistakable, on the left side of my face. And at the same instant, on the other side, I felt Sandy's fingers stroking my cheek.

They're lying, I thought. *They're just trying to make me feel better.*

'Well, Freya?' Dad said softly.

And then I got it. I suddenly saw how the story had to end—the only right answer. *Touch the one you love the best.*

Still with my eyes closed, I reached out quickly, touching Sandy's face with one hand and Dad's with the other.

And what about Mahmoud?

You want a happy ending, don't you? You want me to say that his lip healed up and his teeth grew back and he's going to be a doctor.

But real life's not like that, is it? His teeth are gone for ever—and he doesn't *want* to study medicine. He wants to live out his life in the desert, with a herd of camels and the freedom to travel where he likes. The way his family has done for hundreds of years.

Khadija's doing her best for him. She's bought her family a house and twenty strong new camels. But however rich she gets, she can't end the fighting that tears Somalia apart. Only the warlords and the pirates can do that, by putting down their guns.

She can't change the fact that the modern, citified world doesn't leave much room for boys like Mahmoud, who want to be nomads. And she can't do anything about the global warming that makes the rains fail and dries up the waterholes. Not on her own, anyway. Those are huge issues, involving everyone.

Like I said at the very beginning—we're all connected.

Gillian Cross has been writing children's books for over thirty years. Before that, she took English degrees at Oxford and Sussex Universities, and she has had various jobs including working in a village bakery and being an assistant to a Member of Parliament. She is married with four children and lives in Dorset. Her hobbies include orienteering and playing the piano. She won the Carnegie Medal for *Wolf* and the Smarties Prize and the Whitbread Children's Novel Award for *The Great Elephant Chase*.

Isbn: 978-0-19-275589-6

You've got such thin bones. You've got such red blood.
You can't carry on . . . You'll fall.

It's a beautiful, blank wall and Ashley can't resist tagging it—even though she has to climb twenty feet on to a roof to reach it with her spray cans. She reckons she can make it without being caught, if she sneaks out in the dead of night.

But someone sees her. Someone dangerous is watching her every move.

Then the notes start arriving. At first she takes no notice. But the watcher won't be ignored—and his messages are about to turn deadly.

Ashley is balancing on a tightrope. And when she falls, he'll be waiting . . .

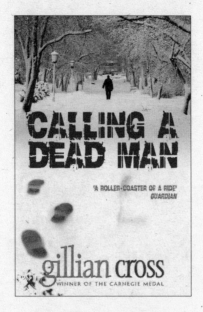

'A ROLLER-COASTER OF A RIDE'
GUARDIAN

gillian cross
WINNER OF THE CARNEGIE MEDAL

Isbn: 978-0-19-275588-9

How did John Cox die?

His sister Hayley thinks she knows, but she wants
to see the place where it happened. With John's friend
Annie she travels to Russia to visit the site of the
explosion that killed him.

But they soon realize that there is more to John's
death than meets the eye. And certain people are
desperate to keep them from finding out the truth.

Meanwhile, deep in the wastes of Siberia, a man with
no memory and a high fever stumbles out of the forest . . .

Isbn: 978-0-19-273163-0

'This play we're doing, it's not true, is it? I mean, there never was a Sweeney Todd who killed people?'

Jackus never wanted to be in the school play, but he didn't have much choice.

Now he sees that what's unfolding on-stage is more than just acting, more than just pretend. Strange things are happening. *Terrifying things.*

Ghostly footprints. Unexplained whispering. The touch of a cold hand in the shadows . . .

What has been woken by the play's dark words? Can Jackus stop it, or are the actors doomed to play out the tragedy to the bitter end?